George Gordon Scott

Clumber Chase

Or, Love's Riddle solved by a royal Sphinx - Vol. I

George Gordon Scott

Clumber Chase
Or, Love's Riddle solved by a royal Sphinx - Vol. I

ISBN/EAN: 9783337137212

Printed in Europe, USA, Canada, Australia, Japan

Cover: Foto ©Andreas Hilbeck / pixelio.de

More available books at **www.hansebooks.com**

—Railways, postages—in a word, all the numerous facilities of the age—have almost annihilated distance, and, as a natural result, caused an individual trade between country customers and London establishments. Those who do not visit town, so as to select and purchase directly, send for patterns from which they can give their orders. But as all apparent advantages on the one hand have more or less their corresponding drawbacks, so this system is not without its bane. Pushing tradesmen make a market by offering goods at lower rates than they can possibly be sold at to realise a fair profit. The bait traps the unreflective, and the result is that the receipts *en masse* are not equal to the tempting samples. There is no new invention in this; it has been practised in wholesale merchandise and by candidates for contracts, as the proverb hath it, since there were hills and valleys. But we grieve to add it is sometimes resorted to by those whom one would credit for more integrity. Ladies, therefore, need exercise caution, and place confidence only in houses of old-established fame, for rapidly-made businesses are not generally reliable. And to what does this assertion amount more than to the fact that nothing great can be effected not only without labour but without time, and that Rome was not built, as the old saying says, in a day? Messrs. Jay, of Regent-street, whose name is well known amongst the few on the list of *bonâ fide* establishments in the metropolis, have adopted a plan for assisting country ladies in choosing for themselves London fashions and fabrics. And their customers may rest assured that they will thus be enabled to obtain goods of every quality, both low and high priced, at the most reasonable terms—that is, the terms of small profits for quick returns—and that they may firmly rely upon the thoroughly corresponding character of samples and supplies.—From the *Court Journal*.

CLUMBER CHASE,

OR

LOVE'S RIDDLE SOLVED BY A ROYAL SPHINX.

A TALE OF THE RESTORATION.

IN THREE VOLUMES.

BY

GEORGE GORDON SCOTT.

"Acerrima proximorum Odia."

TACITUS.

" I love thee to the level of every day's
Most quiet need, by sun and candle light,
I love thee freely, as men strive for right;
I love thee purely, as they turn from praise.
I love thee with a passion put to use
In my old grief, and with my childhood's faith
I love thee with a love I seemed to lose
With my lost Saints, I love thee with the breath,
Smiles, tears of all my life!—and if God choose
I shall but love thee ' better after death.' "

E. B. BROWNING.

VOL. I.

LONDON :

T. CAUTLEY NEWBY, PUBLISHER,

30, WELBECK STREET, CAVENDISH SQUARE.

1871.

DEDICATION.

—

To GEOFFREY ST. JOHN HARTSFOOT, Esq.,

OF

BALDIVALLOCH.

My Dear Hartsfoot,

As in the Tale of "Clumber Chase," I have endeavoured to reproduce your worthy ancestor, *Master Oliver*, I venture, in grateful remembrance of the happy hours passed in our Excursion to Norway last Autumn, to dedicate this Book to you, knowing that I shall thereby insure at least one indulgent critic for the shortcomings of,

Yours ever faithfully,

GEORGE GORDON SCOTT.

Avignon, June 22nd, 1871.

CLUMBER CHASE.

CHAPTER I.

THE " MULBERRY-TREE TAVERN " AND ITS FREQUENTERS.

GOOD DAY, Mr. Pepys?"

"Your most obedient, Mr. Evelyn ; glad to see you in London ; thought you were at Sayes Court, getting rid of your troublesome tenant—Old Benbow—for he did tell me, the other day, when he came to the Office, that he, and you, were at issue about the damage done to the plantation."

"Oh! don't speak of it. Heaven defend me from ever having such another destroying angel for a tenant as the Admiral!" *

"Ah!" rejoined Mr. Pepys, with a deprecatory shake of his ambrosial perriwig, which had that very morning been re-curled, preparatory to a dinner he was going to give on the morrow. "Ah! I did tell him he should confine himself

---

* Heaven was apparently deaf to this pious prayer of John Evelyn's, as two reigns after, in William the Third's time, Heaven, or perhaps its Antipodes, sent him the Czar, Peter the Great, who more sweepingly completed the destruction and deterioration which Admiral Benbow had so vigorously begun.

to shivering his *own* timbers, and leave yours alone."

"Are you steering homeward, or going in here?" said John Evelyn, wishing to evade the disagreeable subject of the destruction of his beautifully laid out grounds and infant plantations, as he pointed up to the sign of a mulberry tree, swinging from a house at Charing Cross, under which was the legend of " GEOFFERY TROUTBECK, TAVERNER."

" Well, I have been so fermented by the morning's news, that I *was* going in here to get a dish of the new China drink,* which they do say is marvellously orderly for the nerves, and a great disperser of vapours.   May I offer you a dish too ?"

" Thank you—' *Ce n'est pas de refus,*' as they say over the water.   But I hope the bad news you allude to is nothing that touches you personally ?"

" Well, it do, and it do not.   The Duke of York has gone and married Anne Hyde, my Lord Clarendon's blowsy daughter—or, at least, has just owned his marriage—for they have been married, I believe, some time."

" Whew !" whistled Mr. Evelyn.   " And the King ?"

" Ah ! there's the rub.   It seems, from Sir

* Tea.

Allen Broderick, whom I met hot from White-hall, and who did give me the whole account, that the Chancellor rather over-acted his part of devotion, and loyalty, and all that. When it is well known that, while apparently to the surprise of everyone, either not seeing, or conniving at the Duke's siege to Mistress Anne, he so played his cards as to take right good care that she should not be anything else *but* Duchess of York. Yet, to the King, with the aid of a Pomander and a pocket handkerchief, he brought tears to his eyes, and raved, and vowed, that he could sooner have forgiven his daughter for being mistress to the Duke, than for her presumption, and *lèze majesté*, in making herself sister-in-law to his most sacred majesty!"

" Ha! ha! ha!" laughed Evelyn, with a little low, quiet laugh, and an incredulous shake of the head. " And what did the king say to *that ?*"

" You know he has always wit in his anger, and truly his wit would seem to be a safety valve on all occasions to his displeasure, for at this *too* great self immolation of my Lord Clarendon, a vivid flash as of lightning seemed to burst through the dark clouds of his face, as with a dry, husky laugh he did exclaim—' Oddsfish ! my lord; now, by St. Anthony! are you trenching upon *our* privilege, by proclaiming that you would rather have had your daughter a *quean* than

in a fair way to become a queen;' and he spelt
out the two words.   But, good Lord!" continued
Mr. Pepys, " to see how men will debase themselves!   It almost makes one hearken to the tale
of my Lord Clarendon's maternal granddam
having been a tub woman."

" Nay, for that matter," rejoined Evelyn,
" given an abject and obsequious courtier, and you
will always find far filthier dregs and dross than the
refuse sloppings of fifty generations of tub women
could bestow.   But pray how is Sir Allen Broderick getting on? and how fares the suit of his
son Gilbert with pretty mistress Dorothy Neville?"
added he, as he followed Mr. Pepys into " The
Mulberry Tree."

" Why, as for Sir Allen, his lick of the Bribe
Jar, though it was to the tune of £30,000, I
don't think has serviced him much, as he has
spent double in breaking of the Seventh Commandment; and, good lack ! the sins of the
fathers truly *are* visited upon the children—for
his evil reputation has fallen like a blight upon
poor Master Gilbert, and done him much dis-
favour with pretty Mistress Dorothy, or rather
with her mother—for I verily believe the girl
loves him, though she is obliged to make as if
she didn't.   Madam Neville is so inveterate
against him; and then a nick-name is sure to
stick to a man tighter than his skin, at all events,

closer than his merits ; and his *sobriquet* of Captain Pomander* has certainly *not* advanced his suit."

" But how came he by such a nick-name, for he seems a manly, honest, sensible, fine young fellow, indeed marvellously so, among our Whitehall fungi ?"

" Why, when the poor boy did return from foreign parts two years ago, he had a curious wrought Pomander that he did have recourse to upon all occasions, even in church, as if even the odour of sanctity were too much for his delicate nerves ; and, moreover, he carried in each pocket a miniature flask, or, as the French call it, *flaçon* of Venice glass, cased in a filligree of fine Brindisi goldsmith's work.   One of these contained syrup of jilly flowers, with which he did always admonish his sack, and the other, essence of barberries, with a few drops of which he did chastise his Rhenish."

" Ah ! I see ; the old story ; the best and quickest seed to sow for making enemies and propagating falsehoods and calumnies is to differ in small things from the herd.   When you rob, murder, or in any other way deface the decalogue,

* A Pomander was what would now be called a *Casolette*, or vinaigrette.   It was a gold, or silver, small filigreed apple, with a branch on the top, which turned on a pivot, and when so turned, the apple opened in quarters, each quarter having a perforated top, and containing aromatic vinegar and other perfumes, and was used as a vinaigrette, or smelling bottle.

as Admiral Benbow has done my plantations, it is
by no means absolutely necessary, by way of in-
suring impunity, to wait for darkness, or affect
secresy; but woe! to the rash mortal who, pre-
ferring pepper where custom and conventionality
use sugar, who has so little deference for public
opinion as to pepper openly."

Here Master Troutbeck, in honour of Squire
Evelyn and the Secretary of the Admiralty,
brought in the " China drink" himself, and
curious was its equipage—a large oval, plain
silver teapot, of the flat shaving-pot style, divided
longitudinally across the centre, for the purpose
of making green tea on one side and black on
the other; while on the outside of this machine
—for such it really was—were two long, plain
spouts, like those of a coffee-pot; but in order
that the black and green teas might not pour out
simultaneously, inside was a sort of silver cap
over the opening of each spout, which was pushed
aside with a spoon when the tea was to be poured
through it; and to the end of each spout on the
exterior was suspended by little chains, like an
old Roman lamp, little perforated silver bowls,
or strainers, to catch any stray leaves or twigs,
and prevent their falling into the diminutive
Japan cups—for none other were then known,
save those which had been imported from China
and Japan, with their compatriot the tea. Flank-

ing each cup was a glass of spring water, and in
case that even these should not be sufficient to
neutralise the disagreeable sensation of the new
" drink "—for it and cream and sugar had not
yet met—were also little silver vine leaves, containing slips of lemon peel, citron, quince, and
angelica, and red Guava cheese, as *bonnes bouche*,
such as children are given in the nursery reward
and punishment system, after some nauseous
dose. Having, with a profound obeisance, duly
consulted the taste of his guests as to colour,
and poured out a cup of green for Mr. Evelyn,
and of black for Mr. Pepys, mine host of the
" Mulberry Tree " left his aristocratic customers in
the coffee-room, to attend to his more profitable
ones at the bar.

" Well," said Mr. Pepys, making a fearful
grimace, which graphically exemplified the
triumph of enterprise over taste, as he replaced
his cup in the saucer, and seized a whole handful
of sweetmeats, " well, I cannot say that I do
think that is a drink that anyone will ever become
addicted to."

" I rather think that we don't know how to
prepare it," said Mr. Evelyn, " and that even if
we did, what we get of the shrub in this country
is not worth preparing, for the Chinese get their
tea fresh as they want it out of their gardens, as

wo pluck our salads, as short a time before discussing them as possible."

" Ah ! that may make a difference, certainly," said Mr. Pepys, taking up his empty cup and minutely examining the blue and white beauties of Cathay pourtrayed upon it. " If the China women be really like these," he added, " there can be no need of any one singing ' Beauty Retire ' to them, for it has retired from them with a vengeance."

" Why, yes," smiled his companion, " they certainly are, as you said, Mr. Pepys, of Her Majesty's Portuguese maids of honour, when first they came over—' sufficiently unagreeable.' "

" Young maidens and true lovers all, buy for one halfpenny the fearful tragedy of Arden, of Faversham, who was cruelly murdered in King Harry the Eighth his time, by his wife, dainty Mistress Alice, and her paramour, Swartz Will; and how it was found out by the blood on the rushes in the cedar parlour; and all of a Sunday night!— on which it's wrong to commit murders—and Swartz Will walks to this day, as I hope you may never do," bawled out a ballad seller, in a shrill, yet hoarse, cracked voice.

" *Ciel ! quel hourvari ! quel vacarme infernal !*" cried a Frenchman, rushing out of the street into the coffee-room, with both hands to his ears,

while he was followed more leisurely by another
arrival, who had remained a few seconds in the
street to buy off the ballad seller with a carolus,
and politely request she would lose no time in
decamping, and joining Swartz Will in his perambulations. The first comer was the *chef* of the
royal kitchens, a somewhat recent importation of
the Comte de Grammont, who had given him the
sobriquet of Horace, Marmite de Casserole, the
man's real name being Horace Mérivale Casanove. De Grammont had long in vain tried
to seduce him from his allegiance at Versailles,
till one unlucky day (for him, Louis Quatorze) the
Grand Monarque had stopped short at his seventh
plate of *purée à lá bisque*, and pronounced it decidedly bad. " Ha! ha !" chuckled the treacherous
Count to himself. " *Maintenant je ferais bisquer
Casanove.*" And that very evening he, with *un-*
due emphases and *in*discretion, repeated the
public affront the king had put upon him, asking
if after *that* he would stay where he was not appreciated ? while in England he would be put
upon a par with the *other* courtiers, seeing that
he had a right to wear a sword, which, being interpreted, meant that Monsieur Horace Mérivale
Casanove's great-great-grandfather, having been
one of the Lyons silk weavers, attracted to Paris
by the splendid offers and immunities of Francis
the First, such as living rent free, being exempt

from imprisonment for debt, and above all, being allowed to wear swords, like nobles or military men—Monsieur Horace Mérivale Casanove had resolved to consider the latter privilege hereditary, much regretting he had no power of enforcing the two former ones also. But when De Grammont perorated his arguments by clasping his hands in supplication, and telling the illustrious Casanove that in transferring his talents to White-hall he would be performing a noble act of charity, for the poor king was so scandalously ill fed ; in short, he concluded, " You have seen his portrait, you have noted his dark, saturnine, deeply lined face ; well, *mon cher, c'est le resultat des cauche mars rentrés ! tout çela vient d'une indigestion en permanence, causé par ses exécrables dîners !*" The pity which had hitherto only simmered for his Britannic Majesty now boiled over, and Horace Mérivale Casanove consented, with the air of a Curtius, to immolate himself on the barbaric altars of English culinary fires ; also, *moyennant*, three thousand livres additional salary. The person who followed him into the coffee-room of the " Mulberry Tree" was Monsieur de St. Evermond. Upon seeing him, Casanove removed his hands from his ears, and having adjusted his sword knot, which somehow or other always wanted something doing to it, he made a profound bow to Mr. Evelyn, and then, with a more familiar, not to say patronising air, turned to Mr. Pepys, and said, laying his fore finger at the side of his nose—

"Ah! mon brave Monsieur Pepys! I have no forgot you; I shall send to you to-morrow, *quatre pâlts, à faire venir l'eau à la bouche de Jules Cæsar quand même il est mort.*"

"Thank you; but no garlic, remember, my good sir."

"*Ah! de l'ail fie donc! c'est de la fausse science, toutes ces sauces, qui vous flattent le palais, pour le moment, et vous disent des injures pour vingt quatre heures aprés—non, non*, I have change all dat, as Monsieur St. Evermond here say, when we saw de serviteurs kneel to place de dish on de royal table, he tought it was to ask the king's pardon for give him so bad dinnère. *Ah! pauvre roi, qui mangait tous les jours, et ne dine jamais. Now*, he say to me, Casanove, *you* have made king of me, for now I live, I reign *veritablement, car maintenant je mange en prince!*"

"So that," said Mr. Evelyn, with a smile, "you will go down to posterity as the second king maker in English history."

"Will you try some of this China drink?" said Mr. Pepys.

"*Bah! C'est un bruvage d'apothicaire;* I keep to de *café—Mme. de Sévigné a tort; ni le café, ni Racine passera.*"

Again, the Duke of York's marriage with the Chancellor's daughter came on the tapis. Monsieur de St. Evermond had not heard of it; said it was certainly not known the night before at Whitehall, where there had been a ball, which ended late.

"Very likely," said Pepys; "but I did have it on the best authority an hour ago, from Sir Allen Broderick, who had but then left my Lord Clarendon, upon his return, after breaking the news to the King." And then he did repeat to St. Evermond the scene that had taken place in the royal closet on the occasion, as he had before narrated it to Mr. Evelyn.

"*Ce pauvre duc,*" said St. Evermond. "He *must* be unlike every one else, and more especially unlike his brother. So he is all for the respectable, and the orthodox."

"Was there any new beauty at the court ball last night?" asked Mr. Pepys.

"That was there," rejoined St. Evermond, "the freshest, fairest, prettiest creature I have seen for a long time—positively a fourth grace! and danced—I mean *danced*—and neither floundered, nor romped, as—pardon me for saying it —your English ladies generally do."

"And yet," said Mr. Evelyn, "one would think the *present* Court ladies were sufficiently *light* to dance well; but who was this new beauty?"

"A young Mistress Neville; to see her dance Trenchmore! is enough to make Terpsichore jealous. And she is the only English woman I ever saw who knew *how* to dance the Branles,* which you English *will* call the Brawls, being so fond of brawls, I suppose; but all lights have their shadows, and this brilliant meteor had the densest of shadows, in a mother who never quitted her, and who looked for all the world like an effigy of Elizabeth Cromwell, the *ci-devant* 'Lady Protectress,' cut out of black velvet and buckram."

"I'll wager six pieces of eight," cried Mr. Pepys, "it was pretty Mistress Dorothy herself; but here comes Silas Titus, who will tell us all about it. Good Lord! to think what supple

---

* English French has always been, not to say *is*—not "French of Paris,' but "French of Stratford-atte-Bowe." THE BRANLES was first introduced into England by Anne Boleyn, from the Court of Francis the First. And as its name comes from the verb *ébranler*, to shake, the proverbial expression of "no great shakes," as applied to anything inferior, or below par, had its source from this dance, and was originally restricted to the designation of a bad dancer. Therefore, Gray is doubly wrong, in his lines, in "A Long Story," when he says—

> "Full oft within the spacious walls,
> When he had fifty winters o'er him,
> My grave Lord Keeper led the *brawls*,
> The Seal and Maces danced before him."

For the "grave Lord Keeper," Elizabeth's dancing Chancellor, was Sir Christopher Hatton, who never lived at Stoke Poges Manor—the scene of "A Long Story." On the death of the Earl of Huntingdon, Sir Edward Coke purchased that Manor, and lived there with "the grave Lord Keeper's" termagant widow, whom he married in 1591; but as her far fiercer fires quite quenched the poor COKE, it is not to be wondered at that she should have incised the name of Hatton on the traditions of Stoke.

grooms of the bedchamber those once sturdy rebels make, while an honest man who has never swerved cannot find room even to cool his heels in an ante-room."

"Because he *is* an honest man, perhaps, Mr. Pepys," said Evelyn.

Before he had finished speaking, Silas Titus pushed open the half glass door of the coffee room, his shoulders shaking with an affected half suppressed laugh, and his love locks thrown back upon his fine *point d'Alençon* collar, beneath his broad-leafed feather-bound beaver hat, while against his glitteringly white teeth he gently knocked, as a sort of accompaniment to his laugh, his gold inlaid ebony cane, for having so recently been a bare headed and barefaced Round-head, he was now, of course, upon the strength of his appointment as one of the grooms of the bedchamber, all that was most extreme, and most finikin, in the shape of cavalier coxcombry.

"*Coque fredouille!*" muttered Casanove, with ineffable contempt; for the Republican antecedents of the new courtier were too tough for his own orthodox royalty to render palatable, by any amount of climbing, bred in courts—at least in court kitchens—as Horace Marmite de Casserole had been.

"Oh! oh! what I would give to see the meeting," said Titus, aloud, pressing both hands to his chest, and bending forward, to convey the idea that he was nearly broken in two from convulsions of laughter.

" How now, Master Titus ? We cry halves in the jest, whatever it may be," said Mr. Pepys.

" Odds life ! sirs, you won't be content with half when you hear it. Monsieur de St. Evermond—*je vous baise les mains*. Mr. Evelyn, were I a tree, you should have all my *boughs*. He ! he ! he ! Mr. Pepys, I give you joy. I thought Madam Pepys' beauty could not be mended, but patches *have* mended it ; she *is !*—" And here he gathered the fingers of his right hand to a point, pressed them to his lips, and then opening them wide, and waving his hand from him as if blowing kiss, suddenly stopped, while Mr. Pepys frowned ; but the next minute, passed a very large pocket handkerchief over his face, and swept away the frown, as a notable housemaid would do a cobweb where it was too much *en evidence*. While Silas Titus, turning on his heel, and perceiving Casanove, extended two fingers to him, saying, " Forgive my not seeing you before. You could not suppose I would intentionally overlook a man who rules the roast ? Ho ! Drawer, bring me a flask of Rhenish, that I may drink Monsieur Casanove's health, and wish his Majesty well over it," added he, seating himself, placing his hat upon the table before him, and tossing his gloves into it, as he again exploded in a fit of laughter.

"We would fain share your mirth if we only knew the cause, and lighten your labours in such a great enterprise of laughter," said Mr. Pepys.

"One moment, my dear sir, till I have recruited my strength with a draught of wine, for if sorrow is dry, mirth, on a warm autumnal morning, is a great deal drier."   Having drained a large goblet of wine as soon as it was brought, "Now," continued he, "you shall hear my adventures," which, though they began in the ordinary way with a petticoat, are only likely to end in a panic! "As I was coming down Spring Garden, about a quarter-of-an-hour ago, I saw a closely muffled female figure, that is, with her wimple closely concealing her face, yet evidently watching me. So, thought I, *a bonne fortune*, and none of my seeking either. I stopped. She stopped; but did not attempt to uncover her face. I went on a few steps, but looked back. She was following. Of course I stopped till she came up; and then, taking off my hat and making her a bow, that would have done equally well for a goddess or a duchess, such a happy mixture was it of deference and devotion, I said, ' Madam, you appear to be a stranger in this great city, can I have the happiness of being any service to you?' ' Eh? my fine sir,' said a shrill voice, in a broad Suffolk

accent, throwing back her hood, and discovering
such a wealth of ugliness! as I have seldom seen
monopolised by one face—for her dark red hair
was square-cut, over a very low forehead, still
Nature was merciful in giving her but *one* eye,
which squinted horribly; the very small allowance
of nose she possessed seemed shrinking backwards, as if it felt that it *could* have no chance
against her enormously fat cheeks and high cheek-
bones, or that it feared it might fall into one of
the many pits the smallpox had dug into those
cheeks, while all that her nose had been defrauded
of in size, had been with additional injustice be·
stowed upon her mouth, and then it was that the
voice, so worthy of the portal from whence it
issued, said, 'Eh? my fine sir, will you please
tu point me the way *tu* the Mall, where the King
du walk *tu* o' mornings?' 'And what may you
want with the King, madam?' for as I had began
madaming her before I had seen her, I could not
be so barbarous as to insult her by saying my
pretty maid now that I had done so. 'Eh? I'm
no madam, but just a poor body, sir.' 'Well,
but you don't answer my question; what may
you want with the King' 'Eh, sir? my business
is wi' the King, and none else; so I can tell it to
none else, if I knew it, which I don't, as it's all
written down for the King.' So a petition,
thought I, and sent through so lovely a pleader

it cannot fail of success. ' Show me the paper,' said I, ' and as I often see the King, I will give it to him.' ' Nay, nay, sir! it is all sealed up, and I was to give it with my *own* hand into *his*, and to do that I was to find him on the Mall.' ' Well, just let me see the outside of the packet ?' ' No, sir, that's ag'in' my orders, and I durst not *du* it; because the quality knows about each other by what they calls their great coats of arms, and if you seen them you'd know who it come from, and no one was *tu du that* but the King.' I thought to myself, with all your apparent sim- plicity, you are as cunning as a six-year-old fox !"

" Nay, for that matter," put in Mr. Evelyn, " thorough and incorruptible honesty, which this poor girl seems to have had, will outwit the most complex cunning any day, just because all cun- ning is shifty, while integrity is immovable."

" Well," resumed Titus, " I thought I'd try her with a golden key, and offered her two pieces of eight, which she refused.   ' I don't want your money, sir; I only want you *tu* tell me the way *tu* the Mall, and how I shall know the king."

" Good lack," interposed Mr. Pepys, " I wonder you did not offer to go with her to see the end of the play."

" No, thank you; I have no fancy for losing my place so soon. The king would have fancied

that I had had the impertinence to preach him an
incarnate sermon before his whole court, taking
for my text—

> " ' Vice is a monster of such hideous mien
> That to be hated needs but to be seen.'

" For as my Inamorata of the black wimple is
evidently an agent acting for someone else, she
may by poetical license be called 'a Vice,' so,
keeping out of the scrape, I gave a hackney
coachman a double fare, seeing he would have no
fair in her, to convey her safely to the entrance
of the Mall; but still, she had a last word with
me. 'Eh! sir,' stretching half out of the window,
as the vehicle was about to rumble off, ' will you
give me a sign like, by which I shall know the
king when I *du* see him?' 'Well, he is a tall,
very dark gentleman; perhaps with a mallet in
his hand, for he is fond of playing at pell mell;
but you'll know him chiefly by all the dogs and
dogesses by which he is always surrounded.'
And at last, amid the grins of the bystanders, and
the winks of the coachman, I despatched this
nymph of the mysterious mission, never having
been so cruelly taken in before."

" Poor soul! I hope she may succeed in her
suit," said Mr. Evelyn.

" I wonder what it is?" queried Mr. Pepys,
biting his nails, as was his wont when perplexed;
"but I dare say I shall find out from the Duke of

York or Lady Jem.   And now tell us, Master Titus, as you were at the Court ball last night, was pretty Mistress Dorothy Neville there ?"

" That was she; and *the* event of the evening, first, from her real, downright, indisputable beauty, and next because she was new, quite new, as it was the first time Madame Neville had allowed her—and that not without unremitting *surveillance*—to breathe what I have no doubt she would call ' that polluted atmosphere.' "

" And was young Gilbert Broderick there ?"

" Gilbert Broderick ! no.   Don't you know that his amiable father, Sir Allen, who is as jealous of him as the deuce—I don't mean with Dorothy Neville, though I dare say he is that too—but with his rich old maiden sister, with whom he is at daggers drawn, and fears she may make Gilbert her heir; and as she is fond of pretty Dorothy, being an old friend of her mother's, Sir Allen is so full of spite and all other meannesses himself, that he feared his sister might be tempted, in order to vex him, to come up from the country for this ball, to smooth matters for Gilbert with Madame Neville; so to mar the plot (if plot there were), he packed poor Gilbert off to Ireland a fortnight ago, as a sort of honorary aide-de-camp to Sir Edward Massy, so that he could not possibly be back till full a week after this ball was over."

" What! is Sir Edward Massy gone to Ireland in any official capacity ?" asked Mr. Evelyn.

" Why, have you not heard that he has vacated his seat for Gloucestershire, and has got some appointment worth a thousand a year in Ireland, and I have no doubt will terminate in a coronet, like so many others."

" Well, in some sort he deserves it, for he has done good service to the royal cause, and they have been honourable services, too," said Mr. Pepys.

" Then," said Evelyn, " he will be one of the exceptions that prove the rule ; for in all times, but more especially in ours, peerages seem to be almost exclusively kept as the rewards for public or private profligacy, or political pliancy; for which reason, I cannot conceive an honest man having anything but an insurmountable horror of what is called public life, seeing what a tortuous, immund cesspool it is, and knowing that in all things—

> ' Our nature is subdued to what it works in,
> Like the dyer's hand.' "

Mr. Pepys, whose prudent face twitched nervously, thinking Mr. Evelyn's opinion as to state patronage was a little too plainly expressed in the now courtly hearing of the ex-Roundhead.

Mr. Silas Titus said, addressing himself to the latter—

" Dear ! dear ! I am sorry for poor Master Gilbert and pretty Mistress Dorothy.   I fear between father on the one side, and mother on the other, there is but little happiness in store for them."

" Happiness—bah !" cried St. Evermond ; " there is no such thing as happiness, or if there is, it is like Lady Castlemaine's dress, which begins too late, and ends too soon."*

" Ah, Monsieur de St. Evermond, *a toujours le mot pour rire*," laughed Casanove.

" But seriously," asked Mr. Pepys of Titus, " seeing Sir Allen Broderick's interest not only with the king, but his position about the Chancellor, don't you think he'll do something for poor Master Gilbert, beyond smuggling him out of the reach of his aunt's and Mistress Dorothy's favour ?"

" Not he, the old flint steeped in pitch ; *proximus sum egomet mihi* is decidedly his motto."

" Good Lord ! to think that men can be without bowels, in this way, for their own kith and kin ; but Master Gilbert has great parts, and I should say double the nouse of his father, for I have seen some of his composures, poetical and other, and I've no doubt he'll be to the fore yet."

" Don't believe it," said Mr. Evelyn, shaking his head."

* For it *was* St. Evermond who said this *àpropos* of Lady Castlemaine's *décolletée* dress, two centuries before Talleyrand, who for another century to come will, no doubt, continue to be accredited with all this sort of *mots ; vu, qu'on ne prete qu'aux riches.*

"Truly," said Pliny the younger; "no man possesses a genius so commanding as to be able to rise in the world, unless these means are afforded him,—opportunity, and a friend to promote his advancement."

"And as for poetry, even when of the highest order, what chance has that sort of genius against the world, the flesh, and the devil, when they are let slip to hunt it? for have we not lived to see John Milton, when he prudently concealed himself till the persecutions against him had abated, advertised for, in 'The Whitehall Gazette,' as '*an obscure fellow, one Milton, late of Barbicon, who is wanted of the law officers, by reason of his treasonable and blasphemous writings against his late most sacred Majesty, and on account of the paltry fellow's own insignificance, we give the following description of his person,' &c., &c.* And as for poetry, I do not think our present manners likely to produce any worthy the name; for as John Milton truly says, ' to write a fine poem, we must *live* a fine poem.' "

" Ah!—Milton—Milton," said Silas Titus, twirling his moustache, " that's the fellow who wrote the ' Iconoclastes,' in answer to the ' Icon Basilike.' Never read it. I mean the ' Iconoclastes;'—all I remember is what Hobbs said of his answer to Salmasius' ' Defensio Regio,' which was that he (Hobbs) did not know whose style was best, or whose arguments were worst.   He! he! he!"

"I should have thought," said Mr. Evelyn, with more sternness and more sarcasm than he was won't to indulge in, "that you might have known a great deal more about John Milton when he was Latin Secretary to the Protector."

"*Pergo ad alios, Venio ad alios, deidne ad alios, Una res,*" muttered St. Evermond, in a low voice only heard by Mr. Evelyn.

"Yes—that is about it," smiled the latter, and then added, taking out his watch, "Gentlemen, I must wish you all good-day, as I must be going, it being our audit day at the Hospital;* I shall be only just in time to take water at Whitehall stairs."

And soon after his departure, the rest of the party then and there assembled, separated, and went their different ways.

* He was treasurer of Greenwich Hospital.

CHAPTER II.

ADAM NEVILLE, the mother of pretty Mistress Dorothy, who had made so brilliant a *début* at the Court ball—according to the unanimous verdict of the three C.C.C.'s—critics, courtiers, and cavaliers—had been a widow—a rich one—for ten years, and therefore beset with many suitors. But she was an eminently practical and sensible woman, the rule of whose life in all things was *to let well alone;* moreover, she was a truly pious woman, and would as soon have thought of committing suicide as of tempting Providence (with her eyes open and her wits sharpened upon the whetstone of experience) by contracting a second marriage. "No, no," she was never tired of observing to all who urged her on the subject, whether the gossips of her own sex or the gallants of the other—"No, no; there is a Spanish proverb which averreth that ' Fate sends almonds to those who have no teeth,' meaning that Fortune never comes with both hands full, for which

reason she seldom sends weeds, except to those
who are too old to enjoy their freedom. I was
young and ignorant, and full of hope, and every
other whipped froth vanity—as young people
ever were, and ever will be—when I gave my
heart to Rupert Neville, for a plaything to batter
about as he pleased, and he soon taught me that
SELF is the only idol that men are never tired
of worshipping, or of sacrificing to ; and yet he
was by no means one of the worst, as his *words*
were always velvet, had he been only minded to
make his actions follow suit. He was not one
of your pompous household tyrants either, puffed
up with grandity, till he conceited himself a sort
of cross between King Solomon and the angels,
that a wife should always approach kneeling (if
not actually on her bodily knees, at least with
spiritual genuflections), such as fell to the lot of
my poor friend, Mary Powell, in Mr. Milton, or
else I should have run away home before the end
of the first month, as she did, poor soul, gloomed
and grumped to death."

Elizabeth Cromwell—the some time " Lady
Protectress"—had also in early life, during the
Sheepscote days of the first Mistress Milton,
been a great friend of Madam Neville's, which
friendship or intercourse (which in so many cases
is the world's synonyme for friendship), had continued up to the revolution, when not only all

the Nevilles, being staunch Royalists, but likewise Madam Neville's father, Sir Charles Wheeler, who, after the restoration, was not made Master of the Rolls, as he was promised, but had to content himself with being made a Privy Councillor and Governor of Nevis. It was, of course, utterly impossible that such an intercourse could continue between the wife of the Protector and the daughter and wife of two such devoted Royalists. But, indeed, without even the interposition of such political earthquakes as revolutions, time and marriage are sad destroyers of early friendships ; and so Margaret Neville had found, for one after another, some blight, or some change, had fallen upon most of her youthful *liaisons*, one of the most cherished and enduring of which had been with Mistress Broderick, Sir Allen's sister, and Gilbert's aunt; but that selfish kill-joy, Sir Allen, having set his face against his son's marriage with Dorothy Neville, wholly and solely on account of the money he would have to disburse for the establishment of the young people, poor Dorothy was no longer allowed to pass weeks with her mother's old friend, Mistress Broderick, at her beautiful seat, Clumber Chase ; nor could Madam Neville's proper pride, or rather self-respect, in no longer allowing her to do so, be in any way reprehended, as she naturally considered her beautiful daugh-

ter a fitting match for far greater *partis* than Sir
Allen Broderick's son ; as, exclusive of her beauty
and a *dot* of ten thousand pounds (at that time
considered a good fortune), she would at her
mother's death, come into that charming place,
THE CHESTNUTS, two miles beyond Richmond,
on the Surrey side, worth a clear thousand pounds
per annum, as well as her house on Birdcage
Walk, overlooking the Mall.   The Chestnuts
was a gem in its way, for it was Madam Neville's
hobby, and kept up with a microscopic attention
to detail, that set off its every advantage.   The
house was an old Tudor house, with a flight of
steps, and a marbled balustraded terrace, branch-
ing off on each side of the lower step of this
flight.   In the large entrance hall, with its
armour, and its mullion windows, and deep window seats, was, in the centre, the immensely
wide polished oak Henry the Seventh staircase,
with banisters two feet broad, and thick tor-
sades, at least three quarters of a yard in diameter, while round this hall ran a covered gallery,
with lattice windows looking down into the hall.
But the grounds—it was, with their velvet lawns,
their plaisaunces, and their square fishponds, and
above all, their long covered galleries of closely
clipped hawthorn, with spaces at symmetrical in-
tervals cut in the sides, like unglazed windows,
such as are still to be seen in the Pope's gardens

and in many other Italian gardens, which constituted the chief attraction of The Chestnuts (so called from an avenue of Spanish chestnuts, a mile and a half long, which led from the lodge to the house), for despite the close clipping of these *charmilles*, or verdant galleries, the hawthorne was still so redundant, and in its own sweet month of May so fragrant, that the nightingales never failed to hold their concerts there; add to which, these fragrant galleries, alike impervious to the hottest sun and the heaviest rains, led down to the river side, where was another marble balustraded terrace, the white steps in the centre of which descended into the water, like those of a Venetian Palazzo, and were ever laved by—

" The gentle ripple of the silver tide."

Dorothy doated upon The Chestnuts—not altogether for the dainty greenery of its plaisaunces, and its affluence of those gorgeously rich old-fashioned flowers, now alas ! chiefly banished to cottage gardens, and remote manor houses, which, like the descendants of their original owners, have gone down in the world, and degenerated into farm houses. Flowers, not only rich to regality in their colouring and prodigality of bloom, but in their spicey, generous, oriental perfume, such as those colossal double

gilly flowers, bowed down as it were by their
rich regalia of ruby flowers, and their delicious
spiced Burgundy odour, which one is *sure must*
make the bees reel when they quaff it! Then
the gentle, suave, almost caressing breath, like a
fairy's kiss, of the delicate green and violet velvet
auriculas, cosily hiding in their lowly sphere
beneath the diffusive prodigalities of large crimson damask, and faintly tinted blush-roses, with
great purple larkspurs coquetting between *them*,
and massive double clove pinks, and variegated
carnations almost as large as garden poppies, or
ribbon *pompoms*, to say nothing of those floral
common people, the humble vassal wall-flowers,
who do their fragrant faithful service in rough,
ungenial seasons, when their patrician superiors
would be afraid to put forth the tiniest tip of
their buds. Yet, much as she loved them, and
carefully as she tended them one and all, it was
not exclusively these that made Dorothy Neville
so fond of The Chestnuts, but perhaps because it
was *there* that Gilbert Broderick had first told her
he loved her; and also, perhaps, because of the
broad river, that silent highway by which all his
Majesty's liege subjects were free to travel—for
though there were a few locks, there were no
keys to exclude them from *that*. Then, too, on
summer nights, so wonderful were the nightingales in their vocalisation, that Dorothy, as she

sat at her casement and listened to them, had on
more than one occasion almost fancied she heard
words to their songs!   But, as for London, oh !
how she hated it—for, in the first place, it was
there that Sir Allen Broderick had first discovered,
and then issued his veto against his son's suit—
and there is an inherent justice (?) in human
nature which always makes us cordially detest
any place wherein we have suffered, or where any
exceptionally untoward event may have befallen
us, the said inherent justice always prompting us
to condemn the innocent place as an accessory
after the fact.   Then, as for its amusements,
even had she cared about them, it was but very
sparingly she was allowed to enter into them, for
staunch royalist as Madam Neville was, she was
truly, and not without reason, unaffectedly horrified at the degenerate and disorderly court the
Restoration had given them ; and never, with her
consent, would either she, and still less her
daughter, have crossed the threshold of Whitehall. But what are women's feelings, or women's
principles, still less their prejudices, when
weighed in the scale against the worldly interests
of the men of the family, or at least what the
men of a family imagine to be their interests ?
And that fierce old cavalier, Sir Charles, her
father, chafed and disappointed as he was at the
pie-crust promises he had received in return for

the battles he had fought, and the blood he had shed in the royal cause, was yet an assiduous courtier; and though the King could in silence, and with unruffled equanimity, have supported Madam Neville's absence from court, having heard of the beauty of Dorothy, he thought fit to honour Sir Charles with a gracious complaint of his daughter and grand-daughter's non-appearance at Whitehall, and a request that it might not continue, so that the old cavalier had laid his commands upon his daughter that she should take Dorothy to the before-mentioned ball; and as Gilbert Broderick had been sent by his father on a wild-goose chase to Ireland with Sir Edward Massy, Madam Neville thought she could not take a less objectionable opportunity for making the, to her, great sacrifice of letting her daughter appear at court.

As for poor Dorothy, knowing that the salt sea waves were rolling between her and Gilbert, her reluctance to the proceeding was almost as great as her mother's; but once amid the blaze of countless wax-lights, magnificent jewels, and the cynosure of admiring eyes, she would have belied her age and sex had she not felt a glow of pleasurable triumph, to say nothing of a certain pardonable vanity of attire: for is not a pretty girl's *first* ball dress beauty's coronation robes? Hers was of the purest white, and most gossamer gauze, over the richest and softest white satin, such as Lely delighted to paint, and as he alone *could* paint; while her *berthe* was entirely of pearls, seamed down the front and back, and on each shoulder, with two rows of fine emeralds—heirlooms in the Neville family. Her luxuriant, burnished chestnut hair, worn *à la Ninon*, as the charming fashion then was, making a perfect Greek cap of richly platted hair at the back of her head, while the light tendril-like ringlets on her forehead, as she gracefully glided through Trenchmore, or bounded in a La Volta, showed, as it caught each changing light, the ripple of gold that ran through the dark sheen of her hair. If she danced her best, and looked her brightest, it was not from the novelty and exhilaration of the scene, and, still less, from the openly expressed as well as whispered admiration that floated round her like an atmosphere. No, of course not; it was only that Gilbert might hear of her, and that his father might see her. Poor child! while she *looked* the very incarnation of all that was joyous and bright, how often she sighed and wished she could have been either in the cool *Charmilles*, at The Chestnuts, or with Gilbert's kind aunt Broderick at Clumber Chase. "Ah!" she thought, "should she ever be *there* again?" And yet, why not? for the kind old lady would not accept this compulsory separation,

caused by her brother's selfish tyranny, as an *es-
trangement*, for she was continually sending her
favourite Dorothy little *souvenirs*, and gifts, books,
confections, distilled waters, conserves of violets,
puptons of quince, marchpane, and all the other
thousand housewifery notabilities that constituted
" Woman's Mission " in those days.

This court ball had flashed like a bright ex-
ceptional meteor, athwart the gloomy monotony
of her now disinherited existence, leaving nothing
but weariness and exhaustion after it. Madam
Neville was cat-like in her stay-at-home propensi-
ties,—like all her contemporaries, she was " cumbered about much serving ;" for all ladies at that
time, even the greatest, were their own house-
keepers ;—not but what she had a very able
deputy, or coadjutor, in her tire woman Rachel
Ruffle—indeed so able, both as to temper and
talents, that she rather ruled Madam Neville with
a rod of iron.   But so equitably and beautifully
graduated is the eternal fitness of things in this
not so bad as it might be, nor so good as it ought
to be world, that in her turn Rachel Ruffle had to
succumb to a reign of terror of her own, in the
person of Bridget Butson, the cook. But though
this *divide et Emperi régime* took up a great deal
of Madam Neville's time, it by no means so
thoroughly engrossed it as to prevent her going
more frequently from home, had she had the in-

clination to do so ; yet she felt that at Dorothy's age it was not fair to debar her from " *The diversions of the Town.*" So she cast about how to combine pleasure with prudence, and was not long in hitting upon a happy expedient, for it so chanced that a worthy gentleman, one Master Oliver Hartsfoot. between whom and herself, in early youth, there had been some love passages, in which he experienced so sad a defeat, it had left him a confirmed bachelor and book worm. Now, as was before mentioned, Madam Neville was a thoroughly sensible, practical woman; so she soon came to the conclusion of what was the use of a sacrificed love, if it could not be converted into a self-sacrificing friendship? And as Master Hartsfoot most conveniently lived at a stone's throw from her own house on the Bird Cage Walk, for he occupied one of those small dingy tenements at what is now called " Storey's Gate," but at that time went by the name of FUNNY JOE'S CORNER, in honour of Joe Collins, of Oxford, the staunch royalist, who had been the concoctor and perpetrator of all the ghostocracy and demonology at Woodstock, which so frightened the belligerent Roundeads, though Joe took good care not to have his authorship of this supernatural opera even suspected till after the restoration, when he triumphantly owned to having been the *deus ex machinâ* of all this devilry,—and as he lived in one of the houses, the place was named after him, though he is no longer "famous in *storey*."

Well, in another of these houses also lived Master Oliver Hartsfoot, bibliomaniac, antiquary, and philosopher, with his cat Slut, his serving man, Noah Pump, and his housekeeper, Alice Merrypin. Now, just a year after the commencement of this history, Madam Neville resolved to utilise all Master Hartsfoot's wisdom, learning, and other virtues, so long stagnant, and lying dormant among books, parchments, Antideluvian pottery, brainless skulls, and marrowless bones; and no sooner decided upon than done. So calling for her wimple, fan, gloves, and a Seville orange, stuck full of cloves against back street smells, the widow sallied forth to Funny Joe's Corner. It was noon when Madam Neville arrived at her quondam rejected suitor's door, and at the same moment appeared Noah Pump coming up from Westminster, from "The Royal Martyr Tavern," where he had been to have the sack jar replenished for his master's dinner; it was exactly like those then in use for the reception of the same cordial beverage, being of white glazed earthenware, with blue borders round it, and the date of the year of its fabrication, in blue figures, on its globular centre, but like everything else in Oliver Hartsfoot's house, it

was an antique, and bore the date of 1458, as will
be seen by the following sketch :—

Noah doffed his purple woollen mushroom-
shaped cap deferentially to Madam Neville, but
not without a slight look and gesture of irrepressible surprise at seeing her not only stopping
at his master's door, but with her hand actually
upon the knocker.

"Good day, Noah Pump," said she, affably ;
" I do not ask if your master is within, as I fear
I have come just at his dinner hour; but if so,
pray tell him I am in no hurry, and can wait till
he has done."

Now, Noah Pump, who was a foster-brother,
as well as a servitor of Master Hartsfoot, and
had lived with him nearly all his life, was so far
initiated into things of the past, as to know
pretty well how matters had once stood between
his master and Madam Neville, and consequently

upon seeing her about voluntarily to franchise the wide gulf of years and invade his master's privacy, he fell into almost as great a tremor and fit of awkwardness as Master Hartsfoot could himself at this unexpected apparition of the still blooming, but erst cruel widow, and it was a second or two before he could stammer out, "Yes—no— that is—I—I'll let him know ; but won't your honor's ladyship walk in ?" and as he spoke, or rather stuttered, he inserted the key in the hall door, and pushed it wide open to let the lady pass.

"Thanks, good Master Pump ; but knowing the store your master sets by his books, and papers, and curiosities, I'll wait in the entry till he has finished dinner."

"No—never ! Surely, Madam Neville, *that* mustn't be ; there ain't no papers, nor books, nor other rubbish in the Cedar parlour, for *that's* kept o' purpose for the Quality, and is furnished Christian-like, with all the beautiful Chevey Chase chairs, as master's mother worked afore he wor borned."

But as the widow resisted even the Christian-like attractions of the Cedar parlour, and reiterated her intention of remaining in the hall— hearing Noah Pump's voice in words of persuasion, to which his vocal organization was by no means attuned in unison, and another, and not

yet forgotten voice, refusing—as it ever had been
—to *be* persuaded, the dining-room door, which
was opposite the street door, suddenly opened,
and Master Hartsfoot, napkin in hand, appeared
at it. He was still a comely, and very benevo-
lent looking man of forty-five ; he wore his own
fair hair parted down the centre, and flowing in
natural curls upon his shoulders ; all his features
were well and clearly cut, and were (that great
secret of all beauty next to expression) remarkably harmonious, his eyes being of the very
darkest hazel, and decidedly handsome, and
though usually pale, he retained one silly habit
of his youth—that of blushing like a girl on any
excitement or emotion. His black dress was so
plain, especially surmounted as it was by a large
plain linen Charles the First falling collar, with
cords and tassels, that it might have appeared
Puritanical, but for the fine texture of its cloth,
and the profusion of rich Venetian black silk
tufts and buttons with which it was ornamented,
and his knee and shoe string tags being both of
highly polished and cut jet, gave, as he moved,
an occasional radiant flash to all this darkness.
No sooner had he perceived *who* his visitor was
(to borrow Noah Pump's words in afterwards
describing the scene to Alice Merrypin), " than
he fell back in a sort of sound-like on a chair by

the side of the dining-room door, as one struck all of a heap."

Not so Madam Neville ; she advanced with all possible alacrity, holding out both her hands, as she said, with a little laugh, half hysterical, half affected, " Good Master Hartsfoot, we are such near neighbours, that we ought not to continue strangers ; and—and, in fact, I am come a begging, for I have a favour—a *great* favour to ask you !"

Master Hartsfoot tried to reply that whatever it might be the favour was granted ; but he tried in vain, for his tongue seemed to have followed the example of his limbs, and he might have fainted outright had not Noah, with great presence of mind, put down the sack, and poured his master out a glass of water, which after he had drank, he was still beholden to the Pump, who led him to the table and pressed him down into his former chair, after which humane gymnastic, the faithful servitor discreetly left the room, closing the door after him, and muttering on his way down to Alice Merrypin's dominions—

" All the world over, two's company and three's none."

So inveterately archæological were Oliver Hartsfoot's tastes that he disdained even the use of modern plates, dishes, or glasses, so that his table presented a really rare, and what in these days would be an invaluable, collection of *Henri Deux* ware, curious old Venetian and German glass, and quaint-shaped flagons, and cups of massive, though somewhat barbaric twelfth-century parcel gilt plate, with enormous gilt chargers and gossip dishes of the same, on his sideboard. Modern forks, as they had then been recently introduced from Italy, found no place at his table, but he had recourse to the assistance of those small Edward the Third forks, no larger, and very like, our nineteenth century pickle forks, only they had but two wide apart prongs, and looked strangely incongruous, flanked by the massive, yet squat Evangelist spoons. Having graciously praised a dish of very fine scallops, dressed with cream, tarragon, and other fine herbs, a *plât* for which Alice Merrypin was famous, and of which even Monsieur Casanove might have died of envy, Madam Neville turned on poor Master Hartsfoot the full blaze of one of her most radiant smiles, as she drew a chair and seated herself three-corner-wise, partly opposite, and partly beside him, saying—

"Now, Master Hartsfoot, if you do not go on with your dinner, just as if I was not here, I shall return home without proffering my request, and saying all I came to say."

Great as the bribe was on the one hand, and

terrible as the threat was on the other, strange
to say, either failed to reassure Master Hartsfoot,
who was becoming visibly more tremulous and
confused ; indeed, so little did he know what he
was about, that when his downcast eyes *did* perceive the napkin in his hand, he was seized with
the overwhelming delusion that his shirt was obtruding itself *en evidence*, and with one nervous
clutch hastily thrust this *serviette incomprise* into
his bosom, but " still they came," at least, he
thought so, as with another desperate effort he
clutched the table cloth, and would have banished
it to the same limbo by one vigorous cram, and
so demolished all his splendid *Henri Deux* ware
and Venice glass, had not the widow, quick as
lightning, not only placed both hands upon the
table, but lent against it, as she exclaimed—

"Take care, Master Hartsfoot ; you'll pull
down all the dinner things !"

Whereupon, as suddenly as he had a minute
before grasped it, he released his hold of the
table cloth, but flushed into such a vivid crimson,
that Madam Neville, cool as a cucumber, and
really pitying the poor man, resumed her seat,
and gently fanning herself, said, in a languidly
drawling voice, as if merely continuing some
ordinary and common-place conversation that had
received no interruption—

" La ! how pretty the orange tips of those scallops look. My Seville orange looks quite dingy beside them. The whole dish looks so tempting that I must ask your cook for the receipt."

The spell was broken, as she intended it should be, and Oliver Hartsfoot, recalled to the duties of hospitality, asked if she would not taste the scallops ?

" Oh ! with pleasure."

And as she studiously kept her eyes on her plate while discussing them, Master Hartsfoot, in due course, recovered his cruelly scared self-possession, more especially as his nervous movements were accompanied by a faint chink not unlike what fairy cattle bells might be supposed, caused by the jet tags of the bunches of ribbon at his knees, and the jet tassels terminating his shoe rosettes, as ever and anon he rose to get her bread, or pour her out wine, or perform some other hospitable office, till *vi et armis*, for she laid one of her hands upon each of his wrists, she pressed him down into his chair, and again declared she would go if he did not continue his dinner; and as he at length obeyed her, she opened her mission, by first dropping her voice to the very lowest cadence of confidential communication, as if the room had been filled with obtrusive listeners, and informing him of the tyrannical and parsimonious conduct of Sir Allen Broderick, and consequently how the suit of Master Gilbert to Dorothy had been broken off. "And what grieves me more," added she, "all intercourse for the present, at least, suspended between me and my good old friend of Clumber Chase, lest her detestable brother should suppose that we were as mean as himself, and that my Dorothy and his son met there."

"Poor young people," retrospectively and sympathetically sighed Master Hartsfoot, and then added, "I know nothing whatever of the young gentleman, *pro* or *con*, but I meet Sir Allen constantly at Garway's, the Greek tea house, in Exchange Alley, and in Paul's Chain, and a more pompous, over-bearing man, I never did meet; which is, indeed, his general character, for all say that he only lives for himself, and thinks the world wide enough for none other, even his nearest of kin, but has a veneer of worldly wisdom, or rather base hypocrisy, which ever makes him act upon the advice of Hamlet, Prince of Denmark, as Will Shakespeare puts it, and causes him to ' assume a virtue, if he has it not.' But how can *I* aid you, my good lady, in such a matter?"

"It is not exactly in that matter," rejoined the widow, coming to the point, "but—but—I need not tell you that our present court is anything but what we had hoped or expected."

"Truly," muttered Master Hartsfoot, simultaneously throwing up his hands and eyes, as if they had been moved by a spring.

" Indeed," continued Madam Neville, " though it is a thing I would not breathe out of this room, or own to anyone but you, the Protector's, with all its coarseness and all its roughness, including his filthy practical jokes, was worth a dozen of it."

" Yea—verily ! a baker's dozen."

" But," she resumed, "though the Court, as it is, is out of the question for my Dorothy, yet, dear heart ! it seems cruel, too, to debar a young creature from the diversions of the town, which I have neither time nor spirits to enter into ; and there is no one, even of my own sex, now that things are as they are between us and our good friend Mistress Broderick, that I could with a clear conscience, and quiet heart, intrust my dear Thea to—but you—dear good Master Hartsfoot." And here the lady paused for a moment, closed her eyes, and vigorously inhaled the cloves in her extemporised pomander, the Seville orange, as much to give poor Master Hartsfoot breathing time as herself before she added—opening her eyes suddenly to their fullest extent, and aiming them full at Master Oliver, with a large legible placard that said plainly " There's no compulsion, only you *must*," with a protocol, in her most dulcet accents, and a gentle clasping of her hands—"Now, dear Master Hartsfoot, if you *would* take her occasionally to the playhouse, the puppet show, Vauxhall, the Mulberry Garden, or Mary la Bonne, or by water, when there are French horns, theorbos, and viols, on the river, I should be so vastly indebted to you."

Had a thunder bolt suddenly burst through the ceiling, and, after pulverising his *Henri Deux* ware, Venice glass, and Richard the Second plate, requested him to be its partner in the BRANLES; or had an earthquake invited him to mount its wave, and without waiting for whip or spurs, take a canter to the other side of the equator, it is doubtful whether poor Master Hartsfoot *could* have felt more utterly astounded, dumbfounded, and flabbergasted than he did by Madam Neville's friendly and modest little request, for already did he feel incipient nausea at the Playhouse, odours of sawdust, lamp oil, and orange peel, and, with an internal groan, wish that when Lord Buckhurst removed Nell Gwynne from that sphere of action, he had at the same time exterminated all the other orange girls. Already did he in imagination feel blinded by the lamps and flambeaux at Vauxhall, and labour under a permanent attack of deafness from viols and theorbos, while hopelessly gored between complex dilemmas of French and other horns. But Madam Neville, having once seized, never relinquished her prey, and gently placing her hand upon his, said, still looking into his face, so as to cut off his retreat on every side—

" But you *will*, won't you, good Master Hartsfoot ?" With the weak and the overpowered, though it is a letter longer, ' Yes ' is always an easier monosyllable to pronounce than ' No,' and accordingly the poor springed, vanquished, utterly defenceless archæologist, uttered a faint ' Yes,' only adding much more energetically, this being a last struggle as it were to get free of the meshes, " that he feared he should be but dull company for the young lady."

" It's not for company," said the widow, re-assuringly, " it's for safety, respectability, and —and—for convenience. You need never open your lips, and I'll tell Dorothy never to speak to you, so that I'm sure you will be most agreeable and comfortable together."

And with such an assurance of extenuating circumstances, Madam Neville rose to depart, in order to leave the poor condemned, if not to digest his dinner, which her advent and its result rendered almost impossible, at least to digest her proposition, and his promise, and its consequences. He led her to the street door in silence and sadness, he bowed over the hand she offered him repeatedly and profoundly ; but word spoke he none. He watched her till out of sight, and

then, returning to the dining-room, he sank down
into a chair, faintly groaning, " The Lord be
good to me ;" and there sat, so long and so
silently, that Noah Pump at length came unsum-
moned to ask if his master had not rang. It is
but justice, however, to Oliver Hartsfoot to state,
that from that out he religiously fulfilled his
extorted promise— even to sending Madam
Neville every morning a list of the *Diversions of
the Town*, to know which Mistress Dorothy would
select for the day's or evening's programme ; and
he grew so fond of his charge, that his fetters
daily became less galling, though it is at the
same time quite certain that, before he was six
months older, poor Master Hartsfoot had anticipated the late Sir Cornewall Lewis some two
hundred years, and was most decidedly of opinion
" that life *would* be very tolerable if it were not
for its *pleasures !*"

CHAPTER III.

IT was about two years after Oliver Hartsfoot had been broken to harness as *Cavaliero Cervante* to pretty Dorothy Neville, that, taking his matutinal walk through Westminster Hall, to pick up any crumbs of news that might have fallen from the *Quidnuncs* who haunted it, that he encountered Mr. Pepys, not looking so *debonnaire*, and thoroughly contented as usual; but, indeed, quite the contrary, as if the times, like his wig, were all awry. Master Hartsfoot, nevertheless, resolved to join him, as not being only the very epitome of news from court, camp, and city, but also a perfect *catalogue raisonné* of all the diversions of the town.

" Your servant, Mr. Pepys," said Oliver, with a low bow.

" Good day, Master Hartsfoot? I saw you t'other evening at the Duke's house, with pretty Mistress Dorothy Neville. I did feel truly sorry for her and young Gilbert Broderick, and, indeed, at the time did tell my wife to write and condole with her, which she did; but, good Lord! the letter was so false spelt, and out of grammar, that I was ashamed of it, and would not let her send it.   I do wish I could propound another, and a better match, for pretty Mistress Dorothy, if it was only to spite Sir Allen."

"I don't think she would accept the best match in England, for she's not one of your light o' loves," said Master Oliver.

"Tush!" quoth Mr. Pepys, "I do conceit, Master Hartsfoot, that these altering of resolves and shifting of inclinations, have less to do with light of love, than weight of fate.   We all do know how, in Queen Mary's time, that competent man and honourable person, Master Thomas Wotton, the father of his more noteworthy son, Sir Henry Wotton, did in this very Hall of Westminster—and mayhap, in the very steps we are now treading—meet the overthrow of all his high resolves, that if he did ever enter into a second marriage, there were three sorts of persons he was steadfastly minded to avoid, notably—

> 'Those that had children;
> Those that had law suits;
> And those that were his kindred.'

And yet, following a law-suit of his own, in this

very Westminster Hall, what did fate, but set
up a stumbling block in his way, of fair red and
white snares, in the comely proportions of Dame
Elionora Morton, relict of Master Robert Morton,
an esquire, of Kent, herself engaged in several
suits of law ; and it was the observing of her
comportment in hearing one of her causes before
the judges, that Dan Cupid mixed up the oldest
and most potent of his filtres—compounded of
beauty, tears, and pity—and so, treacherously
overcame poor Master Thomas and all his wise
resolves, that soon he did find himself with another suit on his hands—his own to the Widow
Morton.   So that long before the judges had decided his law suit, he had gained his love suit,
and had undertaken not only the supportation of
Dame Elionora, but of Dame Elionora's children, and of Dame Elionora's law-suits.   Go to !
—Master Hartsfoot, it's one of the most frequent
and most scurvy tricks of fate, to give us the lie
whenever we do throw up fortifications of impregnable resolves round our hearts.

"But," continued Mr. Pepys, "that's the way
with young folks; *never*, and *for ever*, are the
blockades and raised drawbridges of all their
love affairs, but when they get to our time of
life, Master Hartsfoot," he added, with a sigh,
which, nevertheless, was more dyspeptic than

despairing, " they have grown wiser, and think, mayhap, that the single life is the smoothest."

" This from *you*, Mr. Pepys?"

" Well, yes, from me.   You bachelors only see our wives in patches, precious stones, and satins, with smiles and sugaries to match; but, good lack! when the jewels are exchanged for jealousies, the patches for peevishness, and the smiles for swoundings,* the summer weather is all gone, and the squalls begin.   I find my wife troubled this morning because I did check her last night in the coach for her long stories out of Grand Cyrus, which she would tell, though nothing to the purpose, and in no good manner; and last week, because I had stayed out till three in the morning, she swounded on my return, and when she came to, she treated Pierce, Knipp, and Peg Penn, to all the wenches, hussies, and worse, that ever were.   Though I don't say, but perhaps she do find with reason, that in the company of Pierce, Knipp, and other women that I love, I do not value her, or mind her as I ought."

" Oh! Mr. Pepys, it's hard lines for a wife to have her husband making an institution, as it were, of ' OTHER WOMEN THAT HE LOVES,' and neglecting her in their company."

" I don't say—I don't say to the contrary,"

* Fainting fits.

acquiesced Mr. Pepys, waving his hand, as if to thrust back the disagreeable subject, and what he also did *not say*, though he thought it, as the fact was too recent to be forgotten, how the week before he had packed Mrs. Pepys off into the country with £2, and on the same day after her departure, had presented Mrs. Knipp with £5. " I don't say to the contrary ; and for that reason, whenever she swounds, raves, or scolds, never a word say I, and, poor wretch! I must own, that cheese cakes and cream at Islington, or some other diversion, soon bring her round. But, good lack! I'm not the only one ; a fine hurricane there was before the whole Court last night at Whitehall.   Who'd ever have thought that the Queen would have plucked up such a spirit; my Lord Brouncker, who brought me to town this morning from Greenwich, in his coach and four, told me all about it.   It seems that, while the Queen was at cards, the King, who was walking up and down the room, sneezed two or three times, whereupon, the Queen laying down her cards, turned round full upon Lady Castlemaine, who was overlooking the game at a little distance from the card table, and said, in a voice loud enough to be heard by everyone—

" ' Really, Lady Castlemaine, you must not keep the King out so late at night.   You see what severe colds he gets.'

"At this the Castlemaine, with all the effrontery in the world, and an attempt at an innocent look, of which she has long lost the knack, said, throwing up her eyes and her right hand, in which was her fan—

"'I! your majesty? If the King stays out late it must be somewhere else, for he *never* stays late at *my* house.'

"This was too much even for the King, who, going up to her, whispered in her ear what every-one else says out loud, that she was the most impudent woman in England, and bid her leave the room and go back to her lodgings in Pall Mall; but Lord Brouncker says he's no doubt the King will let her keep her house and all its costly treasures, and that in three days they'll be just as good friends as ever."

"Good heaven," said Master Hartsfoot, throwing up his hands and eyes, "and yet people wonder I never go to such a Court, but follow Seneca's prophetic advice—

    ' Ingentes dominos et claræ nomina famæ,
      Illustrique graves nobilitate domos,
       Devita, et longè cautus fuge ; contralie vela,
        Et te littoribus cymba propinqua venat."

"Which only shows," said Mr. Pepys, "that all lords, great people, and frequenters of courts and palaces, were as little worth in Seneca's time as they are in ours, and no doubt will continue to

be so as long as the world lasts. As I take it, the
substance of things, animate and inanimate, in
all ages do remain the same; it is only their external fashionings that do change, for which reason, though manners, and customs, and laws,
and opinions may, and do, change in each succeeding age, still human nature remains radically the
same."

"There is something in that, certainly," rejoined
Oliver Hartsfoot, " for there can be no doubt that
the child-fables of infant states, when got hold of
by the youth of the same states—which are the
poets—become mythologies, and passing on till
they reach the crafty, middle age of nations, they
are converted into creeds; but as all things move
in a circle through the great course of ages, they
at length again resolve themselves into their
original elements, while what is called history
must ever remain the great romance of time."

" Ah !" said Mr. Pepys, " with episodes as long
and as wearisome as those in Grand Cirus."

Perceiving that he had struck out a little beyond his companion's depth, Oliver Hartsfoot
said—

" By the way, Mr. Pepys, as you are a man of
plays and shows and diversions, can you tell me
how they are giving ' The Moor of Venice ' at
the Opera House? for I hear they have changed
' Romeo and Juliet ' for that."

"Well, I really cannot. I saw ' Romeo and Juliet' there, and it was mighty well done, Juliet being enacted by an uncommon pretty woman; but I have no wish to see the other, for to tell you the truth I heretofore thought much of ' Othello, Moor of Venice,' esteemin it a mighty good play, and I read it again the other day, going by water to Deptford, but having so lately read 'The Adventures of Five Hours,' this ' Othello' seems a mean thing."

Such rank blasphemy did this seem to Master Hartsfoot, that had Mr. Pepys taken an arquebuse and shot him through the heart he could scarcely have staggered more; so, remarking that the chimes were striking twelve, he hastily took leave of Mr. Pepys, for whom, however, fate had other adventures of five hours in store. Now it so happened, that among the many *mauvais plaisants* at the Court of " the Merry Monarch," no two were more disappointed at the secresy preserved by the King touching the purport of the Suffolk girl's communication to him on the Mall than Killegrew and Silas Titus; more especially the latter, who, as her editor, as he called himself, thought he had a right to know her mission, but all he did know, was what he had gleaned from the courtiers; to wit, that her advent on the Mall, and the way in which she had accosted, or rather besieged the king, who, though never

so ill bred as his courtiers, having really a chivalric gallantry towards all woman, including even
the old, and the ugly, and who seemed as much
amused as his satellites at this rare specimen of
unhandsomeness, but, nevertheless, took the letter
she presented to him, enclosed in an envelope of
violet velvet, dantily embroidered in a bordering
of golden oak leaves, all save the address—

"To His Most Excellent Majesty,
         King Charles the Second."

which was embroidered in small seed pearls.

When the King had broken the seal, and read
the letter with the greatest attention, he re-folded
and replaced it in its costly envelope, which he
then put, not in his pocket, but thrust it for
greater security into his bosom; then turning to
the bearer, said—

"We will send a written answer by a special
messenger before sun-down, meanwhile you may
say that our royal word is pledged to fulfil all
that is required of us in that letter."

"And then," added Killigrew, who was the
narrator of this scene to Silas Titus, he cast a
circular glance round at us all—for you know the
poor man never possesses his own effigy on even
the smallest piece of metal—and said, "Can any
of you lend me ten caroluses?"

Sir Allen Broderick was the first to evince his

devoted loyalty, by opening his purse strings—a
folly he is never guilty of to his own relations, or
to his poorer fellow-creatures—and said, as he
handed the plethoric little gold mine to the
King—

"Your Majesty spoke of sending a special
messenger somewhere before sun-down; can I
have the honour of being of any use?"

"Not exactly," said the King, who appeared
consumedly amused at the proposition, and
stooped down to flip some imaginary speck off
the point lace trimming of his boot, in order to
hide his mirth. "Not exactly, Sir Allen; but
later in this matter we shall most likely require
your assistance."

Sir Allen bowed, backed, and appeared to drape
himself in the amplitudes of a more than even
ordinary pomposity, while the King counted out
ten caroluses before handing him back his purse,
and then turning to your beautiful nymph of the
black wimple, which there ought to be an Act of
Parliament passed to prevent her ever raising, he
said—

"So faithful an Iris should not go unrequited,"
and placed the ten gold pieces in her hand, at
which her cheeks grew almost as red as her hair,
though, like Ophelia's "rue, with a difference,"
as she dropped a really not ungraceful curtsey,
saying—

“ I cannot—thanking your Majesty all the same—but I dare not; we are never allowed to take vails.”

“ But, my good girl,” laughed the King, “ in this big city of ours, these are considered *prevails*. So you see, you will not be infringing your orders, which were only against vails.”

But her resolution was not to be shaken ; yet with a good breeding that might have shamed many more highly born, she accepted *one*, as his Majesty’s picture given by himself.

The King, waving his hand to her as she walked away, exclaimed—

“ Instead of Sir Allen Broderick’s ten caroluses—oddsfish !—but I’d give my own three crowns to have the power of saying NO, and sticking to it, as that poor country wench does.”

“ Ah, well,” yawned Silas Titus, “ as we are not likely to get any fun out of this wimple mystery, that promised so much, I am determined to take it out of old Pepys, if you will help me, Kil—”

“ Not if it’s to carry off Mrs. P—, now that she’s just got her coach, for I really cannot be a party to your aping your betters in that way ; the Duke of York *might* resent it, as a personal skit upon his brother.”

“ Nothing of the kind, Kil, for *that* would be a skit upon myself; for while carryings on are so easy, carryings off are always troublesome and expensive.   No, I have long had the converslon of at least *one* of the Portuguese maids of honour to Protestanism at heart, and Pepys is, or rather *shall* be, the man to do it, or rather to attempt it; and you and I will be the unseen spectators of the *warm* reception he will get from the Charming Doña Mariquita, Dolores Zampaya."

"Delightful!" roared Killegrew, clapping his hands.   "But do you think our portly-pompous, pre-eminently decorous friend, the secretary, can be springed into such a mare's nest as that?"

"Only you leave him to me; don't be—at least, don't seem surprised at anything I say, except to endorse it all.   I'm now on my way to waylay him, for I know he nearly daily walks in Westminster Hall about this hour," and so saying, on they walked, and scarcely had Oliver Hartsfoot quitted him, before the two conspirators joined their intended victim.

"So, Colonel Titus, any news of your nymph of the black wimple and her quest of the King, that you were telling us about the other day at The Mulberry Tree?" said Mr. Pepys, always on the look out for gossip.

"Pooh! a mere flash in the pan, ending in smoke, by all I can hear," rejoined Titus.

"Still water runs deep," said Mr. Pepys, sagaciously shaking his head. "Your disparage-

ment of an adventure that opened so promisingly,
do remind me of a thing Mr. Batelier lately told
me, how he, being with some others at Bordeaux,
making a bargain with another man at a tavern
for some clarets, they did hire a fellow to thunder, which he had the art of doing, upon a deal
board, and to rain and hail—that is make the
noise of ; so as did give them the pretence of
undervaluing the wines, by saying this thunder
would spoil them, which was so reasonable to the
merchant, that he did abate two pistoles a ton
for the wine in that belief."

" I can assure you, my good Mr. Pepys, there
was no deal board, or other thunder, in this
affair. My nymph, as you obligingly call her,
simply brought a letter to the King, which he
read, pocketed, and paid the bearer (as usual,
out of someone else's pocket) for bringing. At
least, Killigrew tells me this was the *alpha* and
omega of the whole affair, for you know I was
not an eye witness to it. But there *is* a matter
that has made some stir at Court, that I wanted
to consult *you* about, as you may do good service ; but first, as you are such a constant church
goer, which church would *you* recommend to anyone wishing to join a congregation ?"

Mr. Pepys, thinking that he knew his company pretty well, and all *they* could want at any
church, replied, tucking through a button hole

one of the ends of his laced cravat, so as to display the pattern to more advantage, " Well, I
always find the prettiest women at St. Michael
and All Angels ; and at the French church, the
parson's three sisters are uncommon handsome !
especially in the nose."

" In fact, they are all Angels," laughed Killigrew.

" Now, *do* be serious for once," said Titus, re-
provingly, " particularly on a serious subject ;
the fact is, Mr. Pepys,"—lowering his voice to a
strictly confidential pitch—" one of the Queen's
Portuguese maids of honour has a strong inclination to forsake the errors of Popery, and become
a member of the reformed Church ; but she has
no opinion of any of *us* about Whitehall, so as
to chuse an instructor, but from all she has
heard, and what she has seen of you, would have
great faith in your councils."

" Seen of me !   Why, where did she ever see
me, to know it was me ?"

" Well, the other evening she went to Moor-
fields to see Polichinello, which is about the only
one of our public diversions she can understand,
and there she saw you, and was so much struck
by the gravity and wisdom of your deportment
when not laughing at the puppet show, that she
asked who you were, and was also much pleased
with your attentions to your wife."

Mr. Pepy's face twitched, while he ejaculated a faint " Good Lord !" as he added, inwardly, " my wife—why, it was Mercer."

" And," continued Titus, " we thought if she could have some theological discourse with you, her conversion might be managed quietly, without any *esclandre* to irritate her Confessor, for those Jesuits are edge tools to meddle with."

" But, good Lord !" exclaimed Mr. Pepys, now perspiring at every pore, " I don't know a word of the Portingale tongue ; and even my French is far to seek, and worth nothing when found."

" Latin and gestures, my good sir, do wonders, when there is a will on both sides."

" But there is *no* will on my side," protested Mr. Pepys.

" I don't think you'd say so, if you knew how much she admires your ' Beauty Retire,' and how well she sings it."

" Oh ! I have done ' It is Decreed,' I think, much better even, though I do hear on all sides that ' Beauty Retire' hath taken mightily."

" Well, I hope," said Titus, returning to the charge, " it is decreed that you will come to White Hall this evening, at dusk, to save this wandering soul."

" But which of them is it ?" asked Mr. Pepys, not quite impervious to the dexterous thrust about " Beauty Retire."

" Doña Mariquita, Dolores Zampaya."

" Oh! lord! the most ill-favoured of the lot."

" Come, come, be a man; courage! Mr. Pepys," said Killigrew, laying his hands on the quivering Secretary's shoulder. " You have only to fancy yourself Perseus, arming to meet the gorgons, and depend upon it victory will be yours."

" But if I should be seen!—if I should be known!—if the Duke of York should find it out! —if the priests should make a stir, and send the news to the Portugal King that I was intermeddling to upset popery! Good lack! it might breed a war between England and the Portingales, and all our fleet now among the Hollanders."

" Seen! why you were not so timorous when you blackened and smutted your face, and had such high jinks the night before last at Lady Pen's, Mr. Pepys."

" Good Lord! how on earth did you hear that? One might as well have all one's doings published in ' The White Hall Gazette,' things get about so; indeed better, for the ' Gazette' only do come out once a month, and if a man's private diversions get wind in this way, what would it be if the Portingales thought I was intermeddling to upset the Pope!"

" Nonsense, my good sir, there is no analogy whatever between the two cases; it was Peg Pen herself who told me of your revelries, and dress-ings up. the other night at her mother's.   And it is not very likely that any one would tell, since no one but the persons concerned, to wit, your-self, the *fair convert!* Killigrew, and I, would know of your going up the back stairs in the dusk of the evening to the maids of honour's parlour, at the back of the green room, or Council chamber, and you need only carry a few tracts under your cloak."

" Tracts !—Lord !—I have not such a thing in my house.   I did destroy all that Puritan rub-bish directly after the Restoration, thinking them dangerous combustibles to be found in possession of, and even ' Baxter's Shove' I shoved into the fire.   I have nothing in the way of polemics but a large folio Life of Calvin, in Latin."

" The best of all," interrupted Titus ; " mind and bring the folio with you, and then you'll be sure *to carry weight !*"

" Tut, tut, tut," ruminated Mr. Pepys, begin-ning to see more and more into the disagree-able and onerous reality of his position, " I have just bethought me.   My brother John came up yesterday, and is now at my house ; he is a parson, though no great hand at either theology or elocution, for I am always at him to mind his pronunciation, and chastise his voice to better modulation, surely *he's* the fittest to undertake a conversion case ?"

" Out of the question, in the present case, for don't you see, my good sir, it's *you* the lady fancied, and whose judgment she holds in such high estimation ; and a *bonâ fide* clergyman of the established church, attempting the conversion of one of the Queen's maids of honour, might, indeed, infuse a State and national flavour into the affair, which never *could* attach to the friendly intentions of a mere layman—don't you see !"

" Oh ! Lord !" groaned the doomed Secretary. " Well, I'll borrow my brother's cloak and cassock, anyhow."

" Ah ! that's a capital idea !—quite worthy of Mr. Pepys' well-known sagacity, who is well aware that nothing can be done in courts, and more especially *viâ* the back stairs, *without a cloak.*"

" But you'll be there to—to—to introduce me ?" said Mr. Pepys, with a look of despairing helplessness at his treacherous companions, such as a manacled and condemned criminal might cast on the gaol chaplain when arrived at the foot of the gallows.

" To be sure we will," said the pair simultaneously ; " you'll find us waiting for you at nine to night at the top of the back stairs ; but mind how you come up, for the turnings are very sharp ; indeed, a small dark lantern under your cloak would be no bad precaution."

"Oh! good lack! no; for if I was caught it might go hard with me, by leading them into the supposition that I was something in the Guy Fawkes line."

"True," laughed Titus, "always prudent, always to the purpose, and full of forethought, Mr. Pepys. There spoke the astute man, the man of business, and the far-seeing statesman. Doña Mariquita, may not be first cousin to Venus Aphordite; but there can be *no* doubt, after the judgment she has shown in her selection of a mentor, that her pedigree is the same as that of Pallas Athenæ."

"You do give me some content in this matter; still my fears do come to the surface, for there never be wanting busy-bodies and mischief-makers to spoil salvation as well as sport; and, as I said before, if the affair *should* be false interpreted, and it should be twisted into a State plot and breed a war between us and the Portingales, and all our fleet away with the Hollanders—"

"Well, then go home, eat a good dinner, and get Dutch courage by taking an extra glass or two, and I'll bet you the whole English fleet to an acorn that there will be no war, not even a Trojan one, for this Portuguese Helen. So now *addios*, but be sure not to forget the folio."

And these two worthies hurried away, lest Mr. Pepys, who generally made the concrete wisdom of some proverb the text of all his actions, should reflect that "second thoughts are the best," and so change his mind. But Killigrew exploded before they had got well clear of Westminster Hall.

"Hush! for fun's sake, or you'll ruin all," said Titus, placing his hand upon his companion's mouth.

"Well, but," gasped the latter, when they had got fairly into what is now called Parliament Street, still holding his sides, "how on earth do you mean to carry on this pretty plot? for surely you'll never subject a man of Mr. Pepy's respectability to having his face scratched, his wig flung out of the window, and himself after it, by the *gentle* Mariquita, for what she would consider his heretical impertinence?"

"Thomas forbid! I have anticipated everything. He shall never be subjected to such foul usage from any of the fair sex, as he shall not even see, at least, on this occasion, the charming would-be convert. You know, and what is more germain to the matter, *I* know what an admirable mimic you are, Kil, and how wonderfully you take off the maids of honour's confessor, Padre Zancas Padrillo, so I have already ordered you one of his huge hammer-shaped beavers at Holden's, and the rest of the priestly attire at Blagden's. A lank black wig, a pair of round, iron-rimmed spectacles, and equal quantities of lamp-black and verdigris, blent with sweet oil, smeared over your face, to give you a fine olive complexion, will do the rest. You must remain on the top landing, and so soon as you perceive Mr. Pepys ascending, with his folio, flanked by your humble servant, you must begin gesticulating furiously, shaking both your clenched hands at him, and splitting our ears by any jargon you choose to invent on the moment, only plentifully interlarding it with *Los cativomalos Ingleses*, shrieked out in that admirable din, between the chattering of a dozen monkeys and fifty macaws, which you so well know how to deafen your hearers with when taking off Padre Padrillo; and which Mr. Pepys, between his ignorance of the language and his terror of the infuriated Padre, will be sure to take for choice Portuguese."

"Oh! oh! oh! you'll be the death of the poor secretary, Colonel," said young Killigrew, between his paroxysms of laughter.

"Not a bit of it."

"Well, then, at all events," rejoined the other, "you will have to add another act to 'Killing no Murder.'* And how will you manage to account for Zancas Padrillo's having been put *au courant* to Mr. Pepys' proselyting intentions?"

"Oh! that's the easiest part of the affair. I

---

* Colonel Silas Titus was the author of " Killing no Murder.'

shall tell Pepys that from my slight knowledge of Portuguese, I gather from the Padre's furious denunciations, that Doña Mariquita, woman-like, betrayed herself, and that Padrillo then extorted the whole matter from her in confession, but that she had not given up his, Pepys' name, but said it was some English clergyman, whose name she did not know, or at least could not pronounce."

"And what if the King—or, worse still, the Queen should hear the uproar on the stairs ?"

" Oh! the King will thoroughly enter into the joke; and as for the Queen, I shall soon think of some story to satisfy her, and as Lord of the Bedchamber, I have a perfect right to my *entrées* at every back stairs in the Palace; but remember, you are not to continue your vociferations a moment after Mr. Pepys has taken to his heels, which I am very certain he'll lose no time in doing, for fear of that much dreaded war with *the Portingales !* So now, presto ! begone, to rehearse for the evening.

      ' Act well your part—therein the honour lies.' "

And so saying, these two worthies separated, to meet again at nine in the evening at the foot of the back stairs, leading to the apartments of the Maids of Honour. At that time there was no inconvenient lighting, either of streets or

houses, in London; at the first landing of the
said back stairs, flared an oil lamp, out of an
iron sconce, without any glass to shade or pro-
tect it, so that its unrestricted glare cast many
dim, false shadows down the narrow-pointed and
much worn stone stairs, giving just light enough
to "make darkness visible." But precisely as
the Palace clock struck nine, on that dark and
hazy night, poor Mr. Pepys, who was the soul
of conscientious punctuality in all things, might
have been seen by all the cats in the gutter and
on the house-tops, attired in his brother John's
cloak and cassoc, high steeple hat, and round
bob wig, or caxon, and the huge folio of " The
life of Calvin," protruding from under his arm,
walking rápidly, but stealthily, close to the
Palace wall, till he neared the fatal stairs, at the
foot of which the treacherous Titus awaited him,
also cloaked and steeple-hatted. He silently extended his hand, and then, with a deep and
sonorus, though whispered " HUSH !" led the
way up the stairs, followed by his trembling,
though albeit, unsuspecting victim; but no
sooner had they come within three steps of the
first landing, than forth rushed the sham Zancas
Padrillo, like " an embodied storm," and so admirably did he enact his part, and personate the
enraged Padre, that even Titus, who was in the
secret, was for a second almost deceived—so

deafening was his vociferation, so menacing and murderous the electric quivering of his clenched hands, which he only opened to seize the ponderous folio, and raise it above his own head, as if to hurl it with greater impetus at the devoted head of its owner, that poor Mr. Pepys, with a face now streaming like a fountain tree, himself almost *swounded!*   When Titus, standing between him and the mock anathematiser, whispered, at the same time gallantly drawing his sword—" Run! run! my good sir, for your life, and leave me to deal with this mad brute.   I'll make him know that he shall not outrage any of His Majesty's liege subjects in this way; but wait in the street, and I'll come to you the moment I have settled him."   Mr. Pepys did *not* stand upon the order of his going, but went at once, while the two accomplices with difficulty suppressed their uproarious laughter till the poor secretary was safely out of hearing.

" My dear Killigrew," said Titus, " you outdid yourself! and, as they say in France, have covered yourself with glory! The King *must* see the scene either to-morrow or the next day, though unfortunately with the chief actor left out, but I think I could dress the part and do him ; but I must take him back that pretty little book, which I shall, of course, tell him I had the greatest difficulty in rescuing from the infuriated

Padre. I must not, however, return to my friend
the Secretary, under a long half hour, to give him
an idea of the difficulties of my negotiation ; and
this is fortunate, as I am sure in less time than
that I could not recover my gravity.''

Meanwhile poor Mr. Pepys was walking up
and down, his hat slouched over his eyes, his
cloak held before his mouth à *la conspirateur,*
and feeling almost as guilty, and certainly as
frightened, as the most sanguinary conspirator
could possibly have done.

" Good Lord!" thought he, " what a narrow
escape! but mighty handsome of the Colonel, I
must say, to send me safely out of the way, and stay
and deal with the fellow all by himself. I do
hope there will be no bloodshed ; but how fortunate that I was not in my own wig or clothes, or
in any other bravery, but in this quiet cassoc
and caxon, that no one would suspect had me
under them, though I do hope this affair will
bring no discredit on the cloth. I was right to
be so reluctant to enter into it. Truly man pro-
poses, but God disposes. Good lack! how little
one can foresee, not what a day, but even what
an hour may bring forth ; and what fleeting
vapours are all human plans. I had laid it all
out, after doing what good I could to this ill-
favoured Portingale lady, whose soul, it is to be
hoped, is better worth preserving than her face.

Yes, I had laid it all out to go to Heaven,* and have a quiet little bit of supper, and go home early, as if from the office, that my wife might ask me no questions.   But, good Lord! I'm so flustered and shaken at the way things have turned out, that when I have seen Colonel Titus, and heard how he did deal with that mad bull of a Jesuit, I shall slink down to the Dolphin—a mean place compared to Heaven—but hard by, at the river side, where I am not known, but where I do remember that once during the fire we did not fare so badly, or else that we were so sharp set, having had nothing for three days but a shoulder of mutton from the cook's, that we did not think that we fared hardly ; and—" but here Mr. Pepy's cogitations were interrupted by a riotous group of merry makers, male and female, shouting and bearing torches in their hands, one of the party being Orange Moll ; but so little did she suspect the proximity of the august Secretary, that she said as she brushed past him, and nearly endangered his equilibrium—

"Now then, parson, by yer leave, unless you would like to join us."

"Good Lord !" groaned Mr. Pepys, as they

* A place of entertainment so called, situated in Old Palace Yard, on the site of which the Committee Rooms of the House of Commons were erected some years ago. This "coffee-house club," as it was called when it existed, is mentioned in Hudibras as "False Heaven at the end of the Hall." To wit, Westminster Hall.

past on, " what a mercy she did not know me in this trim. But what risks I do run. I do wish the Colonel would come, and hope there has been no bloodshed or bones broke. I wish I had kept steady to my first mind, and refused flatly to have anything to do with the conversion of that ugly Portingale wench. Oh! Colonel, I'm so glad; the Lord be praised! you are safe," added he, suddenly perceiving Titus approaching him, beaver in hand, and mopping his face with his handkerchief, as if removing the hot traces of the fray.

" Well," exclaimed the gallant Colonel, "it has been a sharp bout, but I think I've frightened the fellow nearly out of his ugly skin, and effectually insured *his* silence about the matter."

" Good lack! that do give me great content; but how did you manage that so cleverly, Colonel?"

'· Why, when I could get him to cease his Portuguese jargon, and speak Latin, though you know they pronounce it so differently to us, that I had at first, between that and his passion, some difficulty in understanding him, but at length I made out that Doña Mariquita had betrayed her own yearnings after a change of creed, at which the Padre took alarm, and never ceased till he wormed the whole affair out of her at confession, and that she expected a Protestant gentleman

of great weight and distinction to come and discourse with her on the subject this very evening,
whereupon, throwing myself into a terrible passion, I pointed out to him that *she* had sought
you, and not you her; and then, in order to turn
the tables on him, dexterously availed myself of
your capital idea of *his* assault upon a person of
your distinction becoming a *casus belli* between
England and Portugal."

"Good lack!" interrupted Mr. Pepys, "but I
hope you did not name me?"

"Not for the world; I did not compromise
either you or myself by actually affirming it, but
I left him under the full conviction that it was
no less a personage than the Archbishop of Canterbury, at whose sacred head he had attempted
to hurl this ponderous tome, and whom he had
so soundly abused and so grossly insulted. This,
and the impending war trembling in the balance,
so effectually terrified him, that he soon began
to cry *peccavi;* the more he did so, the more I
held out the difficulties of appeasing you, and
inducing you to be silent upon the outrage
you had received. However, I at length graciously condescended to be mollified, solely *for the
sake of not endangering the peace of the two
countries!* and making him take a solemn oath
never to divulge a syllable of what had passed,
and promising to give twenty pieces of eight to

the poor of the parish ! I·left him, faithfully covenanting on my side that no proceedings should be taken against him."

"I vow to the Lord," said Mr. Pepys, now indulging in a quiet little laugh of perfect safety and release, "you managed this difficult business mighty cleverly, and with great discretion." The words were scarcely out of his mouth, before the sham Padre—who, indeed, had overheard the whole conversation, hidden by a convenient angle of the building—passed close to them, and removing his huge hammer-shaped hat, bowed deferentially down to the very ground, and hurried on as fast as possible.

"You see," said Titus, "how I have brought the fellow to his bearings ; how civil he is, and how frightened he evidently is."

"Good lack ! yes, after being like a mad bull !"

"All Papal bulls are mad bulls," rejoined Titus ; "but I was to play a main of Gleek with the King at ten of the clock, so I must be going."

"Well, Colonel, all I can say is that I am mightily beholden to you."

"Not at all—not at all."

"But you see I was right when I did not wish to entertain the project."

"It was never meant that you should," *thought*

Titus, as he walked back into the Palace; "it was only intended to *entertain us,* which it has done beyond our most sanguine expectations. As for Killigrew, he'd make his fortune at the King's, or the Duke's house."

No sooner was he quit of his gallant friend, than Mr. Pepys, to use his own form of speech, slunk down to The Dolphin, and on his arrival, asked the Drawer what he could have with the least delay for supper?

"Well, your Reverence, there is a fine fresh lobster, and the remnant of a cold venison pasty."

"That will do; let me have them forthwith, and a sack posset with them.   But, ho! stop; bring me first a small tankard of mum."*

"For, good lack!" thought Mr. Pepys, "I am still so flustered by that mad Priest, that I do need something to keep up my strength. But 'tis pretty to see how they do take me for a parson on account of my dress, and how well I do become the cloath."

The drawer soon returned, bearing not only the mum, but the supper.   "That *is* a mighty fine lobster!" said Mister Pepys, but at the same time recollecting how once on board "The Nazeby," when he went with my Lord Sandwich

---

* "Mum," a very rich, strong, and highly spiced German beer—not spiced before it was drunk, but spiced in the brewing, and used chiefly, at that time, by invalids.

to bring the King over from Breda, he had had his dinner spoilt by their bringing him oil, instead of vinegar, with a lobster, he told the drawer to be sure and not make a like mistake. " And," said he, seating himself at table, and tying the napkin round his neck, as if he was going to be shaved, for fear of spoiling his brother John's cassoc, " you may as well bring me the reckoning now, as I am in a hurry to be off, and here is a sixpence for yourself."

Now, whether it was from his previous unusual excitement, the toughness of the venison pasty, which Mr. Pepys declared like one he had some time dined off at his brother Tom's, " was palpable mutton, which was not handsome"—or from the density of the lobster, or the potency of the mum, or the insidiousness of the sack, or from all combined; but certain it is, that no sooner had he supped, than leaning to one side of the high-backed arm chair in which he sat, than he fell fast asleep, dreaming of the most terrible conflicts between himself and Padre Zancas Pedrillo, and that he was belaboured almost to pulverisation with the huge Life of Calvin. What may have ad:led, and no doubt did so, to his terrible physical *mal aise*, was, that he had gone to sleep with a window open at his back, which, through the flimsy red and white check serge curtain, blew in on the back of his

neck all the dense, damp, concrete fog, from the
river ; and with the usual incongruous phantasma
of dreams, at the same time that the priest was
pounding him, he thought he saw Major-General
Harrison, one of the regicides, being hung,
drawn, and quartered at Charing Cross, and
remarked in his sleep, as he had so often done in
his waking hours, that " the general looked as
cheerful as any man could under the circumstances ! " adding a somnolent " good Lord ! and
to think that I cannot even bear up under a
drubbing from this scurvy Jesuit." But after one
still more severe blow from Padrillo, to wit, a
more violent twinge of lumbago, Mr. Pepys was
awoke, by the bellman* crying, " Half-past two
of the clock, and a cloudy morning." Starting
to his feet, and rubbing his eyes, he exclaimed,
" Lord save us !   Half-past two in the morning !"
and then, finding he could not stand upright
without excruciating pain, he added, "good lack !
I am all buckled ! †—how on earth shall I get
home; yet home I must get as soon as possible."
Now, Mr. Pepys never stirred abroad without the
key of his hall door, and it was none of your
little trumpery trinkets, like a modern latch key,

---

* The watchmen of that time always rang a hand-bell—as see
in *Il Penseroso*.
      "Or the bellman's drowsy charm,
        To bless the door from nightly harm."
    † Bent, in which sense buckled is used by Shakspeare, Henry
IV., Part II., Act 1st, Scene 3rd.

but a portly formidable-looking implement, such as would not have discredited the Tower of London, in its palmy days ; so *that* was not the difficulty about his getting home ; the difficulty was how he should account to Mrs. Pepys for his prolonged and solitary absence ; but *that* he must decide upon as he went ; the thing now was to get home ; and in order to do so, to get out of The Dolphin as soon as possible ; therefore adjusting his wig by an exceedingly uncomplimentary triangular piece of cracked looking-glass over the mantel-piece, which leant forward, as if to cast injurious reflections upon every one who passed through the room, he next put on his steeple hat, and seized " The Life of Calvin," from which he had suffered so severely during his adventures of the last five hours ; he then hurried, or rather hobbled, into the street, but with the exercise soon began to find his limbs grow more supple, and at last, that they had conveyed him to his own door, where the lock was too well oiled, and the key kept too constantly on active service to grate in the wards, or make any other unseemly noise. But great was Mr. Pepys' dismay when the portal opened on its noiseless hinges, to perceive his maid servant at the foot of the stairs, with a candle and a glass of water.

" Good lack ! Jane—*you* up at this hour ? "

" Laur, sir ! I took you for Parson John."

" No matter who you took me for; how come you not abed?"

" Laur, sir, madam have been swounding and scolding ever since a little after ten of the clock, and this is the fifth glass of water I've been down for."

" And where's Mercer?"

" She have gone away home to her mother, sir."

" The jade! My wife did well to take time to beat her when she ran away before, at the time of the great fire; and when I can get hold of her I'll baste her with a broom stick, as I did the other girl. You can tell your mistress I've come home, Jane, and that I've been detained by great affairs. I'll just step into my dressing chamber, and put off these things and slip on my night gown* before I go up."

Mr. Pepy's felt intuitively that there was no danger in his wife's illness; indeed, that whatever danger there might be related more to himself, so that there was no occasion for him to hurry, till, like General Harrison on the occasion of his being hanged, drawn, and quartered. he had made himself " as cheerful as a man could be under the circumstances;" and during his in-

---

* What are now called dressing-gowns were at that time called night-gowns; just as ladies' evening dresses were called nig t-gowns also, which they continued to be so called up to the beginning of George the Third's reign.

duction into his "night-gown" and slippers, he took the precaution of recollecting every scrap of gossip he had picked up during the day, as one of various intended peace offerings.

"Tut, tut, tut, my dear," said he, upon entering the nuptial chamber; "Jane do tell me that you are not well. I am so sorry—"

"It is a pretty time of the night, or rather morning, Mr. Pepys, to express your sorrow."

"My dear, I have had horse work of it all day; first at the Parliament House, then at the office, signing a death load of pardons, and it do trouble me to think I get nothing by them. Then all night at Whitehall, on *most unusual business*, with some of the Lords of the Bed-chamber, and—"

"Oh! yes," broke in Mrs. Pepys; "I know all about it. The Parliament House, and the office, and Whitehall, are very convenient doors to lay all your doings at, when junketting and jackenapsing with your Knipps, and your Pierces, and your Pegs—the shameless hussies!"

"I vow to the Lord, my dear, I have never seen so much as the shadows of their whisks;* the last time I see either Knipp or Pierce was when you was with me at Paul's Walk, and I did give you all a pair of plain jessimay gloves a

---

* A peculiar sort of hood, with a cardinal or large tippet attached to it, worn by women at that time.

piece, and you a pair of white ones more than
the rest, which you did take in good part at the
time."

However that may have been, Mrs. Pepys so
stormed and raved *now* that Mr. Pepys could not
for some time bring up his great guns of a pre-
meditated new gown, and an evening at the
King's House on the morrow. Now it is in the
nature of things, that however good cause persons of a suspicious temperament may in general
have for their doubts of an individual upon whom
they are in the habit of exercising this species of
penetration, that it will occasionally happen that
they shoot wide of the mark by aiming at the
wrong time and place; and it is also in the nature
of things, as a pendant to this, that when the
suspected personage, though ninety-nine times
fully justifying the most unlimited suspicion, yet
when unjustly accused on the hundredth, chafes
and writhes under the villanous injustice of the
thing, as if they were " one perfect crysolite " of
injured innocence, and such were Mr. Pepys'
feelings on the present occasion, till in a climac-
teric paroxysm he seized his wig with both hands,
and flung it to the other end of the room, as he
exclaimed—

" I vow to the Lord! you are the most unjust
and unreasonable woman that ever was, when I
do study all I can for your pleasure and diver-

sion. It was only this afternoon I did hear of my she-cousin Potter being come to town, and did arrange with her to go with us to the King's House to-morrow, where they do give " Love in a Tub," and where the King and the whole Court are to be ; and my Lady Castlemaine to have a dress, newly come from Paris, the like of which has never—they say—been seen for splendour ; and having got all my navy money paid, and great promise of more favour from my Lord,* I did conceit that you should have a dress the match of my Lady Castlemaine's, if you were so minded—and it is brave, as they say—and this is the thanks you give me for my pains."†

" Nay, nay, Mr. Pepys, I am always ready to hear reason when you talk reason ; and if I have suspected you wrong I'm very sorry. But when

* Sandwich.

† Mr. Pepys must have considered himself fortunate in escaping so easily on this occasion, as the following details occur in his diary, page 82, vol v., which is another instance how much stranger truth is than fiction. " She (Mrs Pepys) fell out into a fury that I was a rogue and false to her. I did, as I might truly, deny it, and was mightily troubled ; but all would not serve. At last, about one o'clock, she come to my side of the bed and drew my curtain open, and with the tongs red hot at the ends made as if she did design to pinch me with them." To which the editor of the diary adds the following—

" Mrs. Pepys seemed inclined to have acted on the legend of St. Dunstan, who,

" As the story goes,
Once pull'd the devil by the nose,
With *red hot tongs*, which made him roar,
That he was heard three miles and more."

you go out at eight of the clock of an evening, never say where you are going, and don't come home till three in the morning, what *am* I to think ?"

" Not to think about it !" snapped Mr. Pepys.

" Thank you," said Mrs. Pepys, with a resigned sigh, as she wondered what Lady Castlemaine's new dress *could* be like—if it was more splendid than her usual ones ; and then, in order to let bygones be bygones, she said, in her normal piano tone, " Well, my dear, and what news is there stirring ?"

Mr. Pepys, who was by no means sorry that the battle was over—that is to say, fought and won by him, Samuel Pepys, now seated himself beside the bed, mopped his face, and then answered—

" The latest I did hear was from my Lord Sandwich, this morning."

" You mean yesterday morning, Mr. Pepys."

" Well, yesterday morning," frowned Mr. Pepys—" whom I did find in bed, he having been up late with the King, Queen, and Princess, at the Cockpit all night, where the Duke of Albermarle treated them, and after supper, a play, where the King did put a great affront upon Singleton's music, he bidding them stop, and made the French music play, which my Lord says do much outdo all ours. Oh ! and my Lady

Sandwich did give me two bottles of Florence wine for you."

" Is it nice ?"

" Well, I think Sir William Pen did hit it off when he did say it might truly be called a *sensible* wine, and just suited to the times, for it was not *over nice*; and I did add, which caused them great merriment and content, that it was like Ned Kestavin's wife—weak and sweet, yet sharp, and insipid with all. And now, my dear," added Mr. Pepys, too thankful that there *was* such a place of refuge, " let us to bed, for I have to ride as far as Deptford before breakfast, to see the landing of the seven Flanders mares my Lord hath bought." And the worthy Secretary soon slept the sleep of the just, resolving not to enter a syllable of what he called his bout with the Jesuit, in his diary, and still less to let a hint of it escape to his wife; on the same principle that induced Dr. Busby to request Charles the Second's permission to wear his hat in the royal presence, for if ever his boys got it into their heads that there *could* be a greater man in the kingdom than himself, he never should be able to do anything with them.

CHAPTER IV.

Ad suum quemque arquum est quæstum esse callidum.
PLAUTUS.

LES BEAUX ESPRITS, SE RENCONTRENT.

T first Dorothy Neville was not only annoyed, but indignant, that her mother should have hunted Master Hartsfoot out of his lair, " to gallant her forsooth! to public diversions ; what did *she* want of such nonsense, who could not, and would not be amused; as she was thoroughly and hopelessly miserable, why could they not leave her in peace, and let her be comfortably wretched ? " For at eighteen all miseries are of course hopeless, there being no time to remedy or efface them ; it is only at sixty, or on the wrong side of seventy, human wisdom is so matured, as to lay plans, extending into the far future, and so discharge all present incumbrances by drafts on Hope, payable by Time ; the young are no such expert financiers ; *their* moral and psychlogical existence is a from hand to mouth one ; with

them, *more* than sufficient for the day is the evil thereof; they have no horizon; all *their* miseries are bounded by a dead wall. But as nature has provided all animals with instincts, and appurtenances suitable to their position and necessities, so has she provided even the most innocent and artless characters, from the moment Love obtrudes himself into their affairs, with a peculiar and most subtile cunning, which serves them as a scotescope,* enabling them through the most tenebrus darkness, to discover with the most perfect distinctness, objects hidden to all other eyes. For which reason, the fair Dorothy, though indignant at first at her mother supposing that there was anything in this world that she cared to see, now that *her* particular sun had set, yet soon perceived by the aid of the aforesaid scotescope, that dark as all her surroundings were, from the fact of Gilbert Broderick having been forbidden to appear at her mother's house on the Mall, or at The Chestnuts, her only chance of *seeing* him, for she had no intention of *meeting* him, would be at public places, from which no amount of parental tyranny could exclude him. So, albeit, she suddenly became the most docile, tractable daughter in the world, and not only accepted Master Hartsfoot's escort with alacrity,

---

* Scotescope, an instrument enabling persons to see objects in the dark.

but displayed such avidity to go to *every* public place, that it occasionally called forth urgent remonstrances from Master Oliver, not, to do him justice, on his own account, but on hers ; for, vulgarly free and coarsely hybrid as the manners and customs of the day were, he had more than misgivings, that some places of public resort there were, despite their great vogue, and high fashion, which were anything but fitting scenes for a young, pure-minded, and carefully brought up girl, like Dorothy Neville; and he often marvelled thatseeing how listless and *distraite* she for the most part was at such places, that still her eagerness to frequent them did not abate.   Poor Dorothy ! like us all, hers was a shadow hunt— consequently the excitement never flagged, and if she only caught sight of the tip of one of Gilbert's feathers, a flash from his sword-hilt, or heard the clank of his spurs,—let alone ever caught one electric glance from his eyes, or if his cloak touched her sleeve in the press of the crowd, she was amply repaid for three months weary pleasure-seeking, and had an ample provision to exist upon for another three months. For although chameleons do live on air, " good lack !" as our worthy friend Mr. Pepys would say, why they are gross and aldermanic feeders, compared with true lovers ; a race that only became extinct towards the latter part of the eighteenth century.

Such being the state of things, poor Master Hartsfoot became like Sin itself, inasmuch as that he also had *no* holidays. Now it so happens that whenever the masters and mistresses of any two houses have established a great intimacy, the connecting-links of the chain are sure to descend into the lower regions, and render the *liaisons* of the respective servants'-halls and offices, equally close. And as Master Hartsfoot found himself on daily duty at Madam Neville's, of course Noah Pump had equally important affairs to transact (or at least to discuss) daily in Madam Neville's kitchen and pantry, or at her hall door.

And now, she being from home on one particular afternoon, and her butler, Jessop, having just taken in a large box of grouse that had arrived from Scotland, and deposited its contents on the hall table till his mistress's return, stood at the back or street entrance door, with his liveried coadjutor Launcelot Amyot, annotating their master's and mistress's acquaintances, their sayings, doings, goings, comings, &c., &c., as always has been, and always will be, the wont of their order.

"Ah! well, in course the quality knows best," said Noah Pump, in continuation of a foregone conversation; "but I calls the doings as have gone on since the restoration a disgrace to haintient Babylon. Not but what I am main joyful to think as *my* master lives more like a Christian now, and do take a power of diversion, going about with pretty Mistress Dorothy, instead of cobwebbing and moulding his self with them there *save ons* (savans) ; save on's they *are*, sure enough ; at least, they saves on us, and never gives no vails. And all their discourse is about the haintients and the haintients, as I says to my master, after one of these dry-bone, old-iron-and-rag gatherings of the save ons at our house, where they keeps us up till two in the morning ; I says, says I, you'll excuse me, sir, but I've been a thinking, if so be as things goes on as they are a going, what a pretty figure *we* shall cut by the time we becomes the hantients."

"Lord ! Noah Pump, surely you never made so bold with Master Hartsfoot as that ?" put in the orthodox and pre-eminently respectable Jessop.

"But I did though, and he only smiled in his own quiet, kind way, and said, ' Well, you are not far wrong there, Noah.' "

"Well," rejoined Jessop, shaking his head with reproving gravity, and resting the knuckles of both his hands on his hips, with the palms turned outwards, " it's no reason because masters are kind and easy that they are to be taken liberties with, and encroached upon, and I wouldn't for the best tierce of claret I ever bottled, or the oldest butt of sack I ever broached, have taken such a liberty with a master or mistress of mine."

" Aye, but we's fosterers, and was both nursed by the same mother."

" Then, Noah, my man, you should have more mother wit than to treat a gentleman of Master Hartsfoot's standing and acquirements with such unseemly familiarity."

" That's good !" said Noah, " to learn *me* how to comport myself to Master Hartsfoot—me as would cut myself in mincemeat twenty times over for him any day; and if *I* don't know how to respect him, Master Jessop, I should like to know who did, seeing that his goodness is like the latter half of eternity, and has no end, for Parson Stillingfleet told us last Sunday that eternity had neither beginning nor end."

" I must say," put in Launcelot, in order to divert the personal turn the conversation had taken, and appease Noah's rising choler, " I must say I quite agrees with Noah Pump about them there *save ons*, for my father, when I was a boy, lived as butler with old Mr. Selden, where the *save ons* used to have just the same old bone-and-rag meetings, and the same discourse about old books, and about the hantients, as Noah describes as going hon at Master Hartsfoot's ; so that I've seen and *heered* a deal about them ere *save ons* and authors in my time; and, poor *creturs*, hevery allowance should be made for 'em by their *ray*tional fellow creturs, for my belief is, Noah Pump, that they han't got all their buttons."*

" There, you've hit it, Launcelot Amyot; but how can you account for them as *has* all their buttons ; doing sometimes *on*accountably strange, not to say silly things ? Now 1 take it, that if ever woman *had* all her buttons, aye, and all her hooks and eyes to boot, *that* woman is Madam Neville ; and yet they must have been so badly sewn on as every one to have dropped off when she took that born devil, Bridget Butson, for a cook."

" Well, but you know, Pump, it *is* the devil who do send cooks."

" At all events he sent this one, Master Jessop ; but I marvel at Madam's taking her, she having lived with the king's head concubine, my Lady Castlemaine."

" Madam knew nothing about that when she hired her."†

---

* A West of England expression, commonly used by the Devonshire and Somersetshire people to this day, to intimate that a person is not overburdened with sense, and in short, has not half his wits about him.

† It was customary at that time to take servants without any references from the persons with whom they had previously lived, and Pepys, in alluding to this very strange and dangerous custom, says, " 'Tis pity when we copy so much that is bad from the French that we do not copy the good, and take no servants but such as are recommended by the masters they served ; and also, that, before entering an inn or tavern, we do not as the French do, make an arrangement beforehand for our meat and lodging."

"I also marvel that Bridget, getting such enormous wages as twelve pounds* a year from my Lady Castlemaine, she should have ever left her place."

"She said she would not live with any lady who swore at her, were she fifty times the king's mistress."

"Good Lord deliver us! Does she swear, too? But what had she to swear at Bridget Butson for? as she *is* a good cook, and as the devil always takes care of his own, surely he'd do his best for Madam Castlemaine."

"She tells me the way of it was this. One night that the King was to sup at my Lady Castlemaine's. I say one night, though he sups there every night; however, one night in particular the kitchen was flooded, as they so often are at Whitehall Gardens. There was a chine of beef, for one thing, to be roasted for supper. Butson declared that with the kitchen in that state to roast it was impossible, when down comes my lady in the midst of her dressing, with her beautiful hair all over her beautiful shoulders, looking as beautiful as an angel, and as angry as a fury, and stamping her foot at

---

* Long after that, indeed up to George the Second's time, servants' wages were remarkably low, for Mrs. Delaney mentions it with great surprise, the "very high wages Lady Cowper gave her maid," viz., four pounds a year. Just imagine the face of modern *femme de chambre* at being insulted with the offer of four times four pounds a year!

Butson, said, ' Zounds ! woman, though you set the house on fire you *must* roast it."

" And these is ladies and gentlemen ! kings and countesses !" cried Noah Pump, throwing up his hands and eyes.

" That don't follow, Master Pump," ruled Jessop, " they may be the latter, but I deny their being the first."

" Whew ! ladies and gentlemen," whistled Launcelot, " there hain't none made now. My belief is that they went out of fashion with Padua velvet frizzed at the back, of which King James had the last yard to make him a nightgown. And as for the meanness of the quality now a days, it's just past crediting. There's a pretty skinflint for you, that Sir Allen Broderick, with all his *pompostious* grand airs, and strutting and swaggering ; a more scurvy skellum* never had the tormenting of his fellow creturs."

" Hush ! hush !" interrupted Jessop, " if you don't bridle that tongue of yours, Launcelot Amyot, you may chance to want a bit in your mouth before you die ; and in making so free with the name you forget the good lady of Clumber Chase, that is more like an angel without wings than anything else I can compare her to ; and you also forget how near Sir Allen

---

* Skellum—" villain," according to Johnson ; " a mean varlet," according to Tudor lexicographers.

was to being our young mistress's father-in-law."

"No, I don't; but for that matter Sir Allen Broderick is always *near* to every one, and a lucky escape Mistress Dorothy have had say I; though I must own that Master Gilbert is no more like his father than light is to darkness. His mother saved *him*; he favours her, not only in appearance, but in disposition. Ah! poor lady, it was fortunate for her that her skellum of a husband was not long in breaking of her heart, and putting on her out of her misery. But I was just a going to tell Noah Pump how Master Fairlop, the Duke of Albemarle's butler, paid off Sir Allen tre*menjus!* the other day. As birds of a feather flock together, Sir Allen is for ever a going and coming at all hours of the day and night to the Duke's place, near Epsom, and giving no end of trouble to the servants, but never giving on them nothink else; but *always*, when he leaves, going through a piece of stage play like, in tapping his pocket and saying, ' I've no money about me; but another time, another time, Master Fairlop;' which Fairlop and all the other servants do think my Lady Duchess have put him up to, for with all her Duchesship Bess Clarges she was, and Bess Clarges she'll remain till the hend of the chapter; and she's just as great a screw as Sir Allen. Lor, if so be as they are only fastened in their coffins with their own screws they'll be screwed tight enough I'll warrant ye.   Well, as I was a going to tell you, one night, about a month ago, after they had waited supper till all hours at my Lord Duke's for Sir Allen, and no Sir Allen came, just as they was a going to bed, about twelve of the clock, comes a loud ringing at the door.   Now you must know Prodgers, the King's *walley-de-sham*, had brought down some papers for the Duke from the King in the afternoon, and wanted to return *immejet;* but the Duke, expecting Sir Allen, pressed Prodgers against his will to stay, and he would have his company back to town after supper. So when they heard this loud ringing so late, besides every servant in the house, the Duke and Duchess, with Prodgers, rushed into the hall, thinking it was some royal express come after Prodgers ; but when the door was opened, it was Sir Allen Broderick, much splashed and bemired, his sword gone, half the feathers round his hat torn away, and one side of his point collar hanging in shreds ; he was terrible out of breath, and had left his horse at the stables before he come up to the house, and after he had *pologised* to the Duke and Duchess—never a servant moving to offer to help him off with his cloak, till the Duke told Fairlop to do so—Sir Allen panted out, 'I have been attacked by highwaymen, and being

only two to four, the varlets have escaped us.'
Here was Fairlop's opportunity, and he did not
miss it; but said in a loud voice, so that everyone might hear, specially Prodgers, who would
be sure to tell the King; but though Fairlop's
voice was very loud his manner was uncommon
respectful, and he made a low bow as he brought
out the words—

" ' What a fortunate thing it is, Sir Allen, that
you never have any *money* about you ; so it's a
comfort to think how the rogues must have been
disappointed.'

" At this they all fell a tittering in so *rumbust-
shus* a way, particular Prodgers, that Sir Allen,
who looked as if he could eat 'em all without
salt—only fortinately looks don't kill—had nothing for it but to stick his hand upon his hip,
fling back his head, and strut into the dining-
room. But the servants says, to see Fairlop's
face and manner, as he thrust at Sir Allen, was
worth all the stage plays as ever was acted, he
being as cool as any flagon of hippocras he ever
took out of a fountain."

" Oh ! that be brave—that be good ; well done,
Master Fairlop," roared Noah Pump, rubbing
his hands and jumping with delight; while even
the decorus Jessop—though he had heard the
story a dozen times before—so cordially detested
Sir Allen Broderick, that " in his heart of

hearts," he always rejoiced at any of his discom-
fitures—past, present, or likely to be, and so
could not refrain from an appreciative chuckle.
But at this juncture their mirth was most un-
seasonably interrupted by a perfect hurricane of
female voices, pitched in *alto*, proceeding from
the kitchen, a large apartment not underground,
but on the opposite side to the dining-room,
looking on the Mall, and entered by one of four
oak doors, in the large square entrance hall.

"May I never drain another cup of canary, if
that she devil Butson is not at it again, in one
of her tantrums," said Launcelot; "for mercy's
sake, go and threaten her with the kucking
stool,* Master Jessop, afore Madam comes
home. They'll fright the quality up stairs, for
Mr. and Mrs. Evelyn, and Mr. Locke, are sitting
with Mistress Dorothy."

"I'm off," cried Noah Pump, stopping his
ears, "for, as Master Butler says, in his fine new
book, where he do pepper the Roundheads so
nicely—

> 'He that fights and runs away,
> May live to fight another day;
> But he who is in battle slain,
> Can never rise to fight again.'

So let me have an account of the killed and

* A seat placed in the middle of a pond, where Scolds were
ducked.

wounded to-morrow, Launcelot ; and I hope as you won't be neither one nor t'other."

" No—no, I'll to the pantry, Noah ; safe bind, safe find."

Jessop hurried to the scene of action ; hastily opened the door, and as hastily closed it after him, and flinging up both his hands, in the attitude of a prelate about to bless, or to anathematise a congregation, enunciated authoritatively, three times the word " Hush !" but to command is one thing—to be obeyed another ; and as Jessop had arrived just at the height of the fray, when the noise and confusion were at their *acmé*, sonorous as his voice was, it was lost, like the murmur of summer air in the loud din of this raging storm, and as the belligerents were all speaking, or rather screaming together, ears were for the time being, a most useless appendage ; therefore, the scandalized Jessop was fain to reconnoitre with his eyes only, as well as he could see, athwart a dense smoke, which, however, was not that of gunpowder, but of sea coal, which had been most unwarrantably invaded by a deluge of boiling water, which, after quenching its rival element, was running over the floor like a stream of black lava, that the two scullions, Alice and Marjory, like twin Mrs. Partington's (limited), were trying to bail out with their mops.   In the midst of this Stygian flood stood Bridget Butson, her face rivalling the fire before its extinction, her cap all but off, her hair, as if from sheer fright, escaping on all sides, her ponderous bust upheaving like the throes of an earthquake, one ruddy arm akimbo, the other like a colossal statue of Bellona, grasping a spit which ran through a haunch of venison, that might, without much imagination, have been taken for a dividend of a recently speared enemy. While the forces, being equally divided, opposite stood *her* opposite in every sense of the term— Rachel Ruffle, long, spare, of the thread paper type in figure, dressed in rich, soft, glossy black silk, the tight sleeves ceasing at the elbows, where a ruffle of plain, clear lawn relieved them, while over her very flat chest was always pinned a tippet of snowy lawn, spotless as her own reputation. Her dark hair was combed back from her forehead in a roll, as it was worn both by men and women in James the First's time, and as may be seen in the early portraits of Dr. Donne; her eyes were of dark hazel, perhaps more stern than mild-in their expression; her features regular, her complexion pale, without being in the least sickly, and the expression of her countenance of that subdued martyr tone that may be called provokingly placid; and, indeed, it was a true index of her character, for she was never out of temper, so far as words or brusque movements indicate that unseemly state, but she had pre-eminently that elixir of prudence which consists in restraining our own temper, only to compel our adversaries into losing theirs, for, as it is quite clear, that in all feuds temper (which is moral blood) *must* be lost on one side or the other, the perfection of strategy is to take care the loss is not on our own side. Now, Rachel Ruffle was perfect mistress of this art; she never raised her voice, much less her hands; so, according to Demosthenes, she was *not* eloquent, for she never used action, but according to Cicero, she was pre-eminently so, for she never spoke without achieving the object she had in view. She could, it is true, use very deadly weapons, but then, like the spiked and poisoned iron hand of the Inquisition, they were always sheathed in velvet; moreover, she always began with a sort of self-abnegating disclaimer, the formula of which was, " I may be wrong," or, " Perhaps its very wrong of me," but—and now she stood in the " Patience on a monument pose," her hands not indeed placidly crossed as usual, for in her arms she held a fat black and tan turnspit dog, who was trembling with a low plaintive moan, for the poor animal, who had not displayed as much alacrity as Bridget Butson thought he ought to get into his wheel, had been the first literally to get into hot water, and had one of his hind paws dreadfully scalded.

The cause of the fray had been Mrs. Ruffle's presuming to come into the kitchen to look after the baking of some marchepane* and some tansey maids of honour she had made, and could alone make in the perfection that her mistress required. Having come at an inopportune moment, when Bridget Butson was straining every nerve to spit the haunch of venison that was to be roasted for supper, and when she was at the same time calling, " Clove, Clove, Clove," the truant turnspit, all over the kitchen, she, instead of responding in a similar tone to Mrs. Ruffle's civil question of " How are the maids of honour and the marchepane getting on, Bridget?" answered in a fury—

" Souse the maids of honour, and you to !"

Now the "act against profane swearing" being just then in full force, with sundry pains and penalties attached to it, Bridget, like all geniuses being a person of infinite resource, had compounded with the devil, and adopted this word souse as a compromise for stronger explicatives, and indemnified herself for the sacrifice, by using it as often as possible. So when Ruffle had inquired touching the progress of her own

* Marchepain, a thin, sweet, almond cake or wafer.

handiwork, the irate Bridget had, with a stamp
of her foot and a clenched fist, vociferated,
" Souse the maids of honour and you too !" and
suiting the action to the word, gave a vigorous
kick to a large kettle of boiling water, which set
the fire hissing and smoking, the maids screaming, and also brought the truant Clove to the
rescue, who got scalded for his pains, and then
contributed his quota to the concert by a shrill
howl, till he ran for refuge into Mrs. Ruffle's
arms, who ordered one of the scullions to scrape
a raw potatoe, which she put into a piece of old
linen, and bound up his poor paw. Now though
Jessop's voice could not possibly be heard in this
uproar, still his presence (of which even Bridget
Butson stood a little in awe, he being Madame
Neville's prime minister) caused a sudden lull in
the storm, when he demanded—

" In the name of wonder, what is all this disgraceful rumpus about?"

Bridget was silent for less than half a second,
only to take sufficient time to pitch her voice in
a lower and more conquered key, and then replied,
pointing the finger of scorn at Mrs Ruffle—

" Aye, ask them as caused it all ; I'm *that*
flustered, and *that* frighted, and that upset, and
all my supper Lord knows where, that I ain't got
no nerves for gossiping and tittle-tattle, like
some people."

F 5

And bere she darted another look like a larding pin at Rachel, who said in her mildest voice, turning to Jessop—

"You know, Master Jessop, how particular madam is about the sweets, which she trusts entirely to me. I had made a batch of marchepane and of tansey maids of honour, the best I think I ever made; I merely asked Butson how they were getting on in the oven, when she flies into one of her sinful passions, kicks down the kettle, scalds poor dear Clove, fills the oven, and washes all my beautiful maids of honour out of their coffins."*

"Souse you! Pity but what you was *in your* coffin too, and then there'd be peace in Israel, as the *scripters* says."

"Oh! Bridget Butson, perhaps it is very wrong of me to say so; but you, being a native of Sandwich, might take warning, and remember it's not so many years ago since your evil-tongued townswoman, Marjory Mossop, was sentenced to carry the mortar† through the town hanging at the end of an old broom across her shoulder, with the bellman going before her ringing his clapper, and telling the people that was what was done to her for abusing Mrs. Mayoress, and saying that she

* The little white paper cases or boxes that rammikins, *fondus,* or small sponge cakes are baked in, were at that time, and in all old cookery books, called " coffins."
† A wooden basket.

did not care for her the value of a raspberry tart !"

At this local anecdote, Bridget placed lance in rest—that is, she put the spit standing against the wall, and with both arms now a-kimbo, made three measured strides across the floor, till she arrived within three inches of the placid Rachel, who valiantly stood her ground, despite the approaching danger.

" What I've got to say, and what you'll please to remember, Mrs. Prim, is THIS. Mrs. Mayoress *might* have been worth a raspberry tart ; but YOU, I don't care for YOU—no, not the *pip* of a raspberry. So, now the sooner you take your brooms and buckets, and your raspberry tarts out of *my* kitchen, the better ; and there's sixpence for you to pay the bellman for going before you the next time you takes a walk. And if so be as you dies of the pip, like Mrs. Dorothy's canary, I hope when you goes farther you won't fare worse ; but I'm *dubious* on *that* score."

" Perhaps it's very wrong of me, but I'm a person of no curiosity about other people's affairs, and from year's end to year's end never think of looking at the address of any letter or parcel that comes to the house. I may be mistaken—and I hope I am—but, if ever I *did* see a person legibly directed to the author of all evil, that person is YOU, Bridget Butson," said Ruffle, hurling this

Parthian dart as she sailed majestically out of the kitchen, carrying Clove with her. Now, though Jessop was honest as the day, and straight-forward as a sped arrow, still, like all the superior sex, he *was* a bit of a moral coward, and consequently in all domestic jars never venturing upon a decided course of adhesion to one side or the other of the opposing factions; but ever temporising more especially in favour of the aggressor. So gently taking Rachel by the back of the arm, before she had reached the door, he said, " Come, come, Mrs. Ruffle, it's only a little after four, so you'll have time to make some more maids of honour."

" Time! Master Jessop. Time alone cannot make, though, as we have just seen, it may mar maids of honour. And I don't suppose, if I was to give the Crown jewels for it, I could get another quart of cream at this hour in London."

And so saying, she closed the door after her, with a mild and subdued imitation of a bang; while Bridget, being thus left mistress of the situation, screamed after her —

" I say, Madam Starch, you be the last new-fashioned kennel I suppose, as you've got the black dog on your back as well as in your arms; but I'm not a going to do turnspit's work for no such trumpery, I can tell you."

" At all events, I hope you *are* going to have

this disgraceful mess cleaned up before Madam comes home and sees it."

" Tilly Valley! Tilly Valley! Master Jessop, you don't expect a kitchen at all hours of the day and night to be like what you calls Puck's Parlour,* do you ?"

" And why not? At any rate what I do expect is that you'll make Marjery set it in order directly, before all those beautifully bright pewter plates and dishes are quite tarnished with this horrible smoke."

" Lack a daisy," rejoined the somewhat cooled down Bridget, resuming the spit, and again thrusting away at the haunch of venison, as the horrible phantasmagoria of madam's having literally no supper flitted before her. " Lack a daisy; there hain't no use in asking *she* to do a hand's turn; she be one of your born dawdles, made, as I always tells her, out of wet blotting paper, who passes their time in bolting of doors with biled carrots, and then wonders how the plague people had got in, when *they* had fastened up the door; people, my belief is, as was made in a hurry, scrambled up any how, and put off with

---

* In Devonshire, where, to this day, the people devoutly believe in fairies it is a common expression to say of any apartment more than usually neat or elegant, '' Why, this is Puck's Parlour !'' thereby meaning to imply that it had been arranged by the fairies. And Jessop being a Devonshire man, often used the expression.

two left hands, all thumbs, and never a finger
amongst 'em."

Here a knock was heard at the hall door.

"Madam's knock, by all that's contrairy!
Run—fly, and Alice, some faggots quick, to re-
kindle the fire; but if she *should* come in say it
was a jackdaw as got down the chimbley, over-
turned the kittle, and made the devil to pay, and
nothing to pay him with; but for pity's sake,
good Master Jessop, *don't* let her come in here.
Tell her there are visitors—quality, that have
been waiting her return no end of time."

"Ah! well," said Jessop, shaking his head as
he adjusted his hands, and pulled down his cuffs
preparatory to answering the door, "I'll do what
I can; but I hope this will be a warning to you
never to be guilty of the like again."

And no sooner had he closed the kitchen door
than Bridget, spit in hand, flew to it and bolted
it—*not* with a boiled carrot.

"To-day is post day,* any letters, Jessop?"
inquired the mistress of the house on entering.

"No, madam; but Sir James Drummond has
sent a box of grouse from Hawthornden—came in
prime order, with ice under the heather, and there
is a real curiosity with the grouse; at least, I never
saw one before—a cream-coloured moor-hen."

---

* At that time the general post came in but twice a week,
and there was no exclusive metropolitan post.

“ Dear me, what a pretty bird. I tell you what, Jessop, he’s fond of everything rare, so send it over to Master Hartsfoot with my kind regards.”

“ Very good, madam, it shall go directly ; Master Hartsfoot *is* upstairs with Mistress Dorothy, likewise Mr. and Madam Evelyn, and Mr. Locke.”

“ Did Mrs. Evelyn walk ?”

“ No, madam, their coach is on the Mall.”

“ Oh ! well, then, have a couple of brace of grouse put into it, and I’ll just go and tell Butson to have the rest potted.”

“ Pardon me, madam, but if you will allow me I’ll tell her, for Mr. and Mrs. Evelyn have been waiting a long time, and Mrs. Dorothy, I know, wishes to ask your permission about going to some public place with Master Hartsfoot,” said that intrepid Leonodas Jessop, as he valiantly defended the pass of the Butson Thermopylæ when his mistress had advanced two steps towards the culinary battle field.

“ Very well, then, that will do,” acquiesced the lady, as she ascended the stairs, and Jessop preceded her, not only as in duty bound to open the drawing-room door for her, but also to convey to the lower regions the glad tidings that she really was safely arrived, and likely to remain there with her guests.

CHAPTER V.

BEAR AND FORBEAR.

MRS. NEVILLE'S greeting of and apologies to her visitors over, Dorothy rose from her large easy chair near the window, and with an *abandon* and familiarity very unusual with well brought up young ladies of that period, who not only addressed their mothers as "madam," but preluded all their sayings and doings, goings and comings, with a low courtesy, threw her arms round her mother's neck, and gently slapping her cheek in a very poor feeble imitation of chiding, said—

"You naughty *mamma*, where *have* you been all this time without asking my leave, or even telling me where you were going?"

"Oh!" replied the happy mother, covering her smiling face in pretended horror with her hands, "I'm sure Mr. and Mrs. Evelyn will be quite shocked at seeing and hearing such a spoiled girl, are you not?" she added, appealing to them,

as she drew a chair next Mrs. Evelyn, and seated
herself.

" Not a bit of it," said Mr. Evelyn, " we are
just fresh from the kingdom of spoilt girls and
autocratic only daughters—the Hôtel Carnivalet."

" Oh! do tell me about Madame de Sévigné
and Madame de Grignon. *Is* Madame de Sévigné
as charming as every one says, and as her letters
are? one or two of which the Comte de Grammont showed me; and is Mme. de Grignon so
beautiful as report makes her out?"

" Well, to answer your questions categorically,
Mme. Sévigné *is* quite as charming as every one
says, and even more charming than her letters—
quant à la Grignon," and here Mr. Evelyn shrugged
his shoulders in a way which showed he had
benefited by his frequent trips to Paris, as he
gave a furtive look at Dorothy, " I confess I
prefer *your* spoils to Mme. de Sévigné's."

" Ha! ha! ha! my *spoils*. I shan't forget
that; but that no doubt is on the score of old
friendship, but I'm sure Mr. Locke must be
scandalised at my *spoils*."

" Not a bit of it, madam; on the contrary I
am quite delighted with it—or I suppose I must
say *them*. That is our great national sovereign
want, that both in our systems and in our no
systems of education we leave the affections
totally uncultivated. We drive our boys early

from home to public schools and colleges, and suppress our girls at a stated freezing point at home, thus early chilling and hardening their ductile and malleable moral nature, the *only* solid and sure foundation for anything really great, because really good. The greater and more highly cultivated the intellect without this broad, solid, moral foundation, the more faulty and contempt-ible I hold the human being. A flagrant instance in illustration of this axiom, we have had very near our own times, in my Lord Verulum. Nothing could be well greater, or more cultivated than the intellect; nothing lower or meaner than the moral. In short, this supremacy of the intel-lectual without a moral equipoise is in ethics what the *Auram Fulminans* is in chemistry, which latter consists in placing a *grain* of gold in a silver spoon, which grain of gold, when fired, gives an impetus to the force of a musket shot, and drills a hole through that silver *downwards*."

"Oh! how true that is," said Mr. Evelyn, "as you have illustrated it by my Lord Bacon, it was that sordid worldly leaven which caused him to betray with such unutterable baseness his friend and patron Essex, and not only to betray, but to sharpen on the accursed whetstone of his intel-lect every weapon for his destruction. I have, I confess, great contempt for those men who, as it is called, *get on in the world*, for it requires such a quadruped form of mind to do so.   Such a crawling under, or leaping over, every barrier which the more upright and conscientious *will not* franchise. I would rather ten thousand times have had my head on the block with noble Walter Raleigh, than safe under the wig of the scoundrelly Sir Edward Coke who sent him there. But, indeed, it often strikes me that the decline and fall of England must ultimately be caused by the underminding dry rot of selfishness and false pretences, that is sapping her social and political foundation."

" Then are you," said Oliver Hartsfoot, " of Harrington's opinion, who predicts in his ' OCEANA,' that France will eventually be *the* country that is the mistress of the world ?"

" I should not at all wonder," replied Evelyn, " that it were so. The French have a *genius of heart* that we never had, and are never likely to have ; for, though the most selfish and self-seeking people under the sun, we have *no* individuality; consequently no originality, being always like the Sheep of Panurge, for treading carefully in ready-made footprints.   The French have one term which sufficiently expresses the moral calibre of the people—*Politesse du Cœur*. Now, we have neither the expression, nor the thing it expresses ; and how should we ? Consideration for others forms no part of our training ; even if

we do a service, we must always do it in our own
way, without any reference to the feelings—or
grant it—to the prejudices of those we pretend
to serve.   On the contrary, if they have a sore
place, we are sure clumsily to probe and make it
sorer.   We make a tremendous parade, too, of
our services, letting the poor wretches to be
served know every step we have taken *as* we take
it, to duly impress upon them the great trouble
they have given us ; and, if we ultimately fail,
why, then, we rather owe *them* a grudge for our
own wounded pride, without one compassionate
thought for their raised hopes so cruelly crushed.
Now, a French person puts all the delicacy in the
world into conferring a favour, even to reversing
the relative positions, and making the obliged
appear the obliger, and begin by throwing themselves into the case of the person they attempt
to serve, so as to *feel* from *their* point of view,
and so studiously avoid wounding as they go.
Moreover, so far from a flourish of trumpets, announcing each move, they say nothing, however
arduous their endeavours may be, *till* they have
succeeded, and then make *nothing* of all the pre-
liminary hardships; and if they fail, why, the
odds are, they will remain silent, rather than
accept thanks for fruitless intentions.   But all
this comes from the early habit of substituting
others for *self.*   French children are, from the

first, taught to be as unselfish, and as well bred,
not only to their parents, but to their brothers
and sisters, tutors, governesses, and servants, as
if they were always at Court, and in the presence; consequently, in France, instead of seeing
families and their incomes split up into infini-
tesimal fractions, you see three generations often
living lovingly, happily, and with perfect personal freedom, too, under the same roof; the
gallant young Musquetaire, or *Talons rouge, quite*
as *galant* and as *aux petits soins* to his old grand-
mother, mother, or sisters, as he would be to the
most charming *marquise* at Versailles ; and the
budding, blushing young girl, quite as will-
ing to leave her reveries, or her *broderie*, to play
at chess, or *faire l'aimable* to *le Grand Père.*
Whereas with us, simply from our selfishness
and our ill-breeding, not only are we in great
haste to rid our homes of our sons and daughters, but in other relationships, seldom, as we say,
can we put up our horses together. I have
known young women become childless widows,
with a mother still living, or a sister, as the case
may be, without either of their means being
large, and if wonder is expressed that they do
not live with their mother or sister, the answer
invariably is—' Oh ! my mother and I, or
my sister and I, cannot hit it off,' which

means in plain English, we are both so selfish and so ill-bred, that we should eternally be interfering with and annoying each other, and the house would be hell upon earth. This *politesse du cœur* practically extends through all classes, from the highest to the lowest. For instance, ask a working man in France the way to a place, not only does he not laugh at the foreigner's bad French, but will leave his work and *go* a mile, aye! or more, to shew the stranger his, or her way; and, if offered pecuniary remuneration for his trouble, would colour with really hurt feeling and say, 'Comment donc, Monsieur; pour si peu de chose?' Whereas, ask one of the same class in England a similar service, and the odds are, he would either make you some rude, disobliging answer, or think it a good joke to send you in a totally wrong direction; or, at least, if he *did* show you the way, would think he never could be sufficiently remunerated for his mighty services; but if a poor foreigner required them, there is no amount of ridicule that would not be added to the hoax of directing him wrongly. There is another thing, too, in England, which militates against all cordiality and sincerity, our innately vulgar straining always to be—no, to appear—something greater and of more importance than we are—a case in point yesterday. I met Mr. Pepys, and condoled with him upon the death of his uncle Robert, adding, that at the same time, I hoped he had derived some pecuniary benefit from it. Here are his words. ' Why, to tell you the truth,' says he, ' he did leave me nothing. But to put a value on myself, I do tell people that he have left me £200 a year, besides ready money and land.' Now, poor Pepys knew well the vulgar Mammon market for which he was catering, and accordingly marked himself with the only figure that would have any value. In France he would have been saved from any such mortgage upon his veracity, or his self-respect—for people would have valued *him*, Samuel Pepys for any good qualities he might possess—such for instance as his real, hard working industry, and his honest zeal in preventing (so far as he can), the king being robbed, while all the other harpies of courtiers are preying on him night and day. And if French society *did* give his uncle Robert's money bags a thought, it would be merely to regret the poor man had got none of them, and to shew him redoubled kindness and attention in order to heal his disappointment."

" Too true," said Mr. Locke, " even my Lord Clarendon was animadverting to me the other day on the increasing degeneration of our manners at all points. He said, when he was a boy,

no one ever thought of keeping their hat on*
(except at dinner), in the presence of anyone
greater, or anyone older than themselves."

"That might have its absurd side, too. For
instance, fancy *your* not keeping your hat on in
my presence because I happen to be ten years
older than you, my *only* pre-eminence," said Mr.
Evelyn, bowing to Locke.

" Nay—nay, my good sir," laughed the philosopher, " I shall denounce you as a papist if you
fling your incense at me in this way, and will
subpœna Mr. Hartsfoot as a witness against you
—for does he not deserve it?"

" Only so far," said Oliver, " as that with those
who are entered for the race of immortality, a
decade or two certainly don't count; but I have
another separate indictment against Mr. Evelyn."

" Yes, yes; I know what it is," cried Dorothy,
" and offer myself as evidence for the prosecu-
tion."

" Then without judge or jury, I say Lord have
mercy upon me, for whatever you lend your countenance to, Mrs. Dorothy, must succeed from
the *primâ facie* evidence."

" Well, prisoner at the bar," resumed Oliver
Hartsfoot, " you are accused of having written

* It was the custom at that time, and had been for centuries,
for men always to dine in their hats; no doubt on account of the
large cold halls in which they dined.

two excellent plays, and yet, most unwarrantably and inexcusably, keeping them under lock and key from his Majesty and his Majesty's liege subjects."

" Who in the name of wonder could have told you that ?"

" Well, one who fancied himself a great judge of the English poets,* from Chaucer down to Waller, and who stoutly maintained that Dryden is a greater poet than Milton."

" Tush !" said Mr. Evelyn ; " where there is no similitude there can be no comparison. Dryden is PRAXITELES ; Milton MICHAEL ANGELO.† But who can the fellow be ?"

" A man of *numbers* himself, and therefore should be a judge of others, our late friend, poor Edward Cocker,‡ when I last saw him at the house that used to be the Young Men's Club in Cromwell's time."

" Tut, tut ; mere trifles, only fit for the closet,

---

* Not only of the British poets, about whom he was an enthusiast, but likewise of all men of letters. He always swore "By the four Johns ;" to wit, JOHN DRYDEN, JOHN MILTON, JOHN LOCKE, and JOHN EVELYN. By the four Johns I won't, or by the four Johns I will, was his invariable mode of asseveration.

† To show what contemporary judgment was respecting poets and poetry, at Cowley's death the then Bishop of Winchester— Dr. George Morley—and Dr. Bates, one of his brother divines, bewailed him (Cowley) as " England's greatest Poet, and as good a Man ;" the latter part of the eulogium being better deserved, may account for the former part, for moral worth *will* tell at the last. Witness Cowley's own summing up of his fellow poet, Crashaw—

"His faith was wrong; but, oh ! his life was right."

‡ *The* Arithmetician.

and never intended for daylight, still less for lamplight.*   When you come to see me I'll show you something much better worth your attention; I mean my wife's paintings, which are really admirable."

"Of that I have no doubt," said Hartsfoot; "*mais l'un n'empêche pas l'autre.*"

"Oh! Mr. Evelyn, your eyes are partial, and others would look upon my poor attempts with more critical impartiality."

"Nay, my dear; you know Mignard's opinion of them in Paris, and also what Lely told you here, and you will allow them not only to be competent, but also impartial judges."

"Well, my dear Mrs. Evelyn," laughed Mrs. Neville, "I really think husbands are not only impartial, but the most impartial of all judges where their *wives'* talents, virtues, or beauty are concerned ; overrating, decidedly not being what they are prone to, and you must be quite aware that your talent for painting amounts to genius."

Mrs. Evelyn smiled and shook her head in negation, while Mr. Evelyn nodded his assentingly.

* Pepys said of these plays : " They are very well, but by no means such great things as Mr. Evelyn do conceit."   But then to be sure that great theatrical critic, Mr. Pepys, also opined that "OTHELLO" was "*a mean thing,*" in comparison of "THE ADVENTURES OF FIVE HOURS."   So, *cæteris paribus,* giving Mr. Evelyn the benefit of that decision, perhaps his plays were very good.

“ *Mama mia*, you have not yet given an account of your wanderings, and the unwarrantable time you stay’d out without leave,” said Dorothy. “ I hope you did not go and see that sensitive being, Mr. Warcupp, the poor wretch who declares that if by accident a rose touches him (the *rose*, not the thorn, mind) his skin immediately blisters !”

“ Who did you say this sapient Sybarite was?” asked Mr. Locke.

“ A Mr. Warcupp; but the best of the joke is, that the other day at dinner at the Duke of Albemarle’s, where the conversation turned on extraordinary antipathies, and of course the old story of Erasmus fainting at the sight of fish was raked up; whereupon the rose-hater, Warcupp, not only announced his unfortunate peculiarity, but *swore* to it; and as silence is said to give consent, every one *was* silent from astonishment till the dessert came, when, the fruit being decorated with roses, the duchess took one and first, at two or three different times, gently touched Mr. Warcupp’s hand; but no blisters appearing she got out of patience, and then *scrubbed* at his hand with as much goodwill as she used formerly to do at the floors; but still, neither by fair means nor foul, could any blister be got to appear.”

“ Ha ! ha ! ha !” laughed Mr. Evelyn. “ So

that henceforth this Warcupp should have the *sobriquet* of Cupid, as he was certainly doomed to *lie* among the roses."

"It is astonishing," said Locke, "how many different phases vanity has. What is called ambition may be defined as nothing but colossal vanity, that of hearing echo repeat one's name; and this Warcupp-Cupid, or stupid, pretending to such a ridiculous and incredible idiosyncracy was nothing but vanity in its minimum phase, to get himself talked about and wondered at for the moment."

"Quite true," assented Mr. Evelyn, "and therefore ambition, though called by the superficial a noble passion, is anything but that, as nothing that has self for its basis, and which sacrifices everything *to* self *can* be noble; on the contrary, it is the worldly leaven of all meanness. Women think they are drawing a trump card when they marry an ambitious man, imagining that *his* advancement in life of necessity means *theirs*. Not so; the thoroughly ambitious—that is thoroughly selfish man—never thinks the world large enough for more than ONE of his own family, and he is that ONE. However well a wife may do for a stepping-stone, he never allows her to appear as a staff.

"I was much amused the other day at hearing of a piece of our Queen's pretty broken English;

they wanted her to ride at the muster of the troops in Hyde Park the showy Arab she had ridden at Greenwich a few days before, and which had been taught all sorts of *manége* tricks and caprioles; but she would not, saying—

"'No, no. I no like him; *he make too much vanity* to make all de people stare at him.' In like manner, your ambitious men make too much vanity, and all for the same reason as Queen Katharine's Arabian, to make people stare at them. So take my advice, Mrs. Dorothy, never marry an ambitious man."

"I'll do better than that, Mr. Evelyn," said Dorothy, blushing to her very temples, "for I'll never marry any man at all. But, Mamina, where *have* you been? and what detained you so long?"

"Well, you little inquisitor, I first went to one of your *protégées*, Anne Lile; and then I got hustled, and jostled, and frighted out of my wits by a set of those horrid apprentices, banded together like a set of mad fanatics as they are, tearing up the Common Prayer book, with their usual cry of 'Porridge! Porridge!'"*

* The meaning of this word is fully explained in a rare contemporary tract called "A Vindication of the Common Prayer against the contumelious slanders of the Fanatic Party terming it 'Porridge.'" An extract from this pamphlet will be found in a note to Sir Walter Scott's "Woodstock," vol. 1st, p. 22, ed. 1834. Brother Ignatius could tell how the enlightened Londoners flavour *his* porridge for him in the nineteenth century!

" Ah !" said Oliver Hartsfoot, " I fear, Mr. Locke, you may write ' Letters on Toleration,' but that they will long continue sealed letters to men's passions, prejudices, and above all, to their ignorance."

" Aye, the latter is the worst enemy, being father to the two former, and a long progeny of other stumbling blocks, and barriers, and blinds, and shutters for excluding the light."

" Yet," rejoined Hartsfoot, " when we remember that in the physical world, five years are necessary to bring one ray of light from Sirius to our earth, though travelling at the rate of twelve million miles in a minute, we cannot wonder that moral light should at *least* take equal time before it can penetrate the nebulæ of the human mind; and as for Christianity, long as its *dawn* has been, we can never hope to see it in its meridian till all sects are abolished by being merged in *it.*"

" That is true," said Evelyn; " more especially when we remember the very foul and questionable sources to which we owe our so-called reformed religion, the unbridled lust of a tyrannical King, and the equally unscrupulous concupicence of an apostate Monk; for as to the errors and abuses of Popery (and what dominant State Church, with a plethora of wealth, and an inebriety of power, has *not* its errors and abuses?)

Europe was quite ripe to expose and secede from
them ; had Henry the Eighth never indulged in
the regal recreation of decapitating his wives, or
Martin Luther never broken his *solemnly binding*
—however erroneous—vows, and caused the Nun
Catherine Bora to break hers, two pieces of
sacrilegious perjury which we should never have
ceased to revile, had it not suited our sectarian
partisanship to coalesce with the apostates. Just
as in like manner, while ceaselessly inveighing
against the Pope's supremacy, and the unscrupulous occult dealings of the Jesuits in the sub-
version of all laws, human and divine, in their
sapping and mining labours in families, we
carefully and conveniently suppress Pope Martin
Luther and other Protestant Divines (including
' the mild Melancthon's') dispensation to Philip
Landgrave of Hesse, who had married Catherine
of Saxony to enable, that is to *authorise!* the Landgrave to commit bigamy, by marrying his mistress,
Margarite de Staal. The staunch Protestant
Landgrave's piety being something *à la Henri
Huite,* of such a profound and peculiar kind, that
on his recovery from a severe illness, he had
scruples about his *liaison* with this lady, and so
resolved, as it has been the world old custom of
men to do, to submerge one sin by a greater ;
and in order to obtain his object, memorialised

his *protégé* Luther, that his mistress might receive the public honours of his lawful wife—
which precious document he fortified with the
authority of the Old Testament, and in it, as a
quid pro quo, made such liberal promises, not
only of continued, but increased patronage of
Luther, and the Protestant divines, that they,
headed by Luther and Melancthon, instantly held
a conclave to consider the proposition; and, after
first unanimously deciding what a terrible thing
it would be for them to lose the powerful protection of such a patron, had their moral vision so
cleared by this view, that they lost no time in
unhesitatingly adopting that of the Landgrave;
and so, without keeping him in unnecessary
suspense, soon furnished him with the requisite
' DISPENSATION !' The document is, of course,
far too voluminous to quote *in extenso;* but one
paragraph of it is too material to my argument
to be omitted; it is as follows. After innumerable other *fiats* in favour of the royal Bigamarian,
it says—' We ought not to care greatly for what
the world will say, provided our own conscience
is clear: *Nec carandi aliorum sermones, si rectè
cum conscientiâ agatur*. It is thus that we approve
of the proceeding in question, though only in the
circumstances we have just indicated—for the
Gospel has neither recalled nor forbidden what

the Law of Moses permitted with regard to marriage.'* As for the poor heart-broken Landgravine, in vain *she* appealed to the sensual bibolous Protestant Pope, not to let her be put in subjection to her husband's mistress, in this public, authorised, and exceptionally offensive manner. His only and his reiterated reply was, 'It is a wife's duty to *be convenient and to make all things convenient to her husband,* so I hope you will show every consideration and attention to your *colleague!*—the new Landgravine.' Now, I appeal to you, and to the whole world, if the college of Jesuits, and all the Popes whoever wore the Tiara, ever obtruded *their and the church's infallibility,* in a way at all approaching to this ' Dispensation ' of Martin Luther and the

* It has been said that " the world knows nothing of its greatest men." Perhaps it would be nearer the truth to say it thinks little of its greatest men, and finds it convenient to ignore, or to forget them ; the desperate singleness of purpose, and incorruptible sincerity of all REAL greatness being to all wordliness, and its concomitant pliant corruption, the greatest and most impracticable of all impediments and stumbling-blocks, for which reason the sensual and subservient Luther has come down to posterity as a model Reformer ! while the really holy, self-abnegating apostolic SAVONAROLA, who, like another Elijah before Ahab, constrained Charles VIII. to quit and spare Florence from the same havoc that had ravaged Milan, is comparatively unknown. But then to be sure *he* broke no vows in order to marry a Nun, a proceeding which better tallied with, and pandered to earthly corruption. And *he* told his contemporaries in the Catholic church that, by their neglect of the Scriptures, and their multiplicity of ceremonies, " they had neglected and abandoned CHRIST, and gone back to MOSES." While LUTHER, ever sensuous and self-seeking, was wiser in his generation, and in giving the Landgravine of Hesse a dispensation to commit bigamy, approved of, and counselled his neglect of Christ, and going back to Moses. But then *Savonarola was* a noble martyr, while LUTHER was only an apostate monk.

Protestant divines? And see how much wiser, in his generation, the Protestant Pope was than the Roman Pontiff under similar embarrassing circumstances—for it was the latter's steadily and conscientiously refusing to grant a like ‘ DISPENSATION ’ which made our *pious* monarch Henry the Eighth throw off his supremacy, and gave us our ‘ glorious reformation !’ which still strongly needs more reformation. As for Calvin, I think the man and his whole career *so* infamous, that I always feel as if I wanted to rinse my mouth after polluting it with his name.”

“ Truly,” said Locke, “ Butler has summed up the whole question in a couplet, where he says men—

> ‘ Compound for sins they are inclined to,
> By ———ing those they have no mind to.’

I don't at all wonder at Casanove, the King's cook, being puzzled by our tangled web of secrets, and exclaiming, ‘ *Ciel ! quel Pays—deux cents religions ! que deux sauces !*’ By-the-bye, the mention of Casanove naturally reminds me of Whitehall.   Have you heard Rochester's last ?”

“ No,” said Mrs. Neville, “ one never hears the last of my Lord Rochester.”

“ Ha! ha! ha! Very true; but here is his last, and by no means his least. It seems that the Duchess of York had, last night, as usual, all sorts of games, among others ‘*des petits jeux*.’   I

don't vouch for their being exactly *jeux innocents.*
Among others, they were to say, in pairs, what
they would like to be. Lady Castlemaine said,
pointing to a very magnificent Chinese vase,
given to the Duke in Holland, 'I'd like to be
that vase.' 'And I,' said Sir Allen Broderick,
who was her pair on the occasion, 'would like
to be a horse.' 'Tush!' said Rochester, in a
stage whisper to young Killegrew, 'a distinction
without a difference—for the lady would still only
be a rare *jade*, and Sir Allen would continue a
screw.' At which the King laughed louder than
anyone; but the jade and the screw not at all.

"I wonder," said Oliver Hartsfoot, "considering poor Lady Broderick's unforgotten repartee,
that Sir Allen is not rather shy of bringing horses
on the tapis."

"What was that?" asked Mr. Locke; "I don't
remember ever having heard it."

"Why, Sir Allen, for a wonder, had once given
his wife a very beautiful Andalusian mare, of
which she was excessively fond, and one day, as
they were with a large party going out hunting,
and he having said something to her which she
did not hear, from being in the act of patting
the mare's neck, he got into one of his Bashaw
furies, and stamping and frowning, said before
all the assembled guests—'D—n that mare; I
wish it was at the bottom of the sea, since you

think of nothing else, and cannot attend to *me*, madam.'   The poor lady was so nettled at being so spoken to, or rather so publicly insulted, that she summoned for the nonce sufficient courage to reply, in a perfectly audible voice—'Nay, Sir Allen, poor Sunbeam is only my day mare, but you will always be my *nightmare!*' which raised such a laugh at Sir Allen's expense, that he was fain to make good his retreat into the house; but you may be sure the poor lady paid dearly for this sally, and fared the worse for it all the rest of her short life."

"A pity," said Mr. Evelyn, "but she had used whip and spur to her brutal nightmare."

"My dear Mr. Evelyn, you forget," said Mrs. Neville, "Martin Luther's verdict on the score of wifely duty to the poor Landgravine of Hesse, and also as Molière more tersely puts it—

> ' La femme, elle n'est la que pour la dépendence,
>   Du côté de la barbe, est la toute puissance.' "

Here Master Hartsfoot involuntarily passed his hand over his chin, as if making a silent protest that *he* had no beard.

"Ah!" laughed Mr. Evelyn, "no doubt poor henpecked Molière feels brave when he writes those axioms, touching things as they are, and wherein he feels that he is one of the few exceptions that prove the rule, for a kinder, better, or more gentle natured fellow never lived.   And his wife, like my Lady Castlemaine, is also another ' rare jade' that might be added to my Lord Rochester's collection."

" By-the-bye, I did hear one piece of news out," said Mrs. Neville, "which is that the chimney* money is to be taken from the King, and an equal revenue of something else is to be found for him; at least, the people are to be recommended to buy off the tax of chimney money for ever, at eight years' purchase, which will raise the King a present sum of £1,600,000, and the State be relieved from all burden. The debate upon it is adjourned till to-morrow, and the day after Parliament will be prorogued, and our sapient Solons return to their usual course of idleness."

" Well, for my part," said Mr. Evelyn, " I am of the opinion of Pliny's witty friend, *satius est oliosum esse quam nihil agere !*"

" Quite true," laughed Mr. Locke and Oliver Hartsfoot.

" I protest against your abominable Latin, by which we poor ignoramuses lose all the good things," said Dorothy.

" Well, then, my dear young lady, in plain English, what I said at second hand was, àpropos

* Among the innumerable expedients to remedy poor Charles the Second's chronic and incurable impecuniosity, a tax of two shillings a year had been levied on all chimneys throughout the United Kingdoms.

of the prorogation of the Parliament, that it is better to be idle than to *do* nothing."

" I confess I often speculate," said Locke, " upon what posterity will or *can* say upon our terrible dearth, not only of great, but of average men."

" Or," smiled Oliver Hartsfoot, " as my man Noah Pump says, ' Good Lord! what a pretty figure *we* shall cut by the time we becomes the *hantients !* ' "

" Ha! ha! ha! I'll give my friend Noah an angel for that the next time I see him," said Mr. Evelyn ; " but it really is deplorable ! to see how the King's business is done, or rather *not* done, with the exception of poor Pepys, who all in taking most legitimate and constant care of number one, *does* work, and does economise his department of the revenue, so far as it is possible to do so, under that most extravagant, and therefore ruinous of all conditions, whether to empires or individuals—*the want of funds.* But for all the rest, it may be said of them, with scarcely an exception, that they are the most *efficiently useless*, and the most thoroughly *un*trustworthy set of officials that ever hung about a court, or cumbered a State."

Dorothy, who during this conversation had resumed her seat at the open window, and before her embroidery frame, where she had just finished

a moss rose, most exquisitely shaded and broken
at the stem, as if from the weight of a most vel-
vety-looking burglarious bee, who was rifling it
of its sweets, now took advantage of the momen-
tary silence, and placing her little gold thimble,
like a cap of liberty, on the top of her embroidery
needle, and twirling it about, said with a sly
twinkle in her eye and a smile on her lip, both
directed as letters of marque to Master Hartsfoot, while her words were addressed to her
mother—

" Mother dear, we—that is Master Hartsfoot
and I—wish to go to the Bearward, by the Bank
side to-morrow evening.   May we ?"

" May you !   My dear Thea, you astonish me!
—you, who cannot bear to see a fly drowned, or
a moth singe its wings, to wish to go to such a
vulgar and disgustingly cruel place, where poor
animals—your favourite dogs more especially—
are tortured.   Fie ! child, I could not have believed it ! and Master Hartsfoot too !"

But Master Hartsfoot's part was " to suffer
and be strong."   So he proffered no word of re-
pudiation or defence ; no—he understood the
ocular letters of marque he had received better
than that.

" Well, but dear," said Dorothy, returning to
the charge, " everybody goes."

" And suppose it was the fashion for everyone

to commit murder—and we may come to that, as the only novelty in sin left for us—should you think yourself justified, child, in being a homicide, *because* forsooth others were ?"

" Nay, dear; scarcely."

" And yet, Mistress Dorothy, that is precisely what you do; commit murders by wholesale wherever you go," said Mr. Evelyn.

"No—no, Mr. Flatterer; mine are only revised editions of Colonel Titus's play, and if killing at all, is certainly no murder. But, mamma, I have been to all the other places till I am tired, and I wanted to go there because I've never seen it."

" Oh, true daughter of Eve ! Well, child, I think the best way of punishing you will be to let you go to the horrid place."

" I'm sorry to say," said Mrs. Evelyn, " that all the fine lady's *do* go; but I'm very certain dear Dorothy will never go again if she goes once, for it is quite, if not more cruel, and disgusting than a Spanish bull fight."

Here they were startled by innumerable voices just under the window, on the Mall, all exclaiming—

" Oh ! what a darling—what a beautiful little creature ! it looks as if it had come out of a walnut in a Fairy Tale."

Dorothy, who was at the window, leant a little

more forward, and the others came and stood looking over her shoulder. The King and his usual suite were on the Mall; but the cause of the hubbub was that Colonel Titus had just arrived, carrying in the corner of his velvet cloak a little Blenheim puppy, as they are now called, but a little Duchess dog as they were then named, and hat in hand, had just shown it to the King, saying—

" I have the glad tidings to announce to your majesty that Chloe has just had a son and two daughters, and I have brought you the son and heir to know what names and titles your majesty will have bestowed on it—for it really is a perfect beauty !"

" Let the little creature be called Penderel," said the King, " for it is but meet that the most faithful of animals should be named after the most faithful of human beings; and, mind you, my lords, the compliment is all on the side of the biped."

As he ceased speaking, he happened to look up, and perceiving Dorothy, the King took off his hat, and bowed low, in his own peculiarly graceful manner—for which he was as celebrated as for the grace of his dancing. Her curtsey was equally low, and quite as graceful, as she hastily retreated from the window, blushing like " a red red rose."

“Oh! what I would give,” said she, “for that darling pup.”

“I have no doubt,” said Mr. Evelyn, “you have only to ask and have.”

“Then I’ll be among the select few who ask nothing, and who consequently get nothing,” smiled Dorothy.

Mr. and Mrs. Evelyn now rose to take leave.

“My dear Mrs. Evelyn,” said the hostess, “as I have very unwittingly lost so much of your company, *do* return good for evil by remaining to supper; and I can promise all you gentlemen a haunch of my Lord Keeper’s venison, and you, dear Mrs. Evelyn, some of Ruffle’s Tansy maids of honour, which you so highly approve of.”

“Very many thanks, but we cannot to-day accept your tempting invitation, as we are not staying in London, and must return to Sayes Court, and the roads are so bad, that we don’t like to venture on them after dark; but I have long meant to beg the favour of Mrs. Ruffle to give me the receipt for those incomparable maids of honour, and also of her *beaumanger*.* Mr. Evelyn has got some very fine new sort of Tansy plants, lately from Holland, some of which he destines for Ruffle, and also some rare bulbs for you, which he will send down to The Chestnuts; and a blue tulip for you, Dorothy.”

* What we now call blancmange.

" A thousand thanks, Mr. Evelyn—how very kind of you; won't Thea be delighted with her new tulip. I suppose the very tulips in Holland look blue, after De Ruyter's last exploits," said Mrs. Neville, as she rang to have Mrs. Evelyn's coach drawn up. And when it was announced, and they had taken their departure, she turned to Mr. Locke, who was about to follow them, saying, as she laid her hand upon his wrist, to prevent his rising, " Nay—nay, I really cannot consent to lose *all* my guests, and have such a slight offered to my Lord Keeper's venison."

" That is right, *mama mia;* you secure *your* prisoner, and I'll take care mine don't escape, though you *have* the advantage of having the *best* lock in the world," laughed Dorothy, as she ran to Master Hartsfoot, and forcibly held him in his chair by one little white dimpled hand, while she menacingly held up the fore-finger of the other, as much as to say, " Go, if you dare!" So he did not dare, but remained, which, all things considered, was much more daring.

CHAPTER VI.

"JOY IS BRIEF, AND SORROW IS ITS SHADOW."
ASSYRIAN PROVERB.

THE FLOWER AND THE RIVER.

MIZPAH!

HAVING availed herself of her mother's extorted permission to go to the Bear Garden, Mrs. Dorothy was so afraid of losing a particle of that refined and intellectual *diversion*, that she insisted upon her ever obedient slave of the lamp taking her there early; in reality, that she might the better take a census of the house, by being able to distinguish each arrival separately, but being somewhat ashamed of being seen there herself, she had taken refuge in the eclipse of a black moire dress, and a black lace whisk; a red carnation in her bosom, was the only *point de mire* about her, and that could be hidden at a moment's notice by the cardinal of her whisk, or the friendly expansion of her large green fan, while a pair of brown *peau d'Espagne* gloves concealed the snowy whiteness of her hands and arms, which might otherwise have formed too marked a contrast to her black dress. On setting them down, Lancelot said the coachman wished to know at what hour he should return, but that as the night was fine, he was sure madam would not mind the horses waiting an hour or two, if Mrs. Dorothy preferred it.

"Oh! tell Arnold to wait by all means," said Dorothy; "don't you think so, Master Hartsfoot? for you know the place might be too horrible for us to stay in."

"That was always my great fear," responded the docile Oliver; "however, we can but try."

They had the *pleasure* of being *the* first arrivals, which at least gave them the choice of one of the best, that is to say, of the least bad boxes. The amphitheatre was about the size of the present Haymarket Theatre; the boards composing the boxes were so rough, that the roughness frizzed out through the scant lairs of white paint with which they were smeared, which in its turn was enlivened by a broad band of dingy red paint near the top. The as yet "beggarly account of empty benches" were covered, it is true, with red Utrecht velvet, but not being stuffed, were quite as hard as if they had never encountered this mockery of luxury. At every second box flared a rank oil lamp in an iron sconce, the

effluvia from which, mingled rather overpower-
ingly with the Mosaic of sawdust, orange peel,
tobacco ashes, and other contributions that tesse-
lated the arena below.   The orchestra, then in
the act of " tuning up," consisted of one chroni-
cally asthmatic French horn, a theorbo, a dropsi-
cal big drum, and two fiddles, whose excruciat-
ingly squeaking strings were evidently the two
implacable Nemises of the cats, from which they
had been originally purloined.

" Oh ! how horrible !" said Dorothy, taking the
carnation out of her bosom, and burying her face
in it, to counteract the other perfumes.

" Ah ! I was afraid such a place could not be
in good odour with you," said Master Hartsfoot,
having recourse to his own handkerchief, and
wincing under the sounds as well as the smells,
he not having the same motive as his companion
for sacrificing his nose and ears for the satisfaction, or rather to the hope, of his eyes.   But as
Rochéfoucault amiably observes—*il y'a toujours
quelque chose dans le malheur d'un autre, qui ne
nous déplâit pas.*   So neither Dorothy nor Oliver
Hartsfoot were at all sorry to see enter Mr. and
Mrs. Pepys, the latter looking as pretty as a
very vapid, insipid woman can look, and having
that day given Hailes a last sitting for her
picture (the one which adorns the frontispiece of
the second volume of Mr. Pepys' diary), she still

retained her St. Catherine *pose* and air, draperies, and other accessories, with the exception of the spiked wheel and palm branch, and indeed, it would have been difficult for any other woman to bear the palm where Dorothy Neville was. They were also accompanied by Mrs. Pepys' maid, Mercer.*

"Oh! I'm so glad, Mrs. Dorothy," said Mrs. Pepys, seating herself beside her, "I'm so glad," said she, with that grating want of tact, peculiar to her countrywomen at all times, "to see that you bear up and enter into the diversions of the town."

And Mr. Pepys having made one of his private notes that Mrs. Dorothy was looking prodigious

---

* It appears to have been a strange anomalous state of society in those days. This Mercer, so often mentioned in Pepys' Diary, not only accompanied her mistress and master to places of public amusement, but also dined at table with them ; yet Mr. Pepys indignantly and obstinately refused to let his wife invite her drawing-master, Mr. Brown, to dine with them ; while, on the other hand, he takes his own sister, Paulina, as a servant, but will not allow *her* to sit at table with them. Again, he mentions meeting a strange woman at dinner at Lord Sandwich's whom he thought was a new governess ; but adds, "I afterwards heard she was the housekeeper (!)" And my Lord Sandwich, when intriguing with a Mrs. Beck at Chelsea, where, as Mr. Pepys relates, "He played and sang to his lute under her window, and did forty other sordid and foolish things ; also, as a cloak to his proceedings, sent his daughters to lodge with her ; but when he came there under the pretext of visiting them, packed them off into the Park out of the way." Now I don't for a moment mean to insinuate that "noble lords," or perhaps ignoble lords, and "honourable gentlemen" are not quite as immoral in the present day, or even more so, only there is more veneer and varnish used, more pompous parade and pretension in our very vices, which we dignify with the name of decorum. And as hypocrisy has been called the homage which vice pays to virtue, there never was an age in which virtue had so much homage done her as in the present.

handsome, and did far out-do Lady Castlemaine, and even Mrs. Middleton, and added aloud a supplement to his wife's speech, assuring Dorothy that there would be rare sport by-and-bye, when the bulls did begin to toss the dogs, he left her to his wife's tender mercies, and seated himself next Oliver Hartsfoot, while Mercer looked and listened in dignified solitude on the back seat.

" Why, Mr. Pepys," said Oliver, " you have become such a courtier, that you are always at Whitehall, I hear."

" Only upon business about this Tangier Committee, and in the barge with the King, and the Duke of York, and the Duke of Buckingham, and Sir Philip Warwick to Greenwich t'other day; but, good Lord! to hear how foolish and common these great people do talk—just like other men.   But I did dine at ' The Sun ' to-day with Sir Edward Dering,* and did a good stroke of business by a contract with him for timber, and I was glad when it was over—for I have been terribly out of order all day, and did only come here this evening to please my wife, and giving Mercer the money to pay for us, that I might not break my vow against spending money on wine and public diversions."

* Sir Edward Dering, of Surrenden Dering, Kent, which county he represented frequently in Parliament. He was the second Baronet of his family, and some time one of the Lords of the Treasury. He died in 1684.

Oliver Hartsfoot smiled at Mr. Pepys' very *naïve* way of compounding with his conscience, and still greater *naïveté* in proclaiming it; but merely said he hoped he was not suffering from overwork.

"No, it is only heartburn, brought on from eating some of Mrs. Barbary* Sheldon's wedding cake. Lord! to think what a fine rich match she hath made with one Mr. Wood; but, methinks 'tis strange good fortune to so odd-looked a maid, though her body be good, likewise her hand, and her nature, I do think, be very good."

" Well," said his companion, " after all, that is the chief thing—for nature never wears out, though her gifts, more especially her external ones, do."

Yet a gentle sigh from Master Oliver, as he thought how little Margaret Neville's external gifts had suffered from the wear and tear of time, put in a protest against his words.

" Good lack! I do often wish," resumed Mr. Pepys, " that something could be discovered to

---

* Of course this lady's name, like that of Lady Castlemaine, was Barbara; but there was no act of Parliament against Mr. Pepys always writing and pronouncing it *Barbary*. Indeed, at that time, orthography was by no means the arbitrary and tyrannical thing it is now; but, like poetry, a thing (barring the genius) of pure fancy and imagination, so that every writer wrought under a different *spell*. But it is strange that, in the nineteenth century, even educated Englishmen and women *will* persist in always writing "Tartufe" with two f's, though Molière bestowed but one upon him; but to strike the balance, they as invariably mulct poor M. Laffitte of one of *his* f's.

prevent ugliness in women—for it doth seem to me as unnatural a disease in them as it would be for babies to have the gout. And, Lord! to see how ugly the Duchess of York do grow; she features her mother, my Lady Chancellor, more and more every day."

"Certainly beauty does not flourish among our duchesses—for look at the Duchess of Albemarle; perhaps it is," added Hartsfoot, "that in gaining such a height they become dizzy, which improves no one's looks."

"Oh! that do remind me," said Mr. Pepys, "of a capital story my Lord Carlisle did tell me yesterday. You know that the Duke of Albemarle has become a perfect sot, and now drinks with no one but that fellow Troutbeck—not the taverner, but the other—whom no one else will drink or associate with. Well, t'other night they were hard at it, and the Duke, more than half fuddled, did say—speaking of it as a sort of miracle—that Nan Hyde should ever have become Duchess of York. 'Oh!' says Troutbeck, 'you give me another bottle, and I'll match that with quite as great a miracle.' The wine was brought, and the Duke said, 'Now for your miracle to match mine.' 'Well, then,' says Troutbeck, 'I think it even a greater miracle that our dirty Bess should ever have become Duchess of Albemarle!'"

While Mr. Pepys was emptying his always well-stocked wallet of gossip for the benefit of his greatly amused companion, the house was beginning to fill, and Dorothy, all in apparently listening with the deepest interest to a graphic account that Mrs. Pepys was giving her of a long promised pearl necklace of three rows, with which her husband had recently presented her, was sending her eyes on voyages of discovery round the theatre, and at length, standing far back, almost hidden in the shade, she beheld, under the boxes, leaning against a pillar, clad in black velvet, with a heron's plume in his hat, and a white rose in his breast —all her eyes ever went in quest of—for there stood Gilbert Broderick, looking even unusually pale, and by the splashed state of his tan riding-boots, as if he had just come off a journey. The moment their eyes met, Dorothy's whole face was suffused with so deep a flush, that Mrs. Pepys said—

" The heat is too much for you, Mrs. Dorothy ; here is my pomander, and do change places with me—you will be cooler."

But Dorothy, who would not have exchanged her then seat for all the treasures in Europe fused into one universal empire, thanked her, and fanning herself, said it was nothing—in fact she never felt better in her life. And the next moment a floral electric telegraph was established

between that corner of the boxes and the opposite
pillar under them—that is, her red carnation was
once more removed from her bosom, and pressed
to her lips, to which the white rose replied in
somewhat more demonstrative, though silent
fervour. Soon after this, a sort of scaramouch
with two monkeys, and a dog to do duty as a
steed for them, appeared in the amphitheatre,
which part of the performance answered to the
clown in a modern circus, who comes to put the
audience in good humour by divers quips and
cranks, before the real business begins.

"Poor darling dog! how intelligent he is,"
said Dorothy, as an excuse for turning her head
completely away from Mrs. Pepys, and fixing her
eyes permanently on the opposite pillars. But,
alas! quarters of hour's, whether *des mauvais
quarts d'heure*, or those " few and far between "
ones, with the essence of a whole life's happiness
compressed into their fifteen minutes, such as
the one Dorothy was now prodigally expending,
must come to an end; and even " a whole wilder-
ness of monkeys"—let alone two—could not go on
for ever performing equestrian feats on and over
a dog's back. So these charming *artistes*, with
their Master of the Revels, had to retire, in order
to make way for the horrors of the evening.
And presently two huge bulls came snorting and
bellowing into the amphitheatre, followed by

grooms carrying the poor dogs that were to be tossed and tortured.

"Oh!" cried Dorothy, giving a faint scream, and covering her face with her hands as she rose, "Master Hartsfoot! good Master Hartsfoot! *do* take me out of this—I cannot bear it!"

While Oliver, who rose with equal alacrity, handed her over the benches, Mr. and Mrs. Pepys in vain assured her that *now* the sport was going to begin, they both, with a hasty "Good-night," hurried out as fast as possible; but arriving so prematurely, not only their own, but no other vehicle was in sight, only a few stragglers among the lower orders. Now if sorrow is proverbially dry, sitting upon a coach box waiting—it may be for hours—is a sorrow which, in all countries, and under all circumstances, coachmen and footmen find peculiarly so (even when it is pouring rain), and as Launcelot and Arnold were no exception to this rule, the fact was they had adjourned to a neighbouring alehouse, much frequented by serious Jehews during the commonwealth, and then known as " NABOTH'S VINE-YARD ;" but which, since the Restoration, had changed both its politics and its title, which was now that of " OLD NOLL'S NOSE "—a colossal effigy of this solitary feature of Cromwell, upon which the artist had not spared his vermilion, now swinging on a sign-board, in mid air, above

its hospitably always open porch; and it was
astonishing how many poor women in the imme-
diate neighbourhood now complained (though
they could never manage to do it) of how their
husbands were led by the nose.

" Dear! dear!" said Oliver Hartsfoot, " this
is very untoward; would you mind walking a
little way—though I fear your shoes are too thin
for that—or would you be afraid to wait here a
few minutes, while I go and look for the coach ?'

" Certainly *not*. What should I fear, dear
Master Hartsfoot? It is a beautiful moonlight
night, and don't hurry," added foolish Dorothy,
" that is, you—I—what I mean is—you may
catch cold, and over-heat yourself by walking too
fast."

Even the muddy river by the bank side looked
beautiful, with the moonbeams playing upon its
sluggish waters; and the two or three common
hackney boats flitting over them looked actually
picturesque, at least so Dorothy thought as she
gazed at them; and she sighed as she did so—
for of love and moonlight, sighs are always the
sequence—when lo! her sigh was answered by
something more than an echo—in short, by
another sigh even more profound than her own—
for she felt its warm breath upon her cheek, and
the next moment her hand was taken and pressed
within that of Gilbert Broderick, who stole off

her glove (lovers are such thieves) in order to press it, hastily thrusting the captured glove into his bosom. But they had hardly uttered each other's names before Master Hartsfoot was seen triumphantly advancing, waving his handkerchief to intimate that he had found the carriage.

" Go, for Heaven's sake! dear Gilbert; I shall never be let out again if we are seen ; the servants will be sure to tell Ruffle, and she will tell my mother; and here comes Master Hartsfoot !" panted Dorothy.

Gilbert Broderick loved too truly to be selfish, and was too *preux chevalier* to compromise his lady love in the most trifling matter, so he instantly passed out quickly into the road, as if quitting the theatre in haste ; but not before the red carnation and the white rose had changed owners.

" I fear," said Oliver Hartsfoot, " you have thought me a long time gone; but I had to hunt them up at an alehouse in the neighbourhood, and the coach will be here in a few minutes now."

" I did not think you were a moment gone. I am sorry you should have hurried yourself so, Master Hartsfoot. What a lovely night, is it not? it makes me feel quite happy !—almost as if one could feel one's wings growing !"

" Well, you certainly *look* quite radiant."

" What does not, in the moonlight, even the muddy river ?"

She had scarcely ceased speaking, when loud screams were heard from the river, and cries of "Boat upset! Man in the water! Quick! Someone with a rope to fling him!" But before any rope could be gone for—much less brought—a splash was heard. A cavalier had doffed his hat, cloak, and doublet, and jumped into the river, striking out towards the sinking man, amid the vociferous cheers of the bystanders. But in the broad flood of silver light, Dorothy saw *who* the cavalier was, and with an uncontrollable impulse and a wild shriek, darted with extended arms two steps forward; but only to fall fainting in Oliver Hartsfoot's arms, which narrowly prevented her falling in the road. He held her, fanning her with her own fan, till the carriage arrived, into which he lifted her. It was full a quarter-of-an-hour before she revived, and by that time Gilbert had reached the land with the rescued man.

"Both men are safe!" said Oliver, thinking that would be the best restorative, though he was not aware at the time that Dorothy had any personal interest in the matter; but attributed her swoon to the sudden shock to her nervous system.

"Thank God!" exclaimed she.

"Here, my man," said Hartsfoot to a poor man standing by, "go and inquire who the two persons are—the man who was drowning, and the gentleman who saved him—and I will give you a shilling."

The man soon returned, saying—

" The man as was near drownded, sir, was Master Jambres Fairbrace, the scrivener of Clifford's Inn ; and the gentleman who did the handsome thing, and jumped in after him, is young Master Broderick, Sir Allen Broderick's son. Thank'ee, sir, much obliged "—pocketing the shilling.

Master Hartsfoot, who now really felt for Dorothy, and knew towards what her anxiety would naturally tend, said—

" He's a noble fellow, and cannot be spared. I'll go and take him to a tavern hard by, and see that he gets into dry clothes directly, and takes a sack posset. As it is yet early, you won't mind sitting here for half-an-hour ?"

Dorothy's only answer was to press his hand and say—

" God bless you ! dear kind Master Hartsfoot."

Launcelot lowered the steps, Oliver got out, and five minutes after she saw him walking rapidly away, holding Gilbert by the arm, as if afraid he would escape from him ; while Gilbert carried his hat, in both his hands, as if it contained something that *he* was afraid of losing— and, indeed, he could not well have worn it on his head, as his luxuriant long chestnut curls were streaming with water like a river god. It was a full hour before Oliver returned, and Dorothy was delighted with the length of his absence—for the longer he stayed, the more he would bring her back of Gilbert. As she was watching for his coming almost from the time he had set out, she perceived him for full five minutes before he reached the carriage.

"Well," said he, as soon as he was seated, the door closed, and the vehicle in motion on its way home—"Well, I took him to 'The Dolphin,' and I did what was wiser than merely making him put on dry clothes—for I made him get into a warm bed, and there take a sack posset, while I despatched a messenger to his lodgings in Pall Mall, with a note to his servant, telling him what had happened, and bidding him come directly to attend upon his master, and bring him fresh linen and clothes to dress with. I was very nearly sending the note to Sir Allen's, at Whitehall Gardens; but fortunately I read out the address, when he told me that tender parent did not give his only son a room in his house."

"So much the pleasanter for his son, I should think," said Dorothy.

"I think so, too; but that does not exonerate Sir Allen. However, thank goodness he does not seem to have caught the slightest cold—for as soon as his ablutions were ended, and he had washed the Thames mud away from his person and hair, and thoroughly dried the latter, he, with great anxiety, investigated the lining of his hat. I thought perhaps he had placed his purse there for safety, previous to his plunge in the river; but he said that was still in his pocket, though all drenched, of course. He seemed thoroughly delighted when he found what he was looking for. I could not exactly, from the other end of the room, see what it was; but it looked to me like a little brown packet and something red."

As Dorothy knew perfectly well what it was, she expressed no curiosity upon the subject, but confined herself to enunciating her very high sense of her companion's great kindness; while Master Hartsfoot repudiated all merit in the matter, saying that no one with any pretension to humanity could but feel deeply interested in so noble, and so, in every way, charming a young fellow; and as good Master Oliver was a genuine and practically sincere Christian, and therefore always " did unto others as he would they should do unto him," and he truly surmised how anxious poor Dorothy would be to ascertain that young Broderick had not suffered from his generous rescue of the scrivener, he added—

" I shall make it a point to inquire to-morrow at his own lodgings how he is."

It is rather too nice and subtile a metaphysical fraction to attempt to analyse, whether had they known it, Gilbert would have been jealous, or Mrs. Neville displeased; but certain it is that Dorothy at that moment felt the most desperate inclination in the world to throw her arms round Master Oliver's neck. However, she resisted the impulse, which was as well—for perhaps even the recipient might not have been pleased to see the daughter so far in advance of he mother.

CHAPTER VII.

IT was about ten days after Gilbert Broderick had rescued Jambres Fairbrace, the scrivener of Clifford's Inn, from a watery grave, that before he was up in the morning, he received a mandate from his father—for all Sir Allen's communications to his son deserved no other name—to attend him at Whitehall Gardens before ten o'clock, so that the poor young man rose, and began dressing himself with much the same light-hearted feeling of alacrity that a condemned felon may be supposed to do in attiring himself on the morning of his execution. Now it was only two evenings before this that the town was ringing with the escapade of the two Sir Allens, to wit, Sir Allen Apsley, and Sir Allen Broderick, having both gone down tête-á-tête to the House of Commons very drunk, and both persisted in speaking at the same time, without any possibility of their being either coughed, laughed,

or hissed down, or even of being forcibly ejected
from the House ;* and Gilbert knew, from bitter
experience, that when anything untoward happened to his father, that on the equitable and sapient educational principle of whenever the Little
Lama of Thibet is guilty of any misdemeanour,
or shortcoming, some other poor guiltless boy is
invariably flogged for his highness's transgres-
sion. So, in like manner, Sir Allen's son was
always made available to bear the brunt of his
father's failures, and his consequent ill-temper ;
and, indeed, but for these, by no means rare
occasions, Gilbert Broderick might have ran the
risk of forgetting that he *had* a father, seeing
that there were no acts of care or kindness to
commemorate that fact. Upon the same evening
upon which the two Sir Allen's statesmen-like
proceedings in the House of Commons were
reported at Whitehall, the Duke of York, all in
boasting of the amount of business he had got
through that morning at Berkshire House, yet
added that it was by no means so much as they
ought to have despatched on account of the Lord
Chancellor's (Clarendon, his father-in-law), continued sleeping and loud snoring, which disturbed
and impeded everyone. Whereupon Killigrew
Père, turning to the King, said—

"Ah ! it is very certain that there is but ONE

* Fact.

man who *could* save the country by really doing
and looking after its business."

" And whom may he be?" asked the King.

" Why, you know something of him, only not
all that people say about him. His name is
CHARLES STUART."

The King smiled, and turned upon his heel;
but never resolved upon appealing to either the
duty or the diligence of this Charles Stuart.
And so matters were let to go on as they were
doing, perhaps on the *nil desperandum* principle of
the Apathetic School of Philosophy, that " when
things are at the worst they mend." *Les Nations
ont la vie durent.* And it is fortunate that it is
so, or every European country during the last
eight hundred years must, in each succeeding
age, have collapsed, owing either to the vice,
utter want of principle, or incapacity of their contemporary great men, or rather so-called great
men, alias successful men, in high positions.
My Lord Leicester, the minion of that worst
bad woman, but fortunate monarch, Queen
Elizabeth, was no doubt called a great man
in *his* day, but La Verita è figlia del Tempo;
and Time and his daughter Truth have sent the
Lord of Kennelworth (the only *worth* he possessed)
down to posterity as an unscrupulous monster of
cruelty and meanness, before whose enormities
even Nero and Caligula pale, and Herod alone

could rival in concrete wickednees. There can
be no doubt that ambition is a sort of mental
alcohol, of which notoriety is the *delirium tremens ;*
and those men who sacrifice everyone and everything to contemporary celebrity, mistake the road
to the Temple of Fame.

Benè currunt, sed extra viam, as Erasmus
has it; so that having taken the wrong way,
if they do arrive at posterity, it is to find
their names not *in* the Temple of Fame, but
only *on* the *colonna infame.* Happy they who
take Geoffrey Chaucer's sound, sage advice in his
" Balade of Gode Counsaile," wherein he exhorts
his fellow men to—

> " Flee from the presse duell with soth-fastnesse,
>   Suffice unto thy good, though it be small * * *
> That thee is sent receive in buxomness,
>   The wrastling for this world asketh a fall."

But Sir Allen Broderick had precisely one of
those hard, narrow, selfish natures, that always
have been, and always will be, " wrastling for
this world," and which never can be brought to
believe that, because they run well, so far as
reaching temporary goals go, that they run the
wrong way. Who, in fact, *will not* remember the
Gospel truth, though it is the eternal text upon
which all time and all nature preach to us, and
all history, sacred and profane, confirms to us
that "If a man live many years, and rejoice in

them all, yet let him remember the days of dark-nesss —for they shall be many—and all that cometh is vanity."* And so they squander and mortgage the morning and noon-tide of life, as to render these inevitable " dark days " still darker, till " the night cometh when no man can work." And when the final reckoning comes, and when these poor short-sighted self-seekers are sum-moned from this world's fleeting pageant to which they so clung, themselves being gone, there is none left to regret them, no, not one.

In a large room, pannelled with oak, with escutcheons exquisitely carved in high relief in the centre of each panel, a polished oak *parquet*, or inlaid floor, partially covered with a fine Turkey carpet, and luxuriantly furnished with ebony and silver cabinets, mulberry velvet hangings, finished with rich deep bullion fringe, as were also the Charles the First chairs, covered with the same velvet; while on one spare oblong table, on which was a Persian carpet, were placed, ready for their owner's use, a high-crowned, grey felt, Cavalier hat, with a broad band of purple velvet round it, and two long drooping grey ostrich feathers, a pair of gauntlet tan gloves, and a basket-hilted sword; at another large carved ebony and silver, luxuriantly-appointed writing-table, sat Sir Allen Broderick, who, to judge by his knit brows, his bitten lips, and his frequent pauses,

* Ecclesiastes chap. xi., ver. 8.

in which he caused the feather of his pen to toy
absently with a group of Naiades, on a magnificent Benvenuto Celini silver-gilt hand-bell that
stood at his right hand, was evidently in the
throes of some unusually difficult composition.
And sooth to say, it *is* difficult to be publicly
one's own panegyrist, and proclaim all one's own
virtues, gifts, and graces ; and the task becomes
still less easy when one has first to invent the
attributes which are to be eulogised. Now the
origin of poor Sir Allen's perplexity on the
present occasion was this. The day before he
had met Dryden, and Sir Gilbert Pickering
nearly at his own door, when he first issued
forth to take his morning walk, the former thinking to please him, as it would have done any
other father, said—

"Well met, Sir Allen, I give you joy!"

"Of what?" said he, hoping it might be some
scrap of Court favour intended for him, of which
he was yet ignorant.

"It is very generous of me to bely the proverb,
which says 'two of a trade can never agree,' but
Hippocrene has many rills, if only one source,
and I really think Master Gilbert *has* found the
source and quaffed from the fountain head. I do
not say it to flatter you, but in all truth I think
his poem—I mean his Eosphoros*—admirable,
and some of his minor poems gems, and so I

* Eosphoros—The Star, that makes it well to wake again.

told him when he consulted me about publishing them."

Now, there is nothing so ill-bred as ill-temper, which is what makes it the most vulgar of all the vices, and Sir Allen Broderick's ill-temper was now on this occasion concrete. First, he was furious to think his son should meditate any such public method as authorship, of making his existence patent to the world, and so " clashing," as he phrased it, with his father. And next, with the bitter, cold jealousy of hate, which always resents, either the fear or the dislike, which it is conscious of deserving, he was savage to think that this son, whom he suppressed so far as possible, and kept at such an unnatural distance, had not *first* consulted and confided in *him* about this matter; for those who systematically violate them all towards others, are invariably wonderful sticklers for the sacredness of " family ties," where their *own* personal pleasure, interest, or convenience is concerned.

So instead of even the conventional courtesy of thanking the laureate for his kind and flattering verdict, he merely growled out—

" Oh ! indeed, I was not aware he indulged in *that* sort of folly."

But he resolved then and there, that his son's effusions should never see the light, unless they issued forth, preceded by a fulsome dedication to himself! and it was the endeavour to announce to the world what certainly *would* be the greatest news he could possibly regale it with, to wit, the tender, and more than maternal care, he had always lavished on his son; and that son's fears that nothing but the halo of his father's loved and honoured name, could induce the public to view his crude productions in a favourable light, which now occupied, or rather pre-occupied that exemplary parent. The great difficulty being at once to carry out the school-boy axiom of " lay it on thick, and some will stick," and at the same time to avoid the Charybdis of what modern schoolboys would call " coming it too strong." But still, on the other hand, Virgil is right— *meus agitat molem*—and it was the mass he wished to inform, or rather to mis-inform, for no one knew better the value of a well-aimed lie than Sir Allen; and that lies should be so potent, is all the fault of Truth; for, as a popular dissenting minister of the present day observed in one of his sermons, "Truth is such an inveterate dawdle, that a lie will travel round the world while she is putting on her boots!"

In the midst of all the difficulties about this literary *tour de force* of the *suppressio veri* and *suggestio falsi*, a door opened at his back, at the other end of the room, slightly creaking on its hinges, as all doors did more or less in those days.

“ Who’s there ?” asked Sir Allen, in a sharp, angry voice, without, however, turning round on his chair to see.

“ It’s me, sur.”

“ Who the bare bones are you ?”

“ Desmond, yer honour.”

“ What the Cromwell brought you here ?”

“ Shure it was your honour’s morning draught and the Botigo,* which is worth nothing if it is not like some people’s temper, scraching hot.”

Now this Desmond was an Irishman whom Sir Allen had taken into his service out of charity, as he said, but in reality because he came for half the wages of his English footmen, and was a fine, good-looking, tall, showy servant, more especially in Sir Allen’s crimson livery, with its white facings and silver lace, and also a large solid silver badge on his left arm of Sir Allen’s armorial bearings, such as only private postillions wear now, but which all serving men wore then. He now entered with a tray with one cover laid, the aforesaid Botigo, a roast chicken, a tankard of ale, and a tall, diaphanic-looking flask of Rhenish wine ; in a word, his master’s breakfast.

“ Will I move any of dem papers, or get another table to put the breakquist upon ?”

“ Go to the d——l,” growled Sir Allen.

* Botigo, a sausage made of eggs, mushrooms, and the blood of the sea mullet.

" Shure I am here."

And having so far relieved his feelings, Desmond placed the tray upon another table, while
he lifted over a small chess table to put it on,
close by his master's chair.

" What o'clock is it," asked the latter.

" Why, thin, be dad! one wud tink I was de
town clock, de way de people does be axing me
de time; and, faix! if me hands had nothing
else to do, like dose of de town clock, but point
to de hours, sorrow a much use it ud be, seeing
de're niver five minutes in the same place."

" Will you hold your confounded tongue and
look for my watch?"

Now Sir Allen's watch was one of the last ab-
surdities that fashion had hit upon, being the
golden model of a duck, which opened underneath, longitudinally in the centre, and within
contained a watch, and this one, not being larger
than a large walnut, was thought an especially
delicate little trinket.

" And where wud I luck for yer watch, sir?
Shure it's in your own pockets you ought to have
it."

" Idiot! look under those papers, and all about
the table. You've seen it a hundred times; it's
a duck in gold."

" That's more of it," muttered Desmond, as he
removed and shook each book and paper separ-

ately, and then replaced them. " Dat's more of it. Shure in Oirland it's in de pond de ducks do be, and not among papers."

Everything had been taken off of the table, but no watch could be found; Sir Allen, therefore, flew into one of his towering passions, and flatly accused Desmond of having stolen it, telling him at the same time that that was his reward for taking an Irish blackguard into his service.

" Och! I don't doubt but you're a good judge of blackguards, sur, but I have not got the watch."

And here he folded his arms and set his teeth, as he followed Sir Allen round the room with his eyes, but neither moved nor uttered another word, nor offered to pick up a single thing as Sir Allen dashed them about, and swept everything off the different tables.

At last, coming to the table, where lay his hat, sword, and gloves, he lifted up the hat, and there was the watch under it, where he himself had placed it, to have it ready when he went out. He was not so much ashamed of himself as provoked and annoyed; but turning awkwardly to the dogged, stolid, immoveable statue in plush, he stammered out—" Oh, I beg your pardon ; I thought perhaps you had— In short, I forgot where I had put it."

" No offince, sur," said Desmond, measuring

his master from head to foot, with a sort of side glance, but still keeping his arms folded; "no offince; shure we were both mistaken, dat's all. You tuck me for a thafe, and I tuck you for a gintleman; and, faix, I'm tinking I made de biggest mistake of de two."

Sir Allen reddened with suppressed rage to the very roots of his hair, and said, " I'm sorry, my man, I was so hasty."

" Och! don't mintion it, Sur Allen. Shure them's the best dispositions. I'm mighty passionate meself, for the matter of that. I might kill you in a passion just, but it ud be over directly, and I'd niver tink a haporth about it de next minute."

Sir Allen felt very much inclined to adopt the same course of " happy despatch," and subsequent oblivion upon his servant; but here the door opened, and the butler announced, " Captain Broderick, Sir Allen." So bidding Desmond leave the room (which he was only too glad to do), seating himself before his breakfast, and unfolding his napkin, he greeted his son with—

" So you are come at last ?"

To which poor Gilbert meekly replied that he had endeavoured to be punctual, as the message he had received was to attend his father before ten, of which it then wanted a quarter. Sir Allen procceded with his meal, never inquiring whether his son had breakfasted, and leaving him standing for nearly all the rest of the *audience*, hat in hand, like a groom, or any other menial, waiting for the orders of the day.

"Ahem!" said Sir Allen, at the end of ten minutes, draining another glass of Rhenish, leaving the roast chicken, to that common, but not on that account more agreeable freak of fate, considerably reduced circumstances, and backing his chair away from the *débris* of his morning repast. "Ahem! the matter upon which I sent for you I will speak of anon; but first, I think it right to tell you that it would have been more decorous, more dutiful, and more befitting *my* honour! to have consulted *me* upon your affairs, instead of laying bare to strangers what should be the sacred arcana of family matters, upon which a FATHER's judgment and authority must be the only eligible umpires."

"Really, sir," rejoined poor Gilbert, in genuine and profound surprise, but changing alternately from red to white, from his chronic terror of his father, "I am so little aware of having done so, that I am quite at a loss to conjecture to what circumstance or act of mine you can possibly allude."

"Oh! you are, are you? Well, they say every poet is a fool, and fools, like liars, have proverbially short memories," observed Sir Allen, with

one of his sardonic sneers, the nearest approach
to a smile that ever flitted over his satyr-like
type of face.

" I do not think in this instance, sir, it is my
memory which is in fault, as it is impossible to
remember what one never did."

" And I suppose it is only a myth of mine,
and that you never went to John Dryden to consult *him* about rushing into print; and—and
summoning the public to your crude crotchets
and moon-struck rhymes ?"

The whole "head and front of his offending"
now rushed in accusing crimson to the poor cul-
prit's face, as taking council of the feather in his
hat, and passing it to and fro through his fingers,
he stammered out—" I did not like, sir, to take
the liberty of consulting you about so trifling a
matter, and one that I was aware you would feel
no interest in."

" *That's* nothing to the purpose.　It's the
want of duty and respect of which I complain,
and the acquainting strangers with one's family
affairs, always an undignified proceeding."　And
here Sir Allen rose, paced up and down the room
in his normal attitude, that of his head thrown
back, and his right hand on his hip, almost a
facsimile of the *pose* in which Cruikshank has
immortalised " Lord Bateman."　After which he
continued, " In the first place, I think it ——

indelicate of you to drag yourself before the public in any way during *my* lifetime. This sort of clashings and helical risings in families should always be avoided. However, upon *one* condition I will allow you to publish your rhymes, that you inscribe them to me with a *proper* dedication, though I should infinitely prefer your not publishing them, or obtruding yourself on public notice in any way. Here"—taking his morning's work from the writing-table—" is a rough draft of what you are to say, the style, of course, to be polished and revised prior to publication."

Gilbert bowed, and took this precious document in profound silence; and when later he read it in the solitude of his own room, he was thankful that he had been left the alternative of not publishing his poems—for he felt only too heavily that his father's name was neither " loved" nor " honoured," and had too keen and conscious a sense of the impious sacrilege of a much aggrieved child, lending himself for the sake of authorly vanity to such a sham, about such a parent; and, indeed, the sacrifice was not so very great, despite Dryden's very flattering encouragement, seeing that the only public he, Gilbert, cared to please, or to pluck fame from, began and ended with Dorothy Neville, who was at once his inspiration and his goal.

" There is another matter also which I intended

speaking to you upon,' resumed Sir Allen, so soon as he had transferred, not, indeed, any of his possessions, but all the virtues he did *not* possess in the aforesaid dedication to his son, " and that is, that I must beg you will not again drag *my* name into the mire, by jumping into the Thames at midnight to rescue capsized scriveners, or other low people. Had it been the royal barge, indeed, or anyone else's of condition, there might have been some excuse."

" Really, sir," said the young man, with a wan smile, " I did not think of first making researches in the Herald's College when a fellow creature was drowning."

" *Fellow* creature ! " vociferated Sir Allen, flinging back his head in a way that seemed to endanger its rolling off on the ground, while his right foot was advanced to the uttermost, his hand grasped his hip, and his elbow was bowed out like the handle of a tea-pot. " *Fellow* creatures ! Such *canaille* may be *your* fellow creatures, but they are *not mine.* Zounds ! sir, have you no respect for the name you inherit ?"

" So much, sir, that by God's mercy I hope never to do anything that may make my children ashamed of the name they will inherit."

Sir Allen chafed at this home thrust ; but as he pre-eminently possessed " the wiser part of valour," he thought it better to parry than to return it. So, fanning himself with his handkerchief, he resumed his seat, and after one or two more sonorous " Ahems!" said, " Sit down, that I may now speak to you about the business upon which I sent for you. You are now two-and-twenty?"

" Three-and-twenty, sir."

" Well, an additional reason why you should be settled."

From its previous violent and almost audible beating, Gilbert's heart now stood still, as the blood receded from his cheeks, and a deadly chill paralysed all his limbs.

"And," resumed his father, " despite all his enemies, my Lord Sandwich appears to have a greater hold upon the King's favour than ever ; and, exclusive of the £8,000 a year he has settled upon him in perpetuity, I have no doubt that his Majesty would give a dower of £20,000, or £30,000, to my Lord's eldest daughter, if she married suitably. Now the money, and my Lord Sandwich's bran new earldom, is the least of it ; but the bedchamber *influence* is everything. Some fools strain after wealth, others after titles, whereas the royal road to them is court favour, which comprises all things. Therefore, you will go to my Lord Sandwich's, at his new house in Lincoln's-Inn-Fields—from me—to offer yourself as suitor to Lady Jemima Montague, telling my Lord that I will do my part, so that we shall not fall out about settlements."

"But, sir, it is the public talk that Lady Jemima Montagu is actually affianced to a son of Sir George Carteret."

"'Sdeath! Sir, I hope you don't presume to compare Sir George Carteret's son to my—I mean—that you don't presume to compare Sir George Carterett to ME!"

"Still, sir, an engagement is an engagement."

"Not when a better one offers."

Young Broderick was so dumbfounded by the cool cynicism of this very common, though seldom openly proclaimed, inverse species of morality, that he remained silent, whereupon his father went on—

"Now, no shilly shallying. You have my orders, and, to save time and trouble, I may as well tell you at once that there is no appeal from them."

"Sir," said Gilbert, with more firmness and decision than he had ever before summoned courage to assume towards his father, "I have always endeavoured to obey you, not simply to the letter, but in spirit; and have tried invariably, not only to avoid displeasing you, but have on all occasions, so far as I was able, to anticipate your wishes. Neither am I one who deem

that God and nature have set the same narrow
limits to filial obedience that the law has ; but,
sir, I would with all due deference and respect,
remind you that I *am of age*, at the same time
that I inform you I *cannot* marry Lady Jemima
Montagu."

Had a thunderbolt literally fallen at his feet
Sir Allen would in all probability have been less
astounded, and he certainly could not have been
more so if, instead of this calm and respectful,
but decided protest, his hitherto passively and implicitly submissive son had suddenly with a sledge
hammer dealt him a violent physical blow. He
positively both gasped and reeled under his son's
unwonted audacity, and as soon as he could
speak, which was not for some moments, he stammered out—

" So *you* will not marry Lady Jemima Montagu? Is that your ultimatum ?"

" It is, sir."

" Harkee, young gentleman ; I'm not to be
defied on all points. I still *will* be obeyed,
since I have the misfortune to be your father, a
circumstance you seem to forget. My Lord Peter-
borough is recalled from Tangier; Lord Dartmouth sails in six weeks to replace him. You
either marry Lady Jemima Montagu, or you prepare to accompany Lord Dartmouth to Tangier,
where you will remain till the destruction of all

the Moorish fortifications and harbours is completed, and which it is calculated will take about
four years ; and mind, sir, not a syllable of the
conversation that has passed this morning between us to your friend Mr. Dryden, or any one
else ; and you are publicly to state that it is *your
own wish, much against mine, that you go to Tangier,*
for I do not chose to have all their d—— tongues
set a wagging against me. So, once for all—
Lady Jemima Montagu or Tangier?"

"Tangier, sir," responded Gilbert, in a clear,
firm, and perfectly audible voice.

"Then Tangier be it," hissed Sir Allen, in a
tone so hoarse and guttural that it sounded more
like an effort of ventriloquism than ordinary
human speech.

"There is one thing I would ask you, sir,"
said Gilbert, looking into his hat, which he held
between both his hands, as if it had been a well,
in which he was searching for truth. "Would
you have any objection to my going down to
Clumber Chase to take leave of my Aunt Broderick before my departure? for I hear her health
is so broken I fear I may not see her again."

And as he thought of all her care and kindness—the only care and kindness he had ever
known since his mother's death, when he was a
child of ten, the tears welled up in Gilbert's
eyes ; nay, they did more, they overflowed and

trickled down his cheeks, at which, upon seeing his father's sneer of ineffable contempt, he hastily brushed them away.

" A very great objection," said Sir Allen; " I don't want you to play the same crooked game against me that *she* did with my Uncle Mortimer, who left her Clumber Chase, and left it unentailed, too ! instead of leaving it in the male line to me, as he ought to have done; for what the deuce do women know about managing landed property?   And what the devil does any woman want beyond a hundred a year and a prayer book ?"

Now, the real truth of the matter was, that Sir Reginald Mortimer, Sir Allen's maternal uncle, having been very early in his career disgusted with his nephew's adamantine selfishness, and shocked at his profligacy, and moreover, thinking that his large paternal estate of Broderick Park, in Yorkshire, was quite suffi-cient for a man who had no sympathies or aspirations beyond self; had left his beautiful place of Clumber Chase, in Suffolk, to his dearly loved niece, Phillida Broderick, whom he well knew—had she little, or had she much—had a deep sense of the responsibility of her stewardship, and only lived to minister to the wants, or to the pleasures of everyone of God's creatures that came within her reach, for she in youth's

early spring, when others cull blossoms, had a
great blight fall upon her life; she had deeply
loved her cousin, the gay, gallant, handsome
Algernon Neville, and for a long time thought
he loved her, till the blow came, and she found
he had only sought her for the sake of her friend
Margaret, Sir Charles Wheeler's most beautiful
daughter, which inedited romance, Margaret
Neville, though now ten years a widow, had
never even suspected. It was Phillida's one
secret, and she was determined it should go a
secret to her grave with her. Oh! what softeners
and purifiers are these moral simooms! True,
they prostrate in the dust and unto death for
the time; but after, all other storms pass lightly
over. Sorrow and disappointment warp and
harden narrow, shallow natures, but affliction is
the appointed training-school of all broad, deep,
and noble ones; and the blow which had so
heavily fallen, and crushed out all hope from
Phillida Broderick's young life, had, like the
bruised bitter herbs for the Hebrew sacrifices,
only brought out in greater fragrance the holy
sweetness of her nature, and gave her that truly
Catholic sympathy, which can only be acquired
by searching in our own hearts for the key to
others' lives. Oh, fate! thou world-old great
dramatist—how stringently thou keepest the
unities of all thy tragedies! Phillida Broderick,

who had begun her life with such a heart-quake, was destined to end it, if not with equal, yet with similar uprootings; as from the tyranny and mean jealousy of that petty domestic Herod, her brother, she was now, in her declining years, deprived of the solace and society of the three beings she loved best on earth—her nephew Gilbert, her oldest and dearest friend, Margaret Neville, and her charming and affectionate little daughter, Dorothy; for the two latter could not, in common self-respect, subject themselves to Sir Allen's insults and suspicions. True, they corresponded with their kind friend of Clumber Chase, " as often as the few and far between," and very irregular and uncertain posts, and " private hands" of that day, gave them the opportunity of doing; but where hearts, and souls, and minds are one, what a poor pale simulacrum of affection are letters ! with hundreds of milestones between each.

When his father had impugned his son's motives in wishing to personally take leave of his aunt, for sordid and selfish ends, the young man replied, with a flush of indignation on his heretofore deadly pale face—

" Sir, were my Aunt Phillida to leave me the whole world, the day *she* left it would be the saddest day of my life."

" Ha ! ha ! a most dutiful and affectionate

speech, I must say, considering you have a father !
who has still to leave the world," said Sir Allen,
with a strange noise, something between a growl
and cachination, while like Miss Kilmanseg's
sire, he—

"Washed his hands with invisible soap,
In imperceptible water."

Curtly adding a moment after, as he suddenly
quitted his seat, and walked over to within a few
paces of his son, then stopping with a sort of
" present—fire ! " manner—" you may go."

Gilbert rose, bowed silently, and withdrew, but
before he had closed the room door after him, Sir
Allen had resolved that *the report should get about*
that the reason of his son's departure for Tangier
was that his addresses had been rejected by Lady
Jemima Montagu ! Albeit, from her very plain
person, uncouth, unformed manners, and totally
uncultured mind, the very last person who would
be likely to inspire such an all-accomplished,
preux Chevalier, as Gilbert Broderick, with a
passion malheureuse; but *that* did not matter a
fico; probabilities were too common-place for Sir
Allen's genius to condescend to manipulate the
*im*probable was what he alone deigned to work
in, and no one knew better from long and
successful experience, that once sound the *wrong*
note to start it with, and it was next to an impossibility ever to get that concrete ass, the public,

into the right key after.   In short, no one could
have written for the benefit of courtiers, diplo-
matists, politicians, authors, and men of the
world, a more compendious and practical physi-
ology of lying than this "CLEVER MAN."

How many dead walls we come to in life, where
we have not even the option of turning back, and
have nothing for it, but either to dash our heads
against them or stand still, and summon resignation and resolution to our council.   But sometimes Fate "writes such bitter things against us"
on these dead walls, that the latter course is not.
at first so easy, till SLEEP, that great catholic
sister OF MERCY, comes, and "draws her small
soft finger through them all."

Could Gilbert Broderick only have been by
some good fairy invisibly transported to his own
room on leaving his father, he felt so utterly
prostrated and exhausted both in body and mind,
that no doubt this Sister of Mercy might have
come to him; but no, he had to go with his
great load of misery, under which he staggered
and reeled like a drunken man, into the garish
light of the busy, bustling, work-a-day world,
with all its pleasure-worshippers, and its mam-
mon-worshippers, to jostle, stare at, and
comment upon him; and whoever yet was
suffering under any abnormal affliction, and
had to drag it with them through the highways

and byeways, that they did not meet the very
person whom they would have gone any distance
to avoid? Gilbert had slowly and mechanically
descended the first flight of stairs, more like a
person in a state of sonnambulism than a waking man, so little was his spirit present with,
and conducting his body, when he caught sight
of his father's servants, clustering and gossiping
round the open hall door; their backs were
towards him, so they had not seen him, but he
felt it so utterly impossible to support either
their wonder, their pity, or even their silent
respect, in his present frame of mind, that he
turned hastily back, as if he had suddenly seen
approaching some terrible and imminent danger.
And when he reached the first landing he sat
down upon a long oak bench, covered with mul-
berry-coloured velvet, which ran along the side
of a large pier-glass that reached from the ceiling to the floor, which bench was placed there for
the use of pages and servants in waiting. He
sat there for full ten minutes to try and collect
his thoughts, and marshal his conflict of painful
feelings into sufficient subjection to enable him
to reach his lodgings, with at least the decency
of external calm and self-possession. He might
have taken longer to do this, only that he heard
a movement in the room where he had left his
father, and dreading another *rencontre* he hastily

arose, put his collar straight, adjusted his hair in the glass, slouched his hat somewhat more than usual over his eyes, and, putting on his gloves, leisurely descended the stairs, purposely clanking his spurs that the servants might hear him, and so stand aside to let him pass. All of which happened just as he wished it, he merely touching his hat à *la militaire*, in acknowledgment of their silent salutations. So there, at least, was Scylla cleared, but, as is too often the case, only to be engulphed in Charybdis, for at his father's very door he was pounced upon with cordial greetings by Mr. Pepys and Tom Killigrew, which latter was laughing more than such a stale *rechauffé* seemed to warrant, at Pepys' wonderful escape, a few months ago, from that infuriated Portuguese *Padre*, and how mighty handsome it was of Colonel Titus to let him (Mr. Pepys) seek safety in flight, while he (Titus) remained to encounter the Jesuit single handed.

" How now, my noble friend," cried Killigrew, laying his hand upon Gilbert Broderick's shoulder. " How now, my noble friend, as they say in the House of Lords, where there is little that's friendly and less that is noble. Like poor Ophelia, prythee "wear thy rue with a difference," boy ; that is, don't wear it *all* in thy face, to make thee look like a solar eclipse. Marry, go home, and perfume thy wit with ' The Romaunt of the Rose,' or sweeten thy humour with 'Melibeus.' ''

Gilbert smiled a wan smile, and got as far as "Ah! Tom, if every one had your spirits—" and then fairly broke down.

"Good Lord!" said Mr. Pepys, coming to the rescue, "to see how a man's humour shall be turned by a straw. The other day, at Berkeshire House, I was more than put out by my Lord Chancellor's snoring, and having of all our business impeded, and my wife giving me sweet sauce with a leg of mutton, so that I was fain to dine meanly off a marrow bone. But I went to the King's house, to see 'The Maiden Queen,' which, indeed, the more I do see the more I do like, and is an excellent play, and so done by Nell,[*] her merry part, as cannot be better done in nature. And I did laugh till I cried, and so home to bed with great content; and as she plays in it again to-night, you cannot do better, Master Gilbert, than be led by me, and go and laugh too."

Here Desmond came out of the house, holding a letter, which he handed to Killigrew, saying—

"Shure, sur, Mister Somerset's French futman, in feaders,[†] cudent find yer house,

---

[*] Gwynne.

[†] This was the same "French footman in feathers" who had occasioned Mr. Pepys sundry vague disquietudes, from being the bearer, on two several occasions, of certain mysterious messages from his master, Mr. Somerset, to Mrs. Pepys, delivered apart, only fortunately, Mr. Pepys "did think there was nothing in it," and there is a great deal in *that.*

and axed me to lave dis wid you, from his master."

Killigrew broke the seal, and found a few lines, merely saying—

"MY DEAR KILLIGREW,—

"I herewith enclose you the French verses I promised you, and hope you will profit by their philosophy; though I confess I am not a sufficiently subtle logician to attempt—and still less in the particular point in question—to wish to prove a positive by a negative.

"Ever yours,

"Till I am someone else's,

"H. SOMERSET."

"By Jove! my dear Broderick, the very prescription for your case," said Killigrew, proceeding to read aloud the verses Mr. Somerset had sent him.

LE VRAI BON SENS, PAR UN QUI EN A FAIT LE FICHU EXPÉRIENCE.

"Je ne veux ni la gloire, ni les succès,
L'ambition, ne me vaut rien;
Que le Ciel m'accorde seulement,
L'esprit libre, pour tout bien.

Loin de moi, tout orgueil,
Que le *bon sens* me mène toujours;
Les vrai besoins sont à bon marché,
Le reste s'en fait, à coup sûr!

C'est pourquoi, à la Providence divine,
Je rends grace de n'avoir plus d'attente ;
Evitant de l'espoir les qui-pro-quos,
La santé, et la sagesse augmente.

En quels soucis ! la vie se passe !
De ceux qui du bonheur ont soin ;
Courage ! donc Malheureux ! puisque sans contredit,
Le *vrai* bonheur, consiste à n'avoir point !"*

"Ha! ha! ha! *le vrai bonheur consiste à n'avoir point!* Ce qui met, le bonheur à la portée de tout le monde!" laughed Killigrew.

"Then," thought Gilbert, though he did not say it, "at that rate I should be the happiest fellow alive!" but he only joined in the laugh of his companions, and then said he must leave them, as he had an appointment, for which he was already late.

"Farewell, my dear fellow!" said Killigrew, pulling an exaggeratedly long face, putting his handkerchief to his eyes, and affecting to cry; "farewell! may every misery attend you, so as that you may possess real happiness! and au revoir, au Château des Tristes Apattes du Desespoir!"

"And don't forget to go and see Nell," cried Mr. Pepys, screaming a postscript after him as he was hurrying away across the Park.

* If I knew the name of the modern author of these clever lines, I would apologise to him or her for ante-dating them a couple of centuries. But, like Moliére in that, though unfortunately in nothing else—"Je prends mon bien partout où je le trouve.—G. G. S."

CHAPTER VIII.

LOVE, LAW, AND PHYSIC.

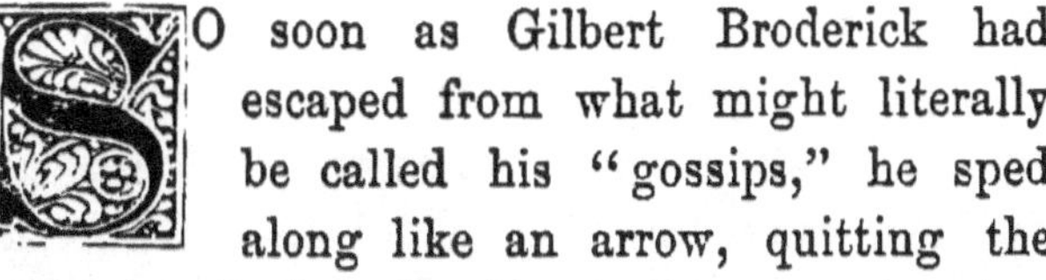O soon as Gilbert Broderick had escaped from what might literally be called his "gossips," he sped along like an arrow, quitting the Park near Spring Garden, and never stopping till he reached his lodgings in Pall Mall, or, as it was called at that time, "The Pell Mell." The door was opened by his landlady, whom he saluted with a courteous, "Thank you; and good morning, Mrs. Swinburn," and then cleared the stairs four at a time, till he reached his bed-room, where he closed the door after him, and turned the key in the lock; but had no sooner done so (forgetting, however, to lock the other door that led into his sitting-room), than his big Mount St. Bernard dog, Monk, who was lying on the floor beside his bed, and his little pet spaniel, Charley, who had made a luxurious nest for himself in the very midst of the down pillow, covered with a fine laced-frilled pillow case, that Mrs. Swinburn always placed on the outside of

"*her* lady's and gentlemen's beds," as a sample
of the snowy and dainty linen to be found within; now both sprang to his embrace, Monk, with
his huge paws, upon his shoulders—Charlie, at
one bound off of the pillow into his arms, with
all the little canine hysterics, caressing greetings,
and desperate efforts to speak—that is, to speak
with *human* parlance, which is so touching in
their true and loving race.   Of course, the little
long   silken-eared, wondrous,   meteoric-eyed,
beauty was called " Charlie," for that name for
dogs at that time was as plentiful as daisies;
and, to do the King justice, he was both pleased
at, and proud of it.

 " So, ho ! my fine fellows," said Gilbert, alternately petting and patting them both, " there
are dark days in store for us ; a horrid ship, with
all its abominations ! for you, my dainty Charlie,
and a broiling tropical sun for you, my poor
hardy Mountaineer Monk !   But, for all that,
we won't part, will we, old friends ?"

 " Part ! I should think not, indeed ; that
would be an infamous shame !" said both the
dogs, as plainly as one pair of large luminous,
bright black diamond eyes, and another pair of
wise, earnest brown ones, could say it.

 " No—no ; I knew you'd say so.   Good dog !
—good fellow !   Down, Monk," and the next
moment the faithful creature had again stretched

himself at full length on the floor beside his master's bed, only this time, instead of lying on his side, with outstretched four feet to sleep, he lay flat upon his stomach, placing his handsome black nose between his two brown fore paws, which is a dog's way of putting on his considering cap.

"And you, Charlie, must go to by-bye again, like a good child, for I am very wretched, and have much to think of," said he, appealing to the little creature, as he still tried to cling round his master's neck, who took him with a gentle force and laid him again on the pillow, as tenderly as if it had been an infant. After which, he took off his hat, laid it on the bed, and flung his gloves beside it, which he had no sooner done, than Charlie, looking half askance towards his master, as if in fear of being forbidden, left his downy nest stealthily, and went and laid upon them. For all dogs are Romeos with regard to the gloves, or any other thing that has touched those they love. The greetings over, and the three friends once more silent, two of them being perfectly satisfied, now that they *saw* all they cared for had come safely back to them—Gilbert threw himself into a large high-backed arm-chair, covered his face with his hands, and groaned aloud. His first thought was of Dorothy; he *must* see her, to break the tidings

of his banishment to her, that she might not hear
it with all imaginable false additions and mis-
constructions.　　And if he could in no way contrive a means of seeing her, there was Master
Hartsfoot; he would write the truth to *him* to
tell her.　　Oh! blessed Providence that had
brought them acquainted.

His next thought was of his good, his kind, his
unselfish, his dearly loved aunt, Phillida; at all
events, thank heaven, to her he could and would
write freely, and minutely, and would pour out,
without let or hindrance, the bitter flood of untoward fate that was sinking his heart.　　But after
these two paramount thoughts, of slight pallia-
tion, the terrible *reality* which he must wrestle
with always came to the surface.　　Four years'
banishment—a semi-eternity!　　What might not
happen in half that time?　　Would Dorothy wait
for him?—that is, would she be let to wait? and
even if she did, and if she was, what might she
be waiting for? perhaps a phantom; for might he
not be killed where carnage was being so plentifully distributed? and even if he escaped lead
and " cold iron," still how many had already
succumbed to the climate; and what right had
he to hope that he would be one of the exceptions?
Well, be it how it might, God was there as well
as here; the issues not only of life and death,
but of all other things, whether great or small,

were in His hands, and His will be done; and though he did not then kneel, he nevertheless prayed with that fervour of sincerity and devotion, with which only the " weary and heavy laden " *do* pray, to Him who has invited them to come to Him, and who has promised to "give them rest." " My God," said Gilbert Broderick, lifting up his eyes, and joining his hands in supplication, " Thy will be done, but with the struggle, send the strength; with the trial, the patience; with the submission, the grace." And much as he loved his Aunt Phillida for whatever else she had done for him, he loved her best of all for having early taught him to "pray always." "You should do so," she would say, "as a matter of gratitude to God, from whom alone all good comes, or can come; and you should do so as a matter of necessity; for had you all the powerful monarchs of the earth for your friends, their power, or even their inclination to serve you, can only come from Him. Besides, earthly friends are not always there, God is. They too, may be false, or may change; God never is the one, or ever does the other. The nearest and dearest friend does not know your whole heart; all its yearnings and all its necessities; all the evil it has yielded to, and all that it has resisted; God *does*, better than you yourself can. For which reason God is even more merciful to us than we are to ourselves, because His knowledge and His power are both infinite ; we have neither knowledge nor power, therefore it is we are unjust, even to ourselves. Oh! my dear child, learn then to *trust*, where you *cannot trace.* Who can? —for truly ' God's ways *are* past finding out,' at least to such poor finite ephemera as we are ; who, at most, only see the knottings, hitchings, and crossings, on the reverse or wrong side of His stupendous work! which has eternity for its woof, and all Time for its warp.'' It was now, in his hour of trial, that Gilbert recalled these lifelong exhortations of one he so dearly loved, and so profoundly respected. The hours, the times, the places, all came vividly before him ; he again saw the deep, earnest, anxious, loving eyes looking into his ; heard the gentle persuasive voice, and felt the little warm, fragile, satiny hand, whose pressure, like an incarnate blessing, emphasized every word. What points are to Hebrew, giving to each word not only its weight and value, but even its peculiar shade of meaning, these looks, and tones, and touches of those we love, are to the words they utter, at once determining their worth, and impressing them upon our hearts. And, as his memory evoked them all, Gilbert answered her as if she had been there, corporeally present. " No, dear best of friends, your child, your pupil will *not* be a coward; he *will* don that spiritual armour wrought from the arsenal of God's word, which alone can guard him through the battle of life, and which your precept and example have kept so bright with constant use." And as he pondered all these things his heart became less troubled, his pulse calmer, his nerves more braced! "Yes," thought he, rising and walking up and down the room, "faire ce qui doit, advient ce que peut? N'est ce pas, chers amis?" and he pulled an ear of both dogs as he passed the four eyes that had been following his every step. As he turned to resume his perambulations, the sitting-room door opened, and Ferrol, his servant, was about to enter, but seeing his master, was going to beat a retreat, with an—

"I beg pardon, sir; I was not aware you had come in. I only came to take the dogs their walk."

"Oh! don't go, Ferrol, I'm very glad you are come; I had something to say to you, and the sooner it is said the better," added Gilbert, re-seating himself, and making the tips of his fingers meet in a sort of *couronne fermée*, as Queen Elizabeth is said to have done when speechless on her death-bed, to indicate that she wished James the First to be her successor.

"How should you like, Ferrol, to go to Tangier?"

" Tangier, sir ?" interrogated Ferrol, with much the same expression of face that he might have assumed had the query been, " How would you like to go to The Tower, *viâ* Traitor's Gate? or to Little Ease? or to The Gate House? The Porter's Lodge? or the Blackhole at Calcutta?" or any other place not exactly celebrated for eligibility or comfort.

" Yes, Tangier."

" Why, sir, that would depend upon circumstances."

" Exactly so ; and I don't think, under any circumstances, I should be justified in taking you away from your friends, and asking you to go to such a place"

" My God, sir, have I done anything to displease you, that you would not take me?"

And the poor fellow's voice was tremulous with emotion.

" Displease me ! No, Ferrol, it is because you please me so well, and I like you so much, and think you in every way such a good, honest fellow, that I consider you worthy of a better fate. There's my Lord Rochester, who has just married the rich Mrs. Mallet, he is in want of a valet ; and if you liked it, I can, I'm sure, most heartily and conscientiously recommend you."

Ferrol's face, which had been radiant at the beginning of this speech, became suddenly over-

cast at the conclusion of it, as he replied, in a
hurt and aggrieved tone—

"As for serving my Lord Rochester, or any
of those Court sparks, I would not do it, sir, if I
was to be made Lord Treasurer for my pains. If
you choose to turn me away, I cannot help it, sir
—for, of course, I have no right to dispute your
will; but if you merely refer the matter to my
option, sir, all I've to say is, that where *you* go,
I'll go."

Gilbert was more than touched by this proof of
affection and fidelity, and so he told him, adding,
however—

"But, upon my word, Ferrol, glad as I shall
be to have you—or rather on that very account—
it seems to me horridly like taking advantage of
your good qualities to let you go with me to such
a detestable place; and then there's the voyage—
I might be shipwrecked!"

"Well, sir, even if it came to that—which, God
forbid!—I suppose there is room for *two* at the
bottom of the sea?"

"And you would not mind going there with
me?"

And Gilbert's eyes filled with tears as he contrasted this great love of his servant with the
total want of it in his father.

"I should think so, sir," was Ferrol's reply.
"In fact there is only *one* place I would not go

to with, or for you; and as I am very certain you will never go *there*, I need not give myself any trouble about it. Whereas, if I lived with my Lord Rochester, or any of the rest of them, that's the very place where they'd want me to go, or drive me to it. Then, sir, there are the poor dogs; though *you* might do very well without me, they could not—for I know and understand all their ways, and I'm certain no one could valet *them* so much to their satisfaction as I do. May I ask, sir, when you intend to sail—that is, by what time I am to have the things ready?"

"My Lord Dartmouth is to sail, I understand, in about six weeks."

"Oh! And it is in his suite you are going, sir?" asked Ferrol, pulling his right ear.

"Yes."

And then, coupled with the sudden over-clouding of his master's face, Ferrol *knew* that this Tangier expedition was some fresh tyranny of Sir Allen's, and in the depths of his heart gave him a benediction—as witches are said to say their prayers—backwards.

And then he began very busily arranging the things on his master's toilet, which really was a work of supererogation, seeing that he had already put them in perfect and most symmetrical order two hours before, and no one had touched them since. At length, when he could *not*—like

a non-plussed Prime Minister—invent any new
combinations, he espied his master's hat on the
bed, which clearly was no proper place for it.
Unfortunately felt—particularly the grey and
brown felt then worn—requires no brushing, but
the velvet band did, and the feathers; it was astonishing how much he found to do to them, and
how minutely he investigated them, as if he had
formed the design of superceding all the plumas-
siers in London.   At last, he walked up to Gilbert, still holding the hat, and giving the feathers
two or three gentle supplementary flips, and said,
with considerable hesitation and embarrass-
ment—

"I ask you a thousand pardons, sir, and I *do*
hope, that with your usual kindness and conde-
scension, sir, you will excuse what I fear is taking a great liberty—though, indeed, *I don't mean
it as such*—but you see, sir, being nearly double
your age, and knowing the world and all its
crooked ways, and dirty blind alleys and cut
throat lanes, better than so young a gentleman
in your sphere of life can possibly do, on account
of never having had your wits sharpened on the
whetstone of necessity, like common people's
children, and, so I know—pray, don't be angry,
sir—though it *seems* a liberty, indeed—indeed, it
is *not*, I do assure you; but I know, sir, how
short of money persons of quality will often keep

their children, more especially their heirs, that *must* have all after them.　And I have a matter of £839 that has been hampering and worrying me these three years, ever since my poor father died, and the produce of the farm was divided amongst the three of us ; and if you *would*, sir, only make use of it, it would be such a relief to my mind—it would, indeed, sir ; for it's lying doing nothing, and truly idleness, whether for money or men, *is* the root of all evil.　And, oh ! sir, for Heaven's sake—for mercy's sake, *don't* go to those money lenders, who not only take all the flesh off your bones, but all the marrow out of them, till they leave you as bleached and as bare as a hundred year old skeleton.　But, *do*, *sir*, in addition to all your others, confer this one more great favour upon me.　You shall never find me ungrateful for it, nor encroach upon it ; indeed, you sha'n't, sir."

And having blurted out the latter part of this speech so rapidly, Ferrol at length paused, from sheer want of breath.

Gilbert was so taken by surprise, and so unfeignedly grateful for the poor fellow's disinterested generosity, and so touched by the true delicacy of feeling, that ran like a golden thread through his blunt speech, that he seized his hand and shook it cordially, as he said, " God bless you, Ferrol, for your kindness ; I almost

wish that I *was* in want of money. It would be
such a real pleasure to accept of help so gener-
ously and freely offered; but I do assure you,
that want of money forms no part of my dis-
tresses just now. However, to complete the
catalogue, perhaps, even *that* may come ;
and should it do so, I *promise you* I'll not
forget the good friend who can and will help
me. But, fortunately, my poor mother's £600 a
year is settled on me."

"I humbly thank you, sir," said Ferrol, bowing as lowly over his master's hat as if it had
been his own; "and if you will only forget the
great liberty my fears led me to take, I never
shall forget, sir, your goodness in so nobly con-
doning it."

Gilbert was about to reiterate the real gratitude he felt to him, when he heard a knock at
the bedroom door; remembering he had locked
it, he now went to it and opened it. It was Mrs.
Swinburne, to say that a gentleman, one Master
Fairbrace, of Clifford's Inn, was in the drawing-
room, and wished particularly to see him. Gilbert really did not want any thanks for saving
Master Fairbrace from supping with the fishes,
and devoutly wished that, at all events, the poor
man's gratitude had gone to the bottom of the
Thames, that he might have had the rest of this
day to himself, as he was in no humour for com-

panionship of any kind; still, as the landlady had owned he was at home, he felt it would be ungracious to refuse to see him; so he desired Mrs. Swinburne to say that he would go to Mr. Fairbrace immediately, and turning to Ferrol, said—

"Now, my good fellow, you can take the dogs out."

"Come, Monk, my man! Come, Charlie, my fine fellow! Now the Mall, and then dinner!" And the next moment Monk, with his fine noble *basso*, and Charlie, with his shrill tenor, were bounding and barking down the stairs before him; while Gilbert, by the other door, walked into the drawing-room, where he found Jambres Fairbrace, a ruddy, regular-featured, good-looking man, of about fifty, dressed—as befitted his calling—in scrupulously new, glossy, fine black broad cloth, a large linen collar, with plain white cord and tassels, such as the Puritans were wont to wear; for sooth to say, the firm of Fairbrace and Evanshaw, of Clifford's Inn, had been the legal advisers of the Protector. His partially grey hair—still more black than grey—was parted down the centre, and hung down straight over his ears, terminating in the faintest suspicion of a curl. And albeit lawyer though he was, there was a singularly honest expression in his whole countenance, more especially in his clear, large, keen grey eyes, where an occasionally merry twinkle shot from them with meteoric brightness and swiftness. His voice was so mellow, round, and perfectly modulated, that had he been a barrister, instead of a scrivener, it would have been quite sufficient ultimately to have led him to the woolsack, even had no other voice seconded it. When young Broderick entered, he rose from his seat, and first making him three profound bows where he stood, as if to royalty itself, he then walked over, and in continuation of this courtly routine, took the young man's hand, which he kissed, saying—

" From the number of days which have elapsed since the night on which you saved my life, Mr. Broderick, you must have thought me one of the greatest ingrates that ever lived, even for a dabbler in the black art! but the fact is, that ever since, I have, till yesterday, been confined to my bed with a severe attack of ague, and this is my first day out."

" I fear," said Gilbert, " that you had to stay too long in your wet clothes ; now, a good Samaritan seized upon me, and made me go instantly into a warm bed ; so I escaped all cold."

" I'm glad of that," rejoined Fairbrace ; " but I deserved to have suffered ten times more for my folly. I had some rather pressing business, and took water at Blackfriar's Bridge, and not finding my usual boatman there, I thought I could manage the craft with a pair of oars myself; so, leaving word with one of the watermen to tell Thompson, the owner of the wherry, that I had done so, I jumped in and pushed off, but soon found the boat had sprung a leak; in fact, the plug had been left out! So that, but for your generous rescue, Mr. Broderick, death was inevitable. Obligations, such as these, sir, can never be either adequately acknowledged or repaid, but they *can* be gratefully remembered. The mouse and the lion is a good fable, with a good moral; and all I can say is, that so long as it lasts, the life you saved is at your service, not only for gnawing nets and toils asunder—for which lawyer's teeth are the only one's sharp enough, and which is my trade—but in every, and any other way, *non*-professionally, that such very humble individuals as I and my family *can* serve you. Pray, sir, remember that you have always a whole family of grateful mice, devoted to your service."

"Really, sir, you quite overwhelm me, and make too much of the assistance I was fortunate enough to render you, considering how very fond of swimming I am."

"And you, sir, make too little of it; for, however fond you may be of swimming, I scarcely think you would select the muddiest part of the Thames at night, with all your clothes on, to indulge in the recreation !"

" Who knows ?" laughed Gilbert ; " variety is charming."

" Ah ! then," said Fairbrace, with the merry twinkle coruscating from the corners of both eyes, " we will leave it so, and suppose that I am out of the question, and that you only meant it as a hint to the fish, always to be well dressed !"

Gilbert laughed very heartily at this sally, and felt himself considerably warming towards his new acquaintance, whose frankness and geniality were after his own heart. After they had conversed for half an hour longer upon the topics of the day, the lawyer looked at a very correct model of a warming-pan in gold, that had been the gift of the Protector, and declared he was not aware it had been so late—nearly one—and he must go, as he had an appointment to dine at The French House, in Charing Cross, with a friend, adding—

" But can I be of any use as to letters or parcels to the country, where I go next week on business to one or two of our clients ?"

" What part of the country ?"

" Why, first to Finborough, to Sir Charles Pettiward's."

" Oh! then, you are going into Suffolk ?"

"Yes; and Norfolk, and after, into Yorkshire."

" Would it be trespassing too much upon your kindness, or rather upon your time, to ask you to leave a packet, somewhat too large to risk by post, at my Aunt Miss Broderick's, Clumber Chase ?"

" Not a bit—not a bit; Clumber Chase is not a stone's throw, as the crow flies, from Finborough. And were the packet as big as Whitehall, so much the better, for I have the same passion for carrying packages as big as houses as you have for swimming in the muddiest part of the Thames, in full dress, late at night."

Gilbert laughed, thanked and shook his new friend cordially by the hand, saying, as he conducted him to the head of the stairs—" I sincerely hope you will have no return of your ague, but if you should, do try a pill made of common cobweb ; I have known it do wonders."

" Thanks, I will; but my wife's jibes, now that I have got well, and she over her fright, are worse than all. She had the impertinence to say to me this very morning, ' Oh! Jambres, you a man of law, and to enter into a concern that wouldn't hold water !' "

CHAPTER IX.

"I WAS SICK, AND YOU VISITED ME."

LL archæologist though he was, Oliver Hartsfoot did not allow himself to be so engaged with the dead and gone (though it must be confessed that he preferred their company,, as to neglect or forget the living and the going. What a blessed thing it is that true sympathy, like its twin virtue true charity, is of unlimited elasticity; otherwise, it would be very apt to snap, from the constant strain upon it from misery to misery, wide as the poles asunder, which brush against it at every turn in this moiling, toiling, work-a-day world. All who have dealt largely and practically—that is wholesale and retail, in the trials, sufferings, wants, reverses, injustice, and oppressions, endured by their fellow creatures, putting their own share of these things out of the question, are fully aware—and none knew this better than Master Hartsfoot— that every-day life furnishes at once more terrible tragedies than ever were represented on any stage, and more improbable romances than fiction ever dared to invent. He also knew the terrible amount of anonymous and inedited wretchedness there is which requires to be sought out: the thousands who, " dig they cannot, and to beg are ashamed;" and who, not coming within the daily routine of orthodox charity, recognised pauperism, and accredited distress,—

" Live, as Saints have died, Martyrs,"

without professional and paraded philanthropy taking any cognizance of them. Among these latter, and their name is Legion, was poor Wenceslaus Hollar, whose talent had earned him a European reputation, and whose industry should have furnished him with a clue to El Dorado, to say nothing of his great patrons, who, if they befriended him at all, should at least have done it effectually ; but patronage in high places always was, and it is to be feared always will be, a most piecemeal and homœopathic affair. Therefore, woe and disappointment are the dividends of all those who invest their capital of HOPE in it. And if " the beginning of anger is like the letting out of water," verily, the beginning of poverty, if not promptly and effectually arrested, is like the opening of a floodgate and the rushing *in* of water, whose torrent it becomes impossible to stem. Oliver Hartsfoot felt this so deeply with regard to poor Hollar's chronic difficulties, that he greatly regretted that he was not sufficiently rich to offer him, and about twenty more equally badly off, a home in his own house, though for that matter, to rescue *all* he felt for, instead of his modest *locale* at " Funny Joe's Corner," he would have required all the palaces, barracks, and hospitals in Europe, joined into ONE, with Fortunatus's purse for his treasury. However, " he did what he could." And oh ! if only *every one* would do likewise what a different world this would be; and without waiting for that inalienable heritage, THE GRAVE, how soon " the wicked would cease from troubling, and the weary be at rest."

Among other efforts to serve him, he was always giving Hollar commissions for original drawings. His last had been for a series of etchings of scenes taken during the Great Fire and the Plague, as well as a larger than the original edition of Hollar's " ORNATUS, MULIEBRIS ANGLICANUS." And having received neither, though bespoken six months back, he feared the poor artist was again struggling in one of his scarcely ever ceasing hand to hand fights, with that most brutal and overwhelming of all athletes, POVERTY! So though the day was not over fine, and the gathering clouds seemed to threaten rain, he thought he would walk down to poor Hollar's ricketty tenement in Axe Yard, and see how he was, and how the etchings were getting on; but he first took out of his escretoire a small leather bag, containing fifty Jacobuses, which he had set apart for their intended price, but wisely thought that perhaps for the want of their presence a little sooner, poor Hollar might be finished before the drawings, for *no* " evil was ever wrought for the want of thought" on the part of Oliver Hartsfoot.

He had not got further than Westminster Abbey when he met Mr. Evelyn, who stopped and spoke to him, full, like everyone else, of the terrible and disgraceful state of affairs; the way everything was bought, sold, and neglected.

" Only think," said he, " it was not disgrace enough to us to let the Dutch take Sheerness, but in our blundering and confusion, and want of all organisation and HEAD, we have sunk below Woolwich some of the king's ships, with considerable stores—the Franklin for one, and another laden to the value of eighty thousand pounds, and the people are in such a state of revolt and disgust that they have cut down the trees before the Lord Chancellor's house, broken the windows, and erected a gibbet with this inscription upon it—" Three sights to be seen, Dunkirk, Tangier, and a barren Queen." And the Chancellor was insulted yesterday in Westminster Hall, about his Dunkirk House, and they say there are regiments ordered to be got together to be commanded by Fairfax, Ingoldsby, Bethell, Norton, Birch, and other Presbyterians, and that Dr. Bates will be at liberty to preach. Now whether this be true or not I cannot say, but I really think nothing but this can knit us together even for a time."

" Surely," said Hartsfoot, " the King will not be so insane, or listen to such ill advisers, as not to summon Parliament at such a terrible crisis?"

" What can you expect with a Lord Chancellor who will do nothing but for money, and who, when the King consulted him about doing so the other day, replied—'Tut, tut! Queen Elizabeth got very well out of her troubles in eighty-eight without summoning a Parliament.' And Mr. Povey, whom I met yesterday, told me that what hath really undone the nation was the Luke of York having made an honest woman of Ann Hyde, who is not even faithful to him. She is carrying on such a game with both young Sidney and young Saville, which the Duke perceives, and they have not spoken for a fortnight. Mr. Povey also told me that, besides her imperious insolence, her extravagance is unbounded, and though the Duke's income is sixty thousand a year, she never spends less than eighty thousand, so that he (Mr. Povey) thought it his duty to carry this account to my Lord Chancellor, and asked his opinion if it should not, in fairness to the country, be brought before the Privy Council?   But my Lord Clarendon, who only thought of screening his daughter's shortcomings, replied that 'no man who loved the king or kingdom would own to the writing of that document.'   Poor Mr. Povey was startled at this, and feared he was undone by his honesty, so that he found it necessary then to show the statement to the Duke of York's Commissioners, who read, examined, and approved of it, so as to cause it to be put into form, signed it, and gave it to the Duke,* and with such a profligate Court and such self-seeking and family ties, and hushing up of family delinquencies everywhere, who can wonder that the country is going to destruction, and that we have become a laughing stock and a bye-word to all other nations?   I understand the King of France (Louis the Fourteenth) said last week that as the Dutch were nibbling at this country and taking it by bits he did not see why he should not take his cousin of England's kingdom outright by a *coup de main*, and Paris is full of caricatures of our king.   The last is his being led with a blue ribband, like a dog, by Lady Castlemaine, while all his pockets

* The Commissioners for regulating the Duke of York's—afterwards James the Second—affairs in 1667, were John Lord Berkeley, Colonel Robert Werden, and Colonel Anthony Eyre. —*Household Book at Audley-End.*

are turned completely inside out, to show their
perfect and literal emptiness."

"It is indeed shocking," said Hartsfoot, " and
fortunate that we have even ONE honest, conscientious clergyman who *does*, and does not
shrink from his duty, for I hear that last Sunday
at Whitehall, Dr. Creeton preached before the
King a terribly denunciatory sermon against the
vices of the Court and the habitual breach of the
Seventh Commandment."

" For which in France Dr. Creeton would have
been called a *Cretin*, considering the sort of
Archbishop of Canterbury* we have, who keeps
as many mistresses—I won't say as the King, for
he at least never has but one at a time—but as
that unredeemed *vaurien*, the Duke of York. It
seems Sir Charles Sedley ran away with *one* of
the Archbishop's sultanas the other day, whereupon that veracious prelate wrote to Sir Charles
complaining of the outrage; as the lady was a
relation of his, the Archbishop felt bound to pro-
tect her honour, to which Sir Charles Sedley
made just such an answer as might have been
expected of *him;* however, it had the desired
effect of quelling his Grace's chivalric punctilio
about his ' relative's ' honour."

" The poor King ! I am really sorry for him,"

* Dr. Gilbert Shelden.

said Hartsfoot, " for I think he *has* some redeeming points."

" Unquestionably he has, but for that accursed and all demoralising WEAKNESS of character which is a moral dry rot that not only undermines anything like virtue or principle in those afflicted with it, but fructifies every vice and evil deed in others, and yet he is not wanting in good councillors either ; at least, in persons who, like himself—

' Never say a foolish thing, and never do a wise one,'

for it was only the other day he was speaking with unfeigned contempt and indignation of the Duke of York being so mastered by his wife, and added that he (the King) would go no more abroad with such a Tom Otter ;* he should be ashamed to be seen with him, whereupon, Tom Killigrew being by, said, ' Sir, pray which is the best for a man to be, a Tom Otter to his wife or to his mistresses ?' But I do pity the poor King, to see how he is preyed upon, not only by those worthless women, but by all the other vultures and harpies by whom he is surrounded. As one instance among a hundred, I asked Mr. Townshend the other day if it was true what I had heard with

* In the play of " Epicine, or the Silent Woman," Mrs. Otter thus addresses her henpecked husband - *Thomas Otter.* " Is this according to the instrument when I married you, that I would be princess and reign in my own house, and you would be my subject and obey me ?"—Act III., Scene I.

great indignation from good, honest, loyal old
Ashburnham, to wit, that the King now had
literally no pockethandkerchiefs, and only three
neck-bands (cravats, or collars), and as many
shirts, adding that the king his father, would have
hanged *his* wardrobe man had he dared to treat
him so. Mr. Townshend said he regretted to
say that it *was* only too true, but the reason of it
was, that those vile rapacious grooms of the
bedchamber every quarter enforced their per-
quisites, and carried off all the King's linen, not
caring how *he* was put to his shifts, or rather put
to doing without them; and that as the linen-
draper was already owed five thousand pounds,
which there was not much chance of his being
paid, he (Mr. Townshend) really could not order
the poor King a fresh supply. Now without for
one moment wishing to palliate that part of the
King's life in which he only too closely emulates
King David, and which in the case of the latter
brought down a curse upon all Judea, as I fear it
will also do upon these realms, yet I cannot
but admire that, unlike most husbands, while
wronging her so essentially, he is so *invariably*
kind, considerate, and respectful to the queen,
really, in all other things, not only consulting,
but anticipating her every wish; so that no wonder that, despite all, she really loves him."

"Well," said Hartsfoot, "when men have

what I am sorry to say may emphatically be called
the vices of gentlemen, it *is* a redeeming point
that they should also have the *manners* of gentlemen, and not brutalise their wives as well as outrage them.   I can only again say that I hope the
king will, at this terrible crisis, summon a Parliament."*

"Yet, *cui bono?* if it is only for the king to
snap his fingers at them, as he did the last time,
dismissing them even without a 'thank you' the
very first day they were assembled; and it's
neither so easy† nor so pleasant for men to come
two and three hundred miles and more, at great
cost and personal inconvenience, merely to be
laughed at, as it were. So I suppose we have
no alternative but to go on in this pull-baker,
pull-devil style, between my Lord Chancellor and
my Lady Castlemaine.   I hear that my Lord
Clarendon lately stopped some grant of two
thousand a year to my Lord Grandison, Lady
Castlemaine's uncle, which so incensed her, that
she sent him (the Chancellor) a most insolent

---

* At that time, and long before, in the time of the Tudors,
Parliament was not the sort of permanent institution it now is,
convening and proroguing itself according to the exigences of the
country, or the straits of the Prime Minister, but was more an
occasional sort of spurt to be evoked or dismissed, at the pleasure
or caprice of the sovereign, and did not as now regularly and
periodically meet for "the dispatch" (or delay) of business, being
alternately prorogued and re-rogued.

† Travelling two or three hundred miles in those days certainly
was a greater undertaking than dining at the Equator and supping
at the North Pole is in our times.

message, in her *broadest style*, and we all know what *that* is; and the king calls him 'the insolent man,' and says that he will not let him speak for himself in Council, which is carrying matters with a very high hand, and shows my poor Lord Chancellor to be in a bad way, unless he can defend himself better than people think he can. Yet his son, my Lord Cornbury, says his father longs for the meeting of Parliament for his own vindication much more than any of his enemies long for it. God grant his expectations as to the results may be justified, but he has indefatigable enemies—in the Castlemaine the chief,—for some grant coming to him the other day to be sealed, which the king had given Lady Castlemaine, the Chancellor refused to assent to it, saying he thought this woman would sell everything in the kingdom shortly ; and this coming to her ears, she sent to him to say that *his* refusal was of no avail as *she had* disposed of this place, and had no doubt that in a short time she would be able to dispose of his (the Chancellor's) place also. Bless me," added Mr. Evelyn, " there are the Abbey chimes striking three. I must say goodbye."

So they shook hands and went their different ways. When Oliver Hartsfoot reached Axe Yard he found the well-known heavy weather-blistered door of Hollar's house in the corner neither open nor shut; that is, it was apparently closed, but not being fastened, on a very slight push opened inwards on its heavy hinges. The dingy hall, or rather passage, looked even more desolate than usual, and the wide, unpolished, worm-eaten oak stairs, seemed as if the indentures in them, worn into perfect bowls, were deeper than ever, while the thick, Henry the Seventh *torsade* banisters, or at least the broad, plain plinth that surmounted them, was polished like a mirror from the friction of the hands of byegone generations that had passed up and down it for so many years. Hartsfoot gently and almost fearfully pulled the blackened and well-worn bell cord by its wooden handle, like that of a child's skipping rope, and the cracked bell, guiltless of wires to convey its appeal to either the upper or lower regions, but hung immediately over the inside of the door, returned a discordant sound that would have been loud, had not its metallic lungs been evidently enfeebled by age.

Master Hartsfoot waited for some minutes, and listened for the heavy-trailing step of old Margery, Hollar's *largo al factotum*, a poor, rheumatic, blear-eyed old woman, who seemed to be a sort of experimental freak of nature, that of an ossified north wind; and while he waited and listened, he contemplated the blades of long grass springing up like prosperous *parvenus* through

the crumbling mortar round the broken door-step;
and when no Margery came ; he began to wonder
if this poor human rush-light had at length burnt
down in her socket, and gone out like all rush-
lights, more especially human ones, not leaving
the world in much greater darkness for her extinction.

At last, upon finding no one came, he resolved
to wait no longer, but go upstairs.   Upon reaching the first landing he knocked at the door that
was Hollar's work room, and where, if at home,
he was generally to be found. After a brief pause
he knocked again ; still no answer; he then tried
to open the door, but found it locked.   But, determined not to go without some further search,
he now ascended the next flight of stairs.   In
the staircase window was an old broken Dutch,
red, urn-shaped flower-pot, with a *bas relief* of
silenas, going one of his progresses, amid grapes
about the size of infant pumpkins, out of which
flower-pot towered, like the Pharos of desolation,
the brown, dry, leafless, withered stem of a wil-
holm geranium. When Master Oliver reached
the first door of the second landing, unmistakeable
signs and sounds of human life reached him, for
there was the plaintive, imploring wail of misery
on the one hand, and that of implacable brutality
on the other.

"Mine goote, sir, I do assure you it ish true ;

I *had* de moneys coming ven de accident happened to my poor man, dat vas so goote as to go for it for me."

"Aye, tell *that* tale to the grasshoppers, and perhaps they may swallow it; but Isaac Ironsides ain't quite so green. Come, Master, I can't stay here all day haggling for what ten minutes would clear out, and my orders is to take *all*, to the bed from under you, which is about the best of the shabby lot; so quick, stir your stumps, up with you, though praps you can't dress till your wallet comes; but that ain't no odds, as I shall be able to help you considerable, as my orders is to take the shirt off your back, and them as returns to first fashions, ain't got no trouble with their dress."

Hartsfoot felt very sick and very indignant, but pretty well knew what was the matter; so, having heard the fellow call himself Isaac Ironsides, he called out, in a civil voice—

"Mr. Ironsides, will you have the goodness to step here a moment?"

"Who the deuce can that be?" said the Sheriff's officer, opening the door, through which his burly form of full seven feet high, and stout in proportion, had no sooner emerged, than Hartsfoot closed it after him, and beckoned to him to come down on the stairs. Seeing a gentleman, the fellow became exceedingly civil.

“ Your sarvant, sir.”

“ I want to know,” said Oliver, “ what is the amount of your claim upon Mr. Hollar ?”

“ Well, you see, sir, business is business, and ourn haint by no means a pleasant business, and we are obliged to act cording to circums*tance*s, or we should never fold our sheep, and—”

“ And you, I suppose, are the gentle shepherd?” interrupted Hartsfoot, “ but I don’t want to hear about that.   I want to know the amount of your claim upon Mr. Hollar, and at whose suit?”

“ At the suit of Jansen Vanderpeerboom, of Crutched Friars, sir, but the *facs* of the case is these—the *horiginal* debt was a bill for twenty pounds, at ten per cent. for six months, but it have run and run, and been put off and off, till it have growed into £43 13s. 6d., and Mr. Hollar promised to pay it to day sartin sure, and when I comes instead of the money, he tries to bamboozle me with a cock and bull story, that he had sent a poor half cripple as does his odd jobs now his old woman is gone—one Roger Marner—yesterday to my Lord Arundel for fifty pounds as was ow- ing to him.   ‘ That’s no go,’ says I, ‘ for my Lord Arundel is away in furrin parts.’   ‘ I know that,’ says he, ‘ but it was to Mr. Ellis, my lord’s steward, I wrote, and he gave Marner the money —some in pieces of eight, some in angels, and the rest in gold Jacobuses—and when poor Mar ner got as fur as Charing Cross, what between the horses and coaches, and a great waggon team that was coming, he hobbled about to and fro to avoid being run over, like one gone off his head, and when at last he reached this house the bag with the money was clean gone.   But,' says Hollar, ' if Jansen will only wait three days longer he shall have the money, he shall indeed.' Now it wasn't likely, sir, that I or any other man in his senses was going to be gammoned in this way."

"Nevertheless, Mr. Hollar told you the exact truth about his having the money in three days, which he certainly could have had for asking, as I owe him more than that, and have this day brought it to pay him.   So, as you came in the expectation of being paid, I suppose you have the receipt about you?   Give it to me, and I will hand you the £43 13s. 6d., that is, if you can give me the six shillings and sixpence change."

" Whew," whistled the amiable enforcer of the law, and then, sticking his tongue in his cheek, he excavated from his breast pocket a large black, greasy pocket book, abstracted from it a stamped slip of paper, and dipping a stumpy pen that had evidently seen much service, and not done any since it left its native goose, he dipped it into an itinerant Lilliputian ink bottle, that dangled viâ a piece of whip cord from his button hole, and on the crown of his greasy hat wrote out a receipt in full for Jansen Vanderpeerboom, by Isaac Ironsides.

And Oliver Hartsfoot, having received the change, requested Mr. Ironsides not to stand upon the order of his going, but to go at once, and accompanied him as far as the first landing, where he looked over the banisters till he saw the hall door form, a very appropriate drop scene (being dark and dirty,) to the bailiff's exit.

If history is always repeating itself, verily fate is always doing so too; that is, she has many rehearsals before the grand finale, for on that very day eleven years after, when poor Hollar was really on his death-bed, and Oliver Hartsfoot had been gathered to his fathers, another and even more brutal emissary of the law stood over the dying debtor, so soon to take the benefit of *the* act that frees for ever, who savagely ordered the dying man to rise.

" I hope to do so in a few minutes," was his mild reply, " only kindly wait, good sir, till then."

But the minister of injustice refused. Well, he seized the body, but the soul had escaped.

*   *   *   *

*   *   *   *

Not knowing if there might not be more of the genus vulture hovering about, Oliver Hartsfoot took the precaution, so soon as he had seen the last of Mr. Ironsides, of going down and locking and bolting the hall door, and then hastened upstairs to the poor sick man's room. Very gently he opened the door, and very gently he crossed the threshold and walked towards the bed. Hollar was lying with his head back on the pillow, his eyes closed, and his wan, worn face upturned. Gently as Hartsfoot walked, the poor sufferer felt his shadow fall across the bed, and murmured, without opening his eyes —

" I am so weak wid dis fever dat I *cannot* rise, but, goote sir, you may take me too if you will not believe me ; but I have told you the truth."

" My dear Hollar," said Oliver, feeling his pulse, or rather feeling for it, for it was almost imperceptible, and he certainly had no fever then, being quite cold; "no one will or can take you, but I take it very ill of you that you did not send to me before you let these wretches outrage you so."

" Ah ! mine Got ! my goote, mine dear Master Hartsfoot ; tank Got I see you once more here before I meet you in heaven. Oh ! how goote, how kind of you to come."

" Now you must not exert yourself to talk, but only to answer me yes or no."

" Ah ! to see you make a' my life come back."

" Where is your old servant ? I am so grieved to see you here so ill, and all alone."

" Poor Madge ! she go ill to de hospital two week ago."

" And never to let me know ? This was not well, Hollar."

" Oh ! dear, goote Master Hartsfoot, you free horse, and I have no spurs, and I should not want but for terrible ting dat happen to poor Roger Marner dat go my message for me."

" Yes, yes, I know all about his losing the money. Now don't exert yourself to talk ; but *why* let yourself go to such a pass ? Surely you, who taught the king and the Duke of York drawing, if they knew it they would not let you be put to such straits."

" Ah ! de poor gentlemens ; dey worse off because dey Prince. De Duke of York, he got spendfast vife ; de poor king, so generous, he leave nothing for himself. De oder day at Council, no paper put for him, Sir Richard Brown call Martin Kingswell, de royal stationer, to know de reason ; and Kingswell say, wid tears in him eyes, he vas ver poor man, wid large children, and he was out of pocket five hundred pounds, and could afford no more. Poor Kingswell ! he tell me dis himself, and bring me a manchet and some sack yesterday."

“ Where are they ?” asked Hartsfoot.

“ Over on drawer.”

Oliver walked over, found the delicate white bread and the sack, poured out a small glass of the latter, brought both over to the bed, and passing his hand gently under Hollar’s neck, so as to raise his head, said—

“ Now you *must* drink this, and eat a bit of bread, for you seem to me to want food more than medicine.”

The poor sufferer did as he was desired, and in a few minutes felt considerably revived, for, indeed, his chief malady was inanition, aggravated by great anxiety of mind.

“ Now,” said Hartsfoot, “ that you seem so much better, if you’ll promise not to be jealous I’ll show you one of my etchings.”

“ Oh ! I shall be so glad. And vat is de subjec ?”

“ Well, I think of calling it the vulture put to flight; but I must get you to help me as to the perspective.”

And so saying, he held up before Hollar’s eyes Jansen Vanderpeerboom’s receipt.

“ Ah ! no ; indeed, indeed, mine goote Master Hartsfoot, I cannot take dat from you.”

“ But you don’t take it from me, it’s your own lawful money—the price of the etchings you are doing for me, and fortunately I brought the money for them to-day, that’s all.”

“ But they are not even finished yet; at least,
de *Ornatus Mulielris* is, but not all de *tableaux* of
de fire and de plague.”

“ That is of no consequence. I only meant
the fifty pounds for the *Ornatus Mulielris*, and,
by-the-bye, that reminds me, here is the change
from Jansen’s receipt,” said Hartsfoot, pushing
the bag (into which he had slipped three more
gold Jacobuses—all the money he had about him)
under Hollar’s pillow.

“ Oh! dear kind, *ever* kind Master Hartsfoot;
you are too good. You break my heart. What
can I ever do for you?”

“ Plenty of drawings I hope ; and I only wish
I was rich enough to give you anything like
what I consider their real value.”

The poor artist said nothing, but two great
tears rolled down his cheeks, and after a minute
or two’s silence, during which Hartsfoot arranged
the pillows and smoothed the bed clothes,
Hollar said—

“ De Lord only knows what state all my drawings and my poor work room are in, for he have
been lock up dese tree week, vile I have been up
here, and I have got de gey onder mine billow.”

“ May I take it? And will you trust me to
see it dusted and arranged every day till you can
return to it? My Alice shall do it, but not without my being there to see that nothing is injured

or disarranged; and every day I will bring you back the key when the room is cleaned, for otherwise all your valuable things may get spoilt."

At this offer, which went straight to his heart, poor Hollar burst into a plentiful flood of tears, which seemed greatly to relieve him, for his *atelier* was his wife, his child, his friend; in a word, his *alter ego.*

" Oh! Master Hartsfoot, if I could only draw a true map of mine heart to show how I loaf you!"

" I don't want any map to convince me of your kindly feeling towards me; but, my good friend, where there is affection there always is obedience, and till you are able to go down stairs again you must obey me implicitly. I'll take the key of your work room, and after that my first injunction is that you turn round and try and sleep for a few hours, and I will send a trustworthy woman—some friend of Merrypin's—to nurse and take care of you, for you must not be left in this way. And what did you say was the name of the man you sent to Lord Arundel's steward for the fifty pounds owing to you?"

" Roger Marner."

" And the day it was lost?"

" Yesterday, about dree of de glock."

" Because I will send an advertisement about it to all the news books;* but still, as I said be-

* Newspapers were at that time called " news books."

fore, I do wish you would appeal to the King, for I am sure it would not be in vain."

" No, no, poor King—free horse, free horse, and I no spurs."

" Being a free horse no spurs would be wanted," said Hartsfoot, as he shut to the shutters, so as to darken the room, and forbidding Hollar to utter another word, he promised to return in the evening, as he left the room, and gently closed the door after him ; and when he reached the hall he took the key out of the street door and locked it on the outside, so that no one might get in, till he could send someone to take care of the house and its master, for which purpose he hurried home, his heart much heavier than when he had left it, and revolving in his mind every possible way in which to serve, that is, to permanently extricate poor Hollar from his grinding poverty, so as to give his rare talent and indefatigable industry fair play; and still the King's patronage ever came to the foreground of these pictures of his imagination, as at once the shortest and least humiliating mode of relief, till he remembered how all things pecuniary were in abeyance at Court, since even one shilling of the wages of the very servants had not been paid since the Restoration, but were all in arrears. There was no doubt that the King would, with his usual impulsive kindheartedness, and his constitutional lavishness, without hesitation bestow either a considerable place or a pension upon his very meritorious and much-to-be-commiserated quondam drawing master; but unfortunately it was almost equally certain that neither the salary of the one nor the annuity of the other would ever be paid; in which case poor Hollar, in addition to all his other trials, would only be subjected to that cruellest torture in all fate's arsenal—A FALSE POSITION. So, before he had reached his own door, Master Hartsfoot decided that there would be no use in asking the King to touch for *this* evil.

"Is Merrypin at home?" asked he, as soon as Noah Pump had opened the door.

"She is, sir, for she is very busy straining calves' foot jelly into some silver moulds that Mrs. Ruffle lent her, as she says they turn out better than from the *chaney* ones."

"Oh! that's lucky; I'm glad she has got some jelly in the house. Send her to me; tell her it's something that presses, and I want her directly."

The directly, however, extended itself into a full quarter of an hour; so that the cabinet council was of necessity delayed, and when the Prime Minister did appear, she was still smoothing her pinners, and the muslin apron beautifully tamboured in a pattern of pansies and bachelor's buttons, with which she had replaced her culinary brown Holland one. Master Hartsfoot, not being too sure that the atmosphere was quite serene, when the quicksilver was at " jelly," said, blandly—

" I am sorry to have disturbed you, as I hear you were busy, Merrypin, but I could not avoid it."

" It's of no consequence, sir; only I fear I smell terrible of lemons and sherry," which announcement she punctuated by placing two fingers of her right hand before her mouth, and giving three little " ahem's !"

" Well, lemons and sherry are both excellent things in their way."

Which, as Mrs. Merrypin was too strict an adherer to truth to gainsay, her master opened the proceedings by placing before her, very graphically, the deplorable and desolate position of poor Hollar, till the tears so incommoded Mrs. Merrypin's eyes, that she was fain, to the crumpling—not exactly of the roses, but of her admirably "got up" apron—to irrigate the tambour pansies and bachelor's buttons with them ; whereupon, Master Hartsfoot asked her if she knew of any competent and trustworthy woman, who could go that very evening to nurse and take care of the poor sick man, and remain permanently as his servant, and he (Oliver) would pay her her wages ?

" Well, sir, I do know an honest, respectable woman as ever was, one Audrey Barton, to whom it would be quite a charity; a widow woman, sir, who has a hard tussle of it to keep life and soul together, with a dead weight of a lout of a boy and a daughter, who does nothing. To be sure, Audrey Barton is rather stricken in years, like myself, but she has plenty of work in her still, and is thoroughly notable."

" Then it would seem that the way the matter stands is this—the mother is notable, and the daughter not able."

" That's just about it, sir."

" But would she leave, or could she leave her daughter ?"

" Oh ! dear, yes, sir ; she's obliged to do that now every day for any odd jobs she can pick up, or else they must starve ; and starvation for one is bad enough, but starvation for two is worse. So, if you please, sir, I'll just step round and bring Mrs. Barton back with me."

" Yes, do ; but stop one moment. I've something else to say to you," said Hartsfoot, who thought it better to strike while the iron was hot, as Mrs. Merrypin was now in such good cue. " Poor Mr. Hollar's work room has been terribly neglected ; in fact, locked up for the last three weeks of his illness, and I have promised to see it cleaned and kept in good order, so that none

of his valuable drawings may be disturbed or
injured, till he is able to get about. Now, what
hour every morning would it be most convenient
to you to come with me to settle the room, till
you have shown Mrs. Barton the way to do it?
And tell her she must not be offended at my
staying in the room while she settles it, as I
should never forgive myself if poor Mr. Hollar
was to miss a scrap of torn paper even, when he
returned to his study.”

Now, if Alice Merrypin had been asked at a
moment’s notice, to dress a banquet for all the
gods and goddesses, however arduous and onerous the undertaking might have been, she would
have felt rather flattered than otherwise ; but her
genius did not lie among cobwebs and litter, and
she felt somewhat taken aback by this question ;
but her love for her master and her natural kind-
liness of nature conquered, and she answered—

“ About half-past nine in the morning—if that
hour would suit you, sir—would be the most convenient to me.”

“ Then half-past nine be it. I suppose it is
too late to make any mutton broth ?”

“ Well, it is for to-day, sir ; but there is some
excellent giblet soup, and that’s worth all the
mutton broth in the world ‘ for putting strength
into anyone that’s ill.’ ”

“ Well, then, we’ll take some of that, and
some of the jelly that Pump tells me you have

made; but not in the silver shapes that Mrs. Ruffle lent you, for we should never take such a liberty with other persons' things as to lend what they have lent us."

"Hardly, sir! I hope I know my place better than to think of doing such a thing," said Mrs. Merrypin, both hurt and surprised that her master should have thought her capable of such want of *savoir vivre;* therefore, perhaps, her curtsey was a shade lower than usual, as she left the room to equip herself for going in search of Mrs. Barton. While he, guiltless of offence, went to his *sanctum* for a "wonderful lamp," that the Marquis of Worcester had given him out of his " Century of Inventions," which, like the vestal fire, he warranted to burn for ever, only without care or replenishing. And certain it was, that it had burnt steadily during the ten years it had been in Oliver Hartsfoot's possession, emitting a dazzling light, almost equal to the then undiscovered Bude light, and the strangest attribute of it was that it emitted scarcely any heat in proportion, as if it had been merely the simulacrum of a flame. This everlasting light was contained in a very small Bhul hand-lantern, with slides to pass over it, so as to shut out the light and render it a dark lantern; and at night it was always Hartsfoot's companion about the dark, dangerous, dirty, ill-paved streets of Old London.

CHAPTER X.

LTHOUGH Oliver Hartsfoot had found poor Hollar much better on his return to Axe Yard the preceding evening, from the few hours' quiet sleep he had got when relieved from that worst of all nightmares, "the man in possession," and cheered by that potent elixir, human kindness, sympathy, and help, in the hour of need. And though Hartsfoot left the poor man still better from the good things Mrs. Merrypin's skill had prepared, and her master's considerate forethought had brought him; still, poor good Master Hartsfoot himself passed a sleepless night, vainly casting about for some channel through which he could effectually serve so gifted, deserving, and hard-working a man, and prevent a recurrence of the horrors of the previous day by not again letting him be subjected to the tender mercies of Jansen Vanderpeerboom and his fellow sharks. True, Oliver was acquainted with more than one professed and pro-

fessional philanthropist, but he knew only too
well, from experience, that they were so im-
mersed in their magnificent theories for the
regeneration, perfectability, and impregnable
happiness of the whole human race, that they
never had either time or inclination to enter into
the vulgar details of individual misery and want.
MAN is their study; but it is in his abstract and
protoplastic state, a most comprehensive, but
not very well defined, or practically working
scheme, strongly resembling Commissioner
Yeh's explanation of "TAOLI."

"What does your Excellency mean by Taoli?"

"What you ought to do is Taoli; what you
ought not to do is *not* Taoli."

"Has Taoli no more extended meaning?"

"Taoli has the most comprehensive meaning;
it comprehends everything."

"Does Taoli teach of a Creator?"

"There are many Taoli. There is Heaven's
Taoli, and Earth's Taoli, and Man's Taoli."

"Are these Taoli's distinct?"

"No; they are all parts of one Taoli."

So leaving the "Taoli" of universal philanthropy in despair, and thinking, with Chanticlear
in the fable, that a grain of millet would much
better serve his purpose than so much sublime,
aggregate, but withal, abstruse philosophy, poor
Master Hartsfoot suddenly thought, "Surely, a

brother artist and compatriot ought, and will have some feeling for him," which was a strong proof of how troubled and upset he was by Hollar's troubles; for in his normal state, Master Hartsfoot had far too logical a mind to jumble what people *ought* to do, with what they *will* do, into a synonyme.

" Yes," said he, following up this last straw he had caught at, " surely Vander Vaes, or Lely, as it now pleases him to be called since his knighthood, seeing the insolent prosperity of his own career, will, out of his superfluity of pelf and patronage, hold out a helping hand to his poor, only less fortunate countryman. But, as we have before said, it was only Hartsfoot's anxiety to serve Hollar that made him on this occasion reckon without his host, for though he might not possess what is called knowledge of the world, systematically living out of it as he did, yet he had a profound knowledge of human nature, which is the raw material of knowledge of the world; therefore, had he had time to reflect, he would have known—none better—that what are called self-made men are *nearly* invariably self-seeking men, who are too pre-occupied in making themselves to spare time or money towards mending the fortunes of others; in short, that those who " get on in the world," as it is called, generally crawl to climb, and are not nice as to crooked or mirey ways, and when at length they *huve* succeeded in attaining the summit of that slippery *Mât de Cocagne* worldly success, and in their *low eminence*, the sun shining on them, and causing the very mire they have accumulated in their progress to glitter, and thus sparkle in the eyes of the groundlings. They do not even give "luck," that golden calf idol of the world, any credit for their rise, but attribute it wholly and solely to their own merits, with a sovereign con‑ tempt for those they deem the poor fools who object to rising by the same means, or to success on the same terms.

Now Hartsfoot thought of all this after, but he did not think of it at the time, and so resolved, so soon as he had superintended the thorough cleaning and dusting of Hollar's work room, and the scrupulous replacing of every scrap of paper where he found it, and had delivered up the key to its owner, promising to take it again every night for the same purpose, that he would call upon Sir Peter Lely and see if he could not in‑ terest him in behalf his poor *confrère*.

The *Date Oleulum Belisario* is, under any cir‑ cumstances, by no means a pleasant task, even when we do not hold out the hat for ourselves; but do what Belisarius *really* did, instead of begging; to wit, spoil other people. It wanted about a quarter to eleven a.m. when Hartsfoot reached the splendid house of Sir Peter Lely, in Whitehall, all the appointments of which were *en grand Seignieur*, perhaps a shade too gorgeous in detail, and thereby betraying the *parvenu*. Two or three coaches had just been sent away from the door, whose occupants had been courteously, if somewhat pompously, informed that Sir Peter could not even see them before that day fortnight, as till then his list of names, inscribed six months ago, was so full that he had not one available minute.

" So," thought Oliver, " this is a bad look out for me, but as the copybook assures us that ' with patience and perseverance we shall succeed in every thing,' now is the time to try the prescription. Fortunately for Hartsfoot, the ' first Lord' in black was now engaged with another coach, and the lackey that fell to his share knew him well by sight, being an intimate of Noah Pump and Lancelot Amyot, Mrs. Neville's footman. So accosting him in the civilest possible manner, he said—

" I am extremely sorry, but I fear, sir, Sir Peter cannot possibly see you to-day ; but if you will enter your name and address in the book it shall be attended to."

" I am in no hurry ; I can wait any length of time, as I have come on very particular business."

Here another footman actually rushed past

Hartsfoot and his colleague, and roared out as he stepped into the street—

" My Lady Castlemaine's coach !"

" If you'll step back here, sir," whispered the good-natured lackey, " you'll see her ladyship."

" Back, back, every one," said the man in black, with a sort of Garter-King-of-Arms authority; not actually touching Hartsfoot, but throwing back his right arm in such a *devise parlante* manner as admirably to represent a pantomimic push, and yet what a work of supererogation was he performing, for Lady Castlemaine had not the slightest objection to being seen, but quite the contrary, and had she been there at the moment would probably have enforced the spirit of Talleyrand's injunction, only slightly altering its formula, and have said—

" *Pas tant de zèle, mon ami.*"

However, a few minutes after, when she did rustle out, affecting to conceal her face in her hood, but letting it slip back accidentally on purpose, which was only natural, as no one ever presented a better *primâ facie* case.

Hartsfoot was not sufficiently in eclipse to hold himself absolved from a bow, which the lady acknowledged, not only with a very gracious smile, which displayed the two rows of pearl within their coral casket, but actually stopped in her onward course and made him a very low courtesy.

“ Ah !” sighed he, “ what a pity that nature should ever be guilty of such discrepancies, and make all angel without and all devil within !”

The man in black, who was in the habit of taking notes, though not of printing them, perceiving how gracious the ruler of the kingdom had been to Master Hartsfoot, as soon as her coach had driven off, turned with an altered manner of extreme *empressement*, and expressed to him his regret that he had waited so long, adding, “ But I really fear it will be impossible for Sir Peter to give you an audience”— those were his words—“ to-day.”

Hartsfoot repeated that his business was urgent, and that he was in no hurry, and could wait, whereupon the man in black—Harbord by name —conceiving that from Lady Castlemaine’s civility the strange gentleman *must* be a greater personage than he (Harbord) was aware of, said—

“ Well, sir, if you don’t mind waiting, for wait I fear you’ll have to do, allow me to show you into the dining room, and suiting the action to the word, he walked across the noble hall and flung open the door of a very magnificent room, about fifty feet long and twenty feet high, and having placed a chair for the stranger, closed the door and withdrew. Now Hartsfoot, like all the town, had heard much of Lely’s splendid mode of living, more especially of the luxury of his plate and other table appointments, which, indeed were spoken of and expatiated upon as one of the London wonders, in an age where with much extravagance there was little luxury even at Court, and no elegance. Still he was not prepared for the *coup-d'oeil* that greeted him on being ushered into this room.

Not only the ceiling was rich in Grinling Gibbon's finest carvings, undesecrated by white paint, but relieved by mosaic compartments in vivid heraldic blues, reds, and gold; but in the centre of the panelled walls hung, suspended by an apparent cord, but still of oak, large bunches of game, hares, pheasants, woodcock, snipe, from the same matchless hand—the fur of the former you were tempted to smooth, while the feathers of the birds looked as if you could blow them away; and some of them, by the cunning of the artist, *had* been turned aside, so as to shew the down underneath; in other panels were grouse and moor fowl, with sprays of heather, which, in all but colour, might have deceived the living birds, as the very breeze seemed still to tremble in their bells. But the *chef d'œuvre* was the sideboard! which was composed of deer, wild boars, and chamois, dead, as the spoils of the chase, lying among the roots, that is at the foot, of a giant oak, whose branches rose on either

side, meeting in a sort of irregular arch at the
top, and so forming the frame of the large mirror that was let into the wall; while in these
branches, amid the leaves and acorns, were innumerable little birds, so life-like in their
anatomy, that the outstretched wings of some
made them appear to be actually flying. This
buffet was laden with the most costly gold and
silver plate, flagons, cups, chargers, salvers,
tankards, many of them gifts from appreciative
admirers, but many more from the owner to himself, yet presented with such becoming modesty,
that they always bore inscriptions purporting to
be the offering of someone else. The curtains
and chairs of this room were of emerald green
Genoa velvet, which had also been embroidered
in Italy, to order, with large silver lilies, and
lined with thick rich padua white silk, and
trimmed with deep silver fringe, which, while it
added to their richness, at the same time considerably lightened them, and toning in so har-
moniously as they did with the light—not dark
—oak wainscoting and carvings, produced a
most charming effect. The sides of the polished
oak floor were bare, but the rest covered with a
most splendid Turnois carpet, of an emerald
green ground, like the curtains, and also strewed
with large white lilies. The table was laid for
dinner, for at that time people dined at noon, or

at latest, from one to two p.m. ; and the table was also worth looking at, not from its mere costliness, but from its luxury of taste.

To begin at the beginning, the napery was of that *thick*, curiously fine, soft, satiny texture, such as in former times (when Hamborough table linen ranked *en suite* with family diamonds, family plate, and family point lace) used often to constitute the gift of royalty, and as such, may occasionally be seen as heirlooms now, but never otherwise. The salt cellars were large branches of red coral, about a quarter of a yard high, surmounted by a large gold conch for the salt. The wine coolers were formed by two gold Bacchantes, with one arm round each other's necks, while in their disengaged hand each held a vintage basket of gold trelliswork of leaves and grapes ; save that round the rim of the baskets the ripe bunches of grapes that came tumbling over were made of the root of the amethyst, which, from its semi-opaqueness, perfectly simulated the bloom of the fruit. In one of these coolers was a bottle of Rüdesheimer ; in the other, a bottle of Vin de Volnay-Mousseux; while vulgar Sack and Xeres were banished to the magnificent limbo of the *buffet*, with humble Mead and Hippocras. Mere show, which may be called the vulgarity of wealth, was offensive to Hartsfoot's innately good and correct taste, and lavish expenditure roused his ire as a crying sin, which, while plausibly affording employment to a few, must, in an indirect manner, occasion want and privation to many. But the beautiful, whether in animate or inanimate things, was his weak point; and he thoroughly revelled in the harmonious and artistic perfection of the room he was sitting in. But there are two distinct kinds of love of the beautiful, and they differ widely; one is a mere sensuous enjoyment of it, quite compatible with the grossest and least imaginative natures; the other is a pschycological appreciation of it, requiring refinement of organization and superior intelligence; and it was through the latter mediums that beauty in every form and shade appealed to the complete and nicely balanced nature of Hartsfoot. And, as he had to wait full three quarters of an hour before gaining admission to the presence of the tutelary divinity of this rare shrine, he had ample time to examine and take in all its details.

"Ah!" sighed he, when at length he sat down after a fourth tour of the room, "I fear SELF is too much studied, and lavishes like all self-worshippers, too much upon its idol, to hope for much help *here*."

And the tears welled up in his eyes as he mentally contrasted the two pictures of poor Hollar's desolate, destitute niche in the world's *tableaux vivants,* and the Court painter's gorgeous scene! But then he *was* the Court painter, and knew how, not only to flatter on canvas, but to canvass flatteringly, the power and patronage of the Laises and Phrynés, whom he transmitted to posterity in such flattering colours, while the other had nothing *but* his genius, his industry, and his honesty—three excellent things to starve upon—*that* made all the difference, and so he starved accordingly.

Master Oliver now looked at his watch, as even the best regulated minds have a trick of doing while waiting, with a vague idea that that process will hasten the arrival of the person or thing waited for. And as the hands pointed to a quarter to one, the fear of Mrs. Merrypin rose up before his eyes, for though upon the whole she was a good and indulgent *guovernante* enough for the housekeeper of a single gentleman, with whom she had uncontrolledly had her own way for five-and-twenty years; still, the line must be drawn somewhere, and as she piqued herself (and with reason) upon her art, keeping *her* dinner waiting was one of the things she could *not* overlook in her master; but just as he had made up his mind to do penance for his sin of *lése-cuisinière,* and go without any dinner at all, a door opened at the other end of the room, which was so masked as to appear like one of the panels, and the great man appeared, palette and brushes in hand, and in his working dress—to wit, a tunic of black velvet, *a point d'alençon*, pointed falling collar, and a black velvet beret upon his head. He bowed where he stood, but made no sign of advancing ; the intruder rose, bowed, and walked over to him, and then bowed again, as he said—

" I have many apologies to make to you, Sir Peter, for this intrusion upon time which I know to be so valuable, more especially as I do not come as a legitimate claimant on it to solicit a sitting."

" Oh !" ejaculated the great man, bowing very slightly, and measuring at a glance his visitor from head to foot, as if seeking some external clue to his errand, " that is fortunate, as *place aux dames*, and I have so many ladies on my list for the next eight months, that as a reply to the gentlemen, I have been obliged to put up a permanent NO in my hall. But perhaps you will not mind coming in here ?" he added, backing into his studio, where pointing to a chair for Hartsfoot, he himself ascended the two steps of the dais, where he enthroned himself on the sitter's chair, falling apparently quite naturally into a very regal attitude, as he graciously continued—" I shall be happy to hear your business."

"My business is rather of a painful nature; in fact, Sir Peter, I have come to try and obtain your powerful interest, and enlist your sympathy in behalf of a brother artist."

The great man slightly knit, and then considerably elevated his eyebrows, as if they were protesting upon his part that really he was not aware that *he* had any *brother* artist! or that any individual of the kind existed within a hundred degrees of consanguinity to him. But all he said was—

"Who is this person?"

"He has the honour of being a compatriot of yours, though he is far from having acquired your proficiency in our language; it is poor Wenceslaus Hollar."

"Oh!" drawled the great man, as he twitched a highly perfumed handkerchief out of his breast pocket, whose cobweb fineness diffused a delicious odour of rose and ambergris through the air before officiating at its owner's nose. "Oh! poor Hollar; I'm afraid there is some great bad management and improvidence there, for he really has a very respectable amount of talent, quite enough to keep the wolf from the door, for a man in his sphere of life, and of his habits."

"As I am cognizant of poor Hollar's indefatigable industry and his almost ascetic frugality, I must beg to differ from you there, Sir Peter; but

the fact is, when a person without friends—I
mean powerful friends, patronage, or opportu-
nities, which the two former can always make—
when a person, I say, begins with a large capital
of poverty, and work and strive as they will, can
only succeed in adding nothing to nothing, the
chronic sum total is—NOTHING REMAINS, and that
is an abyss from which no poor wretch can extricate himself."

"Ah! well, I'm exceedingly sorry for him,
but I'm in a delicate position, and wishing to
preserve my independence" (as so many persons
nobly do when they have thoroughly feathered
their *own* nests) "I have made it a rule never
to ask any favours at Court for anyone."

"Neither should I like my poor friend's honest
self-respect to be wounded by having *favours* asked
for him. My idea was that you, Sir Peter Lely,
being a magnate in your profession, might put
a less fortunate *confrère* in a legitimate way of
making his talents available, for I need not tell
you that the smallest diamond that has the advantage of being set and exhibited by a fashionable jeweller, though of little comparative intrinsic
value, will yet obtain a higher price than an invaluable gem, which is wedged in the darkness
of the mine, and so remains unknown."

"*Peut-être ?*" shrugged the little diamond
which, having been so well mounted, had ob-

tained such fabulous prices. "But what is it in one of your English plays about there being 'a tide in the affairs of men which, taken'—I forget when and where, 'leads on to fortune.'"

"Very true, Sir Peter, but some unfortunates are wrecked upon rocks so steep and so barren that no tide can ever reach them to take advantage of."

"I do assure you," said the knight, crossing his right leg over the left, and passing his hand up and down over his glossy black silk stocking with an air of ineffable complacency and self-laudation, "I do assure you when I first came to this country I did not know a soul; fact, 'pon honour."

"He seems to forget," thought Hartsfoot, "that it is bodies and not souls that have got him on."

"Well but, Sir Peter, you soon knew the King, and that was a royal road to success."

"And Hollar, long before, was drawing master to the King and the Duke of York."

"Yes, I reminded him of that, and wanted him to appeal to them, but he is a very sensitive, delicate-minded man, and knowing the impecuniosity of the royal coffers just now I cannot persuade him to do so."

"Ah! well, if people won't follow up their advantages they have no right to complain."

"Still I think they are to be respected when, to their own hindrance, they draw nice distinctions, and won't *take* advantage of others."

And so saying, finding he had come to a dead wall, and could lead his forlorn hope no further, Hartsfoot rose and apologised for the length of his stay.

"Oh! not at all; I am sorry that I really cannot aid you in any way about Hollar. I'm sorry to hear he is in such straitened circumstances, and if this can be of any use to him—"

And he placed a couple of Jacobuses in Hartsfoot's hand, or rather attempted to do so, for the other drew back with an irrepressible flush of indignation upon his cheek, as if the insult had been offered to himself personally.

"Ah! well, you know best;" and then the great man added, as if under the influence of a sudden inspiration, "I'll tell you what I really might be able to do, perhaps. They have all sorts of little games and things every night at the Duchess of York's; I might propose a raffle for some of Hollar's drawings, at half-crown tickets."

"Scarcely," said Hartsfoot; "that would be very *infra dig*, and for no commensurate relief. Fancy, Sir Peter, having one of your *chef d'œuvres* raffled for!"

He could *not* imagine anything so preposterous! so merely replied, to show his perfect knowledge of the English character, as well of the English language—" Why, you see, as a rule, great people are very reluctant to part with their money, but equally fond of purchasing the chance of obtaining forty or fifty pounds' worth for two or three shillings; and when appealed to for cases of distress—that do not bring with them the *éclat* of *public* charity—invariably search the ledger of their memory to see what *claim* the applicant has upon *them*, and finding none—for mere distress, however extreme, is never considered any—wonder they did not apply to somebody else; while somebody else, in his turn, passes the ' what ought to be done ' on to other somebody else, and so on, *ad infinitum.*"

" Too true," said Hartsfoot, as a quotation ob· truded itself on his mind about " Satan reproving sin," but he, of course, did not utter it; but as he prepared to go, merely looked wistfully towards a large piece of brown *taffeta* that covered a picture on the easel, which his host perceiving, and being in high good humour at having saved his money, even if he had lost his time, pulled it off, and discovered that glorious portrait—*the* picture of Lady Castlemaine.

" Doubtless you know the original ?"

" It's not a painting ; it's the living woman !" exclaimed Hartsfoot, in an estacy.

" Don't, at all events, be too sure that the living woman is *not* a painting," laughed the artist.

" What exquisite hands you do give them all, Sir Peter!"

" I should be no hand at pourtraying fair ladies if I did not."

While Hartsfoot was still rapt in admiration before the portrait, a side door opened from the hall, and the stately Harbord announced—

" Dinner is on the table, Sir Peter."

Thanking him for his courtesy in having let him see that particular picture, which he was aware was never shown to anyone, Oliver Hartsfoot bowed his adieux, and retreated through the side door that the man in black had opened, and left the princely domicile of the SUCCESSFUL MAN with his heart even heavier than he had entered it, to think how completely he had failed in his efforts *there* to serve the unsuccessful man, who had done MORE, so far as deserving success went.

CHAPTER XI.

MOTHER AND SON.——COMPANION PICTURES.——
MOTHER AND DAUGHTER.

T so happened that on the very morn-
ing that Hollar had despatched the
poor old lame man, Roger Marner,
to the steward of his quondam patron,
Lord Arundel, for the fifty pounds that had been
some time due to him, and inadvertently forgotten by Lord Arundel, who had done the poor
hard-working artist many good turns, and
meant to do him many more, Dorothy Neville
had been out with her mother's maid, Ruffle,
and gone her rounds among her own special
pensioners ; so that the basket which the latter
carried, and which had been heavy with
divers packages of little household luxuries,
for those who could with difficulty obtain abso-
lute necessaries, was now quite empty, and

Dorothy so tired that she devoutly wished it had been large enough to hold her, and Ruffle strong enough to carry her.

" *Do*, Ruffle, like a dear good soul, let me get into a hackney coach, or I shall drop," she said, as they were picking their way through one of the narrowest and dirtiest lanes in the purlieus of Westminster, called Catchpole Lane.

"Indeed, Mistress Dorothy, I dare not. It would be as much as my place is worth if madam knew it. She has such a dread of infection ever since the plague, and would not let even one of us servants go in a public conveyence, for fear of contaminating the house after. Perhaps it's very wrong of me to say so, but there's a time appointed for us all, whether it comes by plague, pestilence, or famine, or over gormandising, and sleeping off the effects."

" Of course there is ; so what nonsense to be afraid of infection when it's nearly three years since the plague."

" *I'm* not afraid of infection, madam. I've too many plagues at home with that unregenerated sinner, Bridget Butson; but I *am* afraid to disobey madam's strict orders, and really could not do so on any account, and we shall soon be home now, madam."

As she spoke the rain, which had been long threatening, now descended in torrents.

"Oh! dear," said Ruffle, "I may be wrong, and perhaps it's very wrong of me to say so, but *this* comes, I take it, of my naming that limb Butson, who is always sousing every one and everything, and soused sure enough we're likely to be."

"Ladies," said a poor woman, coming to the door of a miserable-looking hovel, "mine is but a poor place to ask you into, still it will keep you dry if so be you'll condescend to step in till the rain is over."

"Oh! thank you," said Dorothy, darting in, followed with equal alacrity by Ruffle.

Poor and wretched the place unquestionably was, since the rough stones of which the walls were built, like those of a cow-house, or any other out-house, were not even white-washed. A bedstead was in one corner, but without any bedding but some straw and dried fern, and a rug that served at once for blanket and counterpane. On this bed, half lying, half sitting, leaning on her elbow, with her cheek in her hand, was a sickly, lazy-looking girl, watching her mother work. The fireplace, with a sort of cruel irony, was very large, as if for the purpose of letting down as much wind and rain as possible, while the two rusty andirons were drawn closely together to try and keep alight the not very good imitation of fire, composed of nut shells, sticks, and bricks made of ashes, clay and dried leaves, kneaded together with water, and then left to dry—when after much labour, and equal patience, they were induced to ignite and do duty for the more orthodox fuel of wood and coal,* the exorbitant price of the latter placing it quite beyond the reach of many of the middle classes, let alone the very poor. In this " weak invention" of a fire, was a smoothing iron, doing all it could to fulfil its destiny under difficulties, while the poor woman's work was an equally arduous attempt to iron a few rags upon a ricketty three-legged table, made on the model of a joint stool, her ironing blanket being the *débris* of an old flannel petticoat. Still, no sooner had Dorothy and Ruffle entered than she offered them all the hospitality she could, by placing a wooden stool and an inverted deal box near the fire—no, the grate—with many apologies for not possessing a chair, and then, turning to the girl, said—

" Bridget, where's your manners, not to rise when you see gentlefolks ? Fie ! I'm ashamed of you."

" Oh ! pray don't disturb her," said Dorothy, " and do go on with your work, or I shall go back into the rain if we are at all in your way."

* Evelyn, Pepys, and many contemporary writers, mention the terrible fact, of coal being just after the Dutch invasion, £5 10s. a chaldron, from the ships not being able to bring it up the river.

"Dear heart, madam, I hope you won't do that, for you are not in the least in my way. I'm only sorry it's such a poor shelter for you."

And with a natural good breeding, or what Mr. Evelyn would have truly called *politesse du cœur*, the woman resumed her work, or rather made a pretence of doing so, by folding and unfolding the things she had ironed, rather than disturb the ladies by going to the grate for the other iron.

"Your daughter, I suppose?" asked Dorothy, looking towards the girl, who, for want of anything better, had been biting her finger, and staring at her and Ruffle, ever since their entrance.

"Yes, ma'am," sighed the poor woman.

"Have you a husband."

"No, ma'am, it pleased God to take him at the time of the plague; and I often wish that none of us had been parted, but the Lord knows best; we can none of us go without our marching orders, as my poor Joe used to say, he being a soldier."

"Then you have only yourself and this girl?"

"And her brother, ma'am, a lad of fourteen, two year younger than her."

"And what does he do?"

"Whatever he knows how, ma'am, and whatever he can get to do, and neither's much, chiefly running errands and holding gentlemen's horses, and calling the qualities’ coaches at the playhouses, but it’s sore against my grain, if I could help it, his being about the streets so, but beggars mustn’t be choosers ; and as I always tell him to try and be a good boy wherever he is, for God’s everywhere, in the worst places as well as the best, and it’s *us* he takes account of, and not the places we are in. So *they* are no excuse for us if the reckoning is not right at the last.”

“ Well, I’m sure you deserve to have a good son, for he has a good mother.’’

“ Thank you, ma’am, for your good opinion, but such poor creatures as we can’t be good, all we can do is to try hard not to be bad.”

“ Which is the best of goodness,” said Dorothy ; “ but I hope your daughter helps you.”

“ She would if she was able, ma’am, but I’ve never been able to bide at home to teach her much, and she’s not strong, so she only stands about while I and Joe work.”

“ They also serve who only stand and wait,” ejaculated Mrs. Ruffle, casting up her eyes de- voutly as she gave out the above, which may fairly be called the servants’ hall text, and which no doubt she had often found peculiarly satisfac- tory to footmen.

Dorothy could not repress a smile at this word in season, so peculiarly out of season, and in order to hide it, stooped down, and making a holder of her pockethandkerchief, took the iron out of the consumptive fire, and brought it over to the hostess.

" Oh! ma'am," said the poor woman, quite overpowered, "to think you should soil your pretty hand and your dainty handkerchief touching my irons, and waiting on such as me."

" The least I can do is to be of some little use while we keep you away from your own fire," and before the woman could prevent her she took the other iron from the table that the woman had been using, and carried it over to the fire, embedding it in the ashes from whence she had taken the other, a proceeding which greatly shocked Mrs. Ruffle's lady's maid propriety of feeling ; so much so, indeed, that she said, *sotto voce—*

" I may be wrong, and perhaps it's very wrong of me to say so ; but I think, Mistress Dorothy, it's not a young lady's place to do such menial offices."

" Ah! well; but you know, Ruffle, I never *was* in place; so can't be expected to understand the proprieties."

" Oh! the lightning," said Ruffle, placing both her hands before her eyes, while Dorothy called out—

" Put down your iron, good woman, while it lightens so," and as she spoke, a clap of thunder shook the miserable room—if room it could be called—to its very foundation.

"Oh! mother, the thunder!" screamed the girl on the bed; "is God angry with me?"

"Not with you in particular, poor child," said the mother, going over to her, taking her head between her hands, and resting it against her own bosom, while she patted her shoulder as nurses do infants to hush them to sleep; "but goodness knows, He has reason enough to be angry with this wicked city."

To which another loud clap of thunder seemed to assent; while she spoke, the rain came down in such torrents, that a perfect rivulet flowed in under the door, which could do no other harm than to make the clay floor a little damper.

"It is fortunate it rains so, as there will be no danger from the lightning."

"There—hear that, Bridget; the lady says there's no danger while it rains so."

"And poor Joe!" said the girl, "he'll be drowned if he's out in it."

"Joe," said, or rather groaned the mother—"he was born in a storm, has lived in a storm, and ' He who rules the whirlwind and directs the storm,' will take care of him."

While Rachel Ruffles ready cut and dry texts always brought a smile to Dorothy's lips, this poor woman's holy submission and unshakeable trust in God, brought tears into her eyes ; for verily, it was the finest and most touching sermon she had ever heard in her life, and then and there she laid it to heart to ponder on ever after, when she winced at any of her own crumpled rose leaves. While the woman was hushing and soothing the apparently half-witted girl, the door burst open, and in rushed the aforesaid Joe, drenched to the skin, but jumping, capering, and snapping his fingers like a maniac.

"Hoorah, mother ! Charing Cross for ever ! We're saved !—we're rich ! You shall work no more ! Bridget shall wear silk ! and—and I'll be a captain in lace, in father's old regiment !"

"Lord have mercy upon me ! Has the boy gone clean out of his senses ?"

"Not clean, at all events, mother, for I'm up to my knees in mud ; but to show you I'm not raving, what do you think of THAT !" and he flung a small, but bulky and heavy leather bag down upon the table, which returned a metallic chink, and was about to unloose the leather thong that was twisted tightly round its neck, when the mother, pale as ashes, laid her hand upon it, and said, solemnly, fixing her eyes intently on him—

"Joseph Barton, where and how did you come by that money ?"

"Honestly, mother."

"Honestly—impossible ! Gentlefolks don't give bags of money to boys for holding horses and calling coaches."

"Well, I promise you I did not steal it; so, as I told you at first, mother, I came honestly by it, and it is ours."

"Not till I know how you came by it," said she, neither removing her hand from the bag nor her scrutinising eyes from the boy's face.

"Of course you shall; for I'm sure I don't want to make a mystery of the most wonderful piece of luck that ever happened to anyone—at least to us. I had been holding a gentleman's horse for more than an hour at the Mulberry Tree Tavern, at Charing Cross; when he come out he gave me sixpence; it was the only one I had got to-day, and heavy at heart I felt to have no more to bring you home. Well, I waited and waited, to get a chance of crossing over; the place was so thronged with traffic of every kind, coaches, carts, horses, and waggons. At last a clearish moment came; I dashed through the mud as fast as I could tear, and just as I reached the other side, I kicked something, that being covered with mud, I thought was a stone, till I heard it chink ! when I stooped down, and lo ! and behold, it was this bag ! So now, mother, out with your scissors and let us open it."

"Thank God it was no worse !" said Mrs. Barton.

"Worse! Why, you don't suppose, mother, I'd turn thief?"

"No, my boy, I don't," said the poor woman, still tightly holding the bag, as she threw her other arm round the lad's neck and burst out crying. "No, Joe; I thank God that I don't think in His mercy He'd let *that* trial come upon me, for He knows I could *not* bear it. But, my poor boy, we have no right to this money; in short, it will make us poorer, for it will cost us a shilling to have it advertised upon the News Books."

"Oh!" said poor Joe, with a petrified look between resignation and despair, "I never thought of that."

And here for the first time he perceived Dorothy and Ruffle; for, from the darkness, and his great hurry and excitement, he had not seen them on his entrance. So doffing his cap, he bestowed on them his best bow, accompanied by the obligato anterior kick out of his right foot, of all those who like him, have learnt "deportment" about the highways and byeways.

The tears were coursing down Dorothy's cheeks at the scene she had just witnessed between the mother and son. Here, verily God *was* served in truth and in deed, under every trial and every temptation, and under every pressure stretched on poverty's cruellest rack of chronic and hopeless privation. Oh! what were the little holiday velvet clad *toilettées* virtues of the rich, even where they existed, chipped off in small splinters from their superfluities, and gilt with the flattery of parasites, compared to the rigid, unwavering, unrecognised, disinterested, rectitude of this poor woman, with only God for its witness, and His law alone for its motive; for at the moment, in her terrible fear, least the boy should not have come fairly by such a waif, she had completely forgotten the presence of the two strangers, and now that she remembered it, she turned and humbly apologised to them, as if she had been guilty of some unseemly act.

" Pray make no apologies to me," said Dorothy; "I feel grateful to you with a gratitude that will last me my life; but both your conduct and language are so superior to your present position, that you have made me curious; not, I do assure you, with an impertinent and unwarrantable curiosity, but with that of extreme interest in the welfare of one I hope to serve, because one who seems in every way so deserving. May 1 then ask where you were brought up?"

" Aye, surely, madam; I am only proud and grateful to tell it. My maiden name was Audrey Moore; my father was gardener to, and had been bred and born in the service of Sir James Bourchier, whose daughter, Madam Elizabeth, married

—more's the pity!—Oliver Cromwell, afterwards the Lord Protector; and in my lady Protectress's household I was brought up, and served as a laundrymaid, till I married my poor husband, Joseph Barton, colour-sergeant in General Fairfaxe's regiment. And God knows," added she, wiping her eyes with her apron, " had I been her own child, Madam Cromwell could not have taken more care of me; and often and often, now in my bitter struggle for an existence, which, if we were free to choose—which we are not—I'd gladly quit, I think of that dear good lady's words. ' Audrey,' she would say to me, ' in prosperity we can only give God words; and prayer and praise are perhaps all He requires while the sun shines, but as the storm and wreck *will* come more or less to *all*, we should, like the gladiators of old, always be training ourselves for the struggle; for how we *act* under trials and temptation is the *test* of our faith and our lip worship; and often and often in life, we find it harder to *bear* God's will than to do it; for in all action there is relief, but the dull, stagnant, and almost hopeless routine of endurance, it requires ALL our trust in God, and all our moral courage to bear up under them.' And every day of my life I feel the truth of her words, and bless her for them."

" She must, indeed, have been a very good woman. I know my mother has a great regard and respect for her, and I dare say the stories about her parsimony and meanness *are* stories ?"

" That are they, ma'am ; *her* head never was turned by the sort of tinsel Court she'd been much against her will raised to. She gave too much to her suffering fellow-creatures, and there are always only too many of that class *to* give to, to allow anything like waste or extravagance, and for that reason she looked after the Court— as it is called—expenditure, as if it had been the household of a private and not over rich gentleman ; and that of course, by all the hangers-on of such places, who generally fatten on the spoils of their employers, got her the bad word of all such. She was very plain and frugal, too, in her own dress, but then how many hundreds she dressed on the satins, velvets, and jewels she did *not* wear."

" And the Protector, do you think he was really religious, or merely an arch hypocrite, as so many think him ?"

" Well, ma'am, I should say his religion was as like Christianity as a mask is like a human face, there are the outlines of all the features there, but where is the vitality ? that is, the reality ; how can a thoroughly worldly man, caring for and grasping at nothing but power, be a religious man ? because, how can he be a conscientious man? The Protector was a terrible tyrant; it was *in him* to be so. I used always in my own mind compare him to Herod the Tetrarch in a small way, for of course in these days, and in what is called a Christian country, he could not slaughter, poison, strangle, and lie away people's lives wholesale, as Herod did, but so far as the different times and his very different amount of power went, I don't think he left Herod much in advance of him. However, who knows, here we only 'see as through a glass darkly?' And he had the reputation, and I believe deserved it, of conducting the machinery of the government wisely and equitably, for that only requires head work, of which he was quite capable. But the ladies of the family, especially Madam Cromwell and Mrs. Claypole, were as near angels as anything can be on this side eternity, and Master Richard was a dear good gentleman as ever was, and had no vocation for his father's trade, either of usurpation or power."

As Mrs. Barton ceased speaking, a burst of sunshine darted through the miserable lattice, which could not be said to gild, but which certainly did display more saliently all the squalid horror of this place, which the former obscurity had toned down into a fine Rembrandt sort of invisibility.

Dorothy thanked her, not only for her hospitality, but for her anecdotes of the Cromwells, and then said—

"You must let me come and see you soon again, Mrs. Barton, and don't give yourself any trouble about having that bag of money advertised, as I'll have that done."

"Oh! thank you a thousand times, ma'am, and if it is not taking too great a liberty, and encroaching to much on your kindness, *would* you, ma'am, take charge of the bag itself, as you are witness we have not opened it, or meddled with it in any way, and therefore do not know what it contains; and I do not like the responsibility of keeping it in such a poor unguarded place as this, both I and my boy having to be away from the place so much, doing any odd job we can get."

"With pleasure," said Dorothy. "I'll take care of it, and bear witness of your strictly honest and honourable conduct from first to last about it."

And she was about to take up the bag, when Mrs. Barton said—

"Stop, ma'am, let me wrap it in a piece of strong paper, for it may not be quite dry yet, though I see Joe has wiped the mud off of it."

While she turned to look for the paper Dorothy slipped an angel* into Joe's hand, saying—

* An old English coin of the value of ten shillings.

" I'm sorry, my boy, you were disappointed about your prize, but you have a far greater treasure in so good a mother, who brings you up so well."

" I humbly thank you, madam," said Joe, with another scrape, but, albeit, unused to entertaining angels, even ' unawares,' upon looking at the gift, he said, " but you have made a mistake, ma'am, this is an angel, and not a sixpence."

" I did not mean it for a sixpence. Keep it."

" God bless you, ma'am, thank you. Look here, mother, see what the lady has given me. So you see the bag *has* brought us luck after all," said he, as he gave the coin to his mother.

" Oh ! ma'am, God bless you; but this is really too much. It's like robbing you to take all this for your staying half an hour in this miserable place out of the rain. It's a fortune to us."

" Well," laughed Dorothy, " don't you know that it never rains but it pours, and I hope it may be the beginning of better fortune to you, and I think it will. So now good-bye, and thank you very much, Mrs. Barton, for your hospitality, but as I may be for aught you know, a second Judas carrying the bag—so—"

" Oh ! ma'am," interrupted Mrs. Barton, " it is nowhere written that Judas looked, any more than he acted like an angel."

"At all events, it is only right that you should know with whom and where your bag of money is going ; so, Ruffle, just tear a leaf out of your pocket book, and write down the name and address for Mrs. Barton."

Ruffle wrote the name and address, and gave it to Mrs. Barton, who received it with a curtsey and a "thank you ma'am ;" but there was no necessity for that, and she did not read it at the time, as a vulgar minded woman would have done.

The rain had come down in such a deluge, that the at all times dirty streets were comparatively clean, when Dorothy and Ruffle again set out on their way home, and though it was very wet under foot, it was only water, not mud. Knowing how anxious her mother would be at her unusually long stay, coupled with such a terrific storm, Dorothy walked as fast as she possibly could, without actually running, till Ruffle, who deprecated "hurry skurry" of any sort—more especially in her own movements, as it not only flurried her nerves, but what she thought even worse, disarranged her dress—panted up to her and gasped out, "You'll excuse me, Mistress Dorothy, and perhaps it's very wrong of me to say so, but all proverbs are true, and the more haste the worse speed; and you must stop while I pin up your white petticoat, the lace of which is one mass of mud."

" Oh! never mind it, Ruffle; I am all mud, and we'll soon be home now, where I must, and you too, change from head to foot."

" Oh! but, ma'am, what will madam say, to see that beautiful Dresden lace, at four guineas a yard! completely spoilt, and perhaps torn ?"

" Well, I hope she'll say and see," retorted Dorothy, hurrying on, and not giving the horrified Ruffle time to effect the meditated rescue; " how foolish it is to trim shifts and petticoats with Dresden lace; and how much better it would be to spend the money in flannel and linen for those who have neither, as the Lady Protectress did."

"I'm sure, for that matter," said Ruffle—this accelerated speed having put all the verjuice in her composition into a state of fermentation, "madam is one of the charitablest ladies as ever was; and it can't be expected of anyone, that they are to take off their skins, as if they were eels, to give to the poor."

" Dear, how kind of them !" smiled the wicked Dorothy ; "I was not aware that was a practise of theirs, but now I know it I shall have such a respect for them, that I'll never eat another eel pie or *matelotte* as long as I live."

" Oh! Mistress Dorothy," and Ruffle closed her eyes and shook her head, as was her wont over lost sheep, "I may be wrong, and perhaps it's

very wrong of me to say so ; but you know very
well what I meant, and it had nothing whatever
to do with the eels, which are things I can't
abide, dressed or undressed."

Here they reached their own door, at which
they had no occasion to ring, it being wide open,
with Jessop and Lancelot posted at it, looking
out in all directions, while Mrs. Neville was
pacing up and down the hall, in too great a state
of perturbation to do anything else.

" Good Heaven, child ! how you have frightened me ; and where on earth were you during
that terrible storm ?"

" Quite safe and well, dear mother, as you
shall hear ; for I've so much to tell you, and a
great favour to ask you, which you *must* grant."

" I'll hear nothing, and I'll grant nothing till
you have taken off all your wet things ; and you
go and take off yours, Ruffle, and send Phœbe
up with some burnt sack to Mistress Dorothy's
room."

" Phœbe has been up in Mistress Dorothy's room
for the last half hour waiting for her," said
Jessop.

" Oh ! mother, darling," said Dorothy, as they
went upstairs.

" Hush !" said Mrs. Neville, " I'll not hear a
word till you have changed your things." So
Dorothy was obliged to obey, and Phœbe, her

maid, being all ready at her post, with the dry things airing before the fire, the drenched garments were soon changed, and Dorothy comfortably inducted into her dressing-gown, and no sooner was Phœbe dispatched down stairs for the burnt sack, than she flung her arms round her mother's neck, and bursting into tears, produced her credentials of the bag of money, and then told its and Audrey Barton's whole history, so far as she knew it, at which Mrs. Neville was almost as much affected by Dorothy's graphic description, as if she had been an eye and ear witness of the scene.

"And now, *mama mia*," said Dorothy, in conclusion, "the favour I have to ask you is *this*, and if you refuse me *I'll* marry Master Hartsfoot to-morrow, as I know *he* won't refuse *me*, and never see your face again."

"Well, I'm sure!" laughed Mrs. Neville, "after such terrible threats I suppose I shall be bullied into everything."

"Of course you will, like a good, dutiful, and obedient mother, as you have ever been. Now listen to my plan, and sign and seal on the spot, unless you can suggest a better. You know poor Anne Smith, who kept our lodge at the Chestnuts, has been dead these six weeks; you also know that your head gardener, Archy McPherson, at great inconvenience to himself and his wife, has left his own cottage to keep the lodge till you could be suited with a thoroughly respectable trustworthy woman to replace Anne Smith, which you have not yet been able to do. Now it seems to me, though none else have been able to recommend you such a person, Providence has this day done so in the person of that excellent Audrey Barton, and if you could only see the horrible place such a gem is lost in you would understand what a treasure you have found, and what a paradise the lodge at the Chestnuts would be to this poor worthy soul and her family after the bare, dark, miserable dungeon they are now in. Now, if it's YES don't answer me, only kiss me."

Mrs. Neville did *not* answer her, but threw her arms round her dear child's neck and strained her to her heart.

"Ten thousand, thousand thanks, my own dear best of mothers, and now to show you that I have some gratitude in my composition, I promise you," said Dorothy, flinging a saucy smile at her mother over her shoulder, as she walked to an escretoire at the other end of the room, to lock up the bag of money that Joe Barton had found. "Yes, I promise you solemnly that my 'ALLIANCE' with Master Hartsfoot shall be postponed *sine die.*"

CHAPTER XII.

THE RESTORATION.

THE day after Master Hartsfoot had led his forlorn hope to Sir Peter Lely's, he woke with a weight upon his heart about poor Hollar's uncertain future; though, for that matter, even for the best placed and most prosperous, are not all futures uncertain? And a slight pressure upon his conscience, from having for two whole days deserted his post as master of the revels to Dorothy, still *à l'impossible nul n'est tenu*, and as poverty and pleasure, misery and mirth, always have been and always will be moral antipodes, how could he reconcile the two? Nevertheless, he rose an hour earlier than usual, and resolved, after he had seen Hollar, superintended the arrangement of his work room, and breakfasted, that he would don his harness and repair to Mrs. Neville's for his daily orders; previous to which he had the satisfaction of finding his *protégé* in Axe Yard much better, and delighted with Mrs. Barton's care and attention, and with Mrs.

Barton herself; and in his own mind, for he took
care not to express it before his generous friend,
Hartsfoot regretted, as he had so often done before, how that petty tyrant, poverty, ever steps in
between her victims and their wishes, for he had
that morning heard that Marjery (the ossified
north wind) would be able to return to her post
in a fortnight, and he could not help wishing
that he could afford to have kept Mrs. Barton, too,
who was so much poor Marjery's superior in
every way.   But Master Oliver knew nothing of
this ; he merely saw with great satisfaction the
moral and physical improvement of the poor in-
valid, and told him that he had had the bag of
money containing the fifty pounds that Roger
Marner had lost, advertised on the newsbooks,
and that he had no doubt the money would be
recovered, as, indeed, he resolved in his own
mind that someway or other it *should;* after
which cheering assurance he took leave of his
friend and returned home to breakfast, which he
had no sooner finished than he walked to the
glass—a habit he had contracted lately, always
previous to his going to the house on the Mall,
to see that his dress was point device as that of
squire of dames should be, and yet, if all this
care was taken for Dorothy (?) I am sorry to say
it was wasted upon a little undeserving ingrate,
who never remarked what he wore, except that

she thought he always *looked* very nice, and would have thought *him* so had he appeared before her in a flour sack, with holes cut in it for his arms to come through. Having rang to have the breakfast things removed, Noah Pump handed him his hat and gloves, the same he had worn when he went to Axe Yard that morning.

"Not this; the last new beaver Holden sent home."

"It looks very like rain, sir."

Master Oliver was busy arranging the tassels of his collar, so he did not hear this prudent parenthesis; at least, he made no reply to it. Noah brought Holden's last *chef d'œuvre*, arranging the glossy sable plumes, and sighing over them as if they had been those of a hearse. Finding that his master took this piece of magnificence and put it on with no more respect than if it had been his nightcap, Noah thought it his duty to speak out plainly.

"You'll excuse me, sir, but should it rain there goes five pounds ten before a person would have time to sneeze."

"Pooh! Noah," smiled his master, "as you've often heard my Lord Worcester say, we can't counteract the nature of things, and it's the nature of a beaver, you know, to take to the water."

"Yes, sir; but what I'm afeared on is that the water should take to the beaver."

" Bring me a pair of new gloves."

" Lord, sir ! these *was* new this morning; it's all very well for flimsy things like governments to change hands so often, and go from Kings to Protectors, and from Protectors to Kings; but gloves is gloves, and leather's leather, which is much more solider, and so should nat'rally last longer."

" Very true, Noah; but I soiled the gloves you gave me this morning arranging dusty books."

" Hang them books !" muttered Noah, to himself, as he went for the gloves; " they're always kicking up a dust of some kind. If they was mine, I'd dust 'em to some purpose, by adding bell and candle light to 'em ! instead of which, we shall be having them ere Saveons here again next week to make more litter."

As soon as the fresh gloves were brought and put on, Master Hartsfoot issued through the glass door in his dining-room, which opened upon the Mall, and had hardly got beyond its threshold before he met Mr. Locke, who was coming to his house; he offered to go back.

" On no account," said Locke; " I was merely coming to ask you to dine with me and a few more of our friends to-day, at Chatelins, the French house in Covent Garden."

" Thanks—to-day I cannot ; but you know

next week you all sup with me, and Lord Worcester has promised to show us the experiment of igniting water."

" That's a secret that it would be worth the government's while to purchase," rejoined Mr. Locke; " for otherwise, none of our present rulers are ever likely to set the Thames on fire. I hear there was sad work in the House yesterday about secret intelligence, or rather the want of it, and Secretary Morrice told them that he was allowed but £700 a-year for obtaining intelligence, whereas, in Cromwell's time, the Protector allowed £70,000 a-year for it, which statement was confirmed by Colonel Birch, who added that, thereby Cromwell carried in his girdle the secrets and policies of all the European Powers "

" There can be no doubt," said Hartsfoot, " that the secret of all salutary economy, whether in states or households, does not consist in mere retrenchment, and *not* spending, but in knowing when, and where, and how *to* spend; for the most wanton extravagance ever committed, either in states or households, often arises from the not making a necessary outlay at the proper time."

" Unquestionably," said Locke: " but no country can be practically well governed that is only theoretically governed as England is, with a maximum of talk and a minimum of supervision.   No household can go on without a mistress's eye; no business without a master's. With modification, Cromwell was right in his maxim of 'hang well and pay well;' but we waste an immensity of time in making laws too severe to carry out, which is, in other words, offering a premium for evil doing.   In France and Holland, the government at once and effectually prevent adulteration of food and every other species of adulteration, by making the spurious articles that would be used to adulterate them, three times as dear as the genuine ingredients. And false weights and measures are as effectually prevented, by having the delinquent's name and fraud emblazoned in large letters, in his own shop, so as that all who run may read; and no man, consequently, will incur such ruinous disgrace for the sake of a little temporary cheating. Whereas, we sapiently impose a trumpery and inadequate fine upon our rogues, who merely look upon it as paying their way, to secure the right of cheating double tides.   The end of punishment should be amendment, and not mere suffering; and legislation will never be sound and comprehensive till it discovers the art of making it the INTEREST of the mass to be honest and their greatest peril to be the reverse.   And of this art, Cromwell's 'HANG WELL AND PAY WELL' was the nucleus, which being paraphrased,

simply means, let your punishments and your
rewards both be adequate and EFFECTUAL.   But
though we have plenty of blacksmith's forges,
we never seem to learn the art of striking while
the iron is hot in anything, which, I suppose
arises from our national phlegm.   Yesterday,
when it was moved that the King's speech should
be considered, because that in the first part of it,
the league to which he alludes was the only good
public measure of his since the Restoration, yet
no; the spirit of procrastination is so strong in all
our public affairs, that it was voted *nem. con.* that
it should be adjourned till next Friday, *to be considered of.*"

"So Lord Worcester told me, whom I met
last night at the Club in the Pell Mell; and he
also told me of a shocking thing when he was
last in Paris, of some poor man of the name of
Caus, or Caius, or some such name, who was in-
carcerated at *Bicètre*, as a lunatic, who is far
more sane than any of the wretches who shut
him up; his insanity being nothing more than
his maintaining, and, as Lord Worcester says,
most lucidly and logically proving the practicability of utilizing Archimede's old discovery of the
power of steam, so as to propel both vessels at
sea and vehicles on land, at the rate of thirty
miles an hour or more."

"Then, of course he is mad," said Locke;

" for insanity is the stereotyped label, that the
ignorance and prejudice of every age has for all
those pioneers who have the misfortune either to
think, or to make discoveries, greatly in advance
of their own times.   The laughed at, or perse-
cuted 'visionaries,' as they are thought and
called, of one epoch, are the pioneers of science,
who make the great world-wide thoroughfare on
Time's highway for the plodding, practical money
scraping men of succeeding ages to travel by
and traffic on, and what are deemed the Utopias
of enthiasists—so long as they are only in their
germ or seed state of *thought*—grow at last into
laws and statutes ; like acorns, which, as acorns,
are only deemed worthy of being food for swine,
yet when time has fructified them into oaks, then
their utility and importance are found to be in-
dispensable. For that matter, I wonder that poor
Worcester himself, from his almost miraculous
mechanical genius and scientific acumen, has not
been treated to chains and a strait waistcoat
long since."

" It *is* a wonder ; last night it made my blood
boil at the Club, to see a set of asses grinning
and winking at each other, when he was pro-
pounding to me, a certainly very subtle and extraordinary theory that he has, touching the
wondrous and ubiquitous powers of electricity.

He says he is quite certain that if he could only embue half a dozen other minds with his own thorough conception and perception of the subject, he would undertake to convey, through its agency, *almost* instantaneous intelligence from pole to pole!"

" I, for one, don't doubt it," said Locke; " for in physical science, once discover the principle and properties of any agent, and its perfectability and practicability become merely matters of time and study."

" I confess I *should* like," rejoined Hartsfoot, " to live to see the lightning broken to harness!"

" Whether you live to see it or not, depend upon it the electric fluid will be tamed and harnessed before the passions and vices of men are."

" I fear so.   Don't you think poor Lord Worcester is looking very ill?"

" Ah! poor fellow, I don't doubt but he is suffering from the old Cavalier heart complaint of royal ingratitude, just as his coffers have contracted incureable atrophy in the same cause.   I almost wonder that the very stones composing Raglan Castle do not propel themselves from their cement with indignation, and come crashing down upon White Hall!"

"It would certainly seem as if all the cold water in the castle reservoirs* had not been used against the Roundheads, but that the present King had retained a good supply to throw upon the claims of those who had done his father's cause and his own such signal service."

" Do let us return to my house," said Harts-foot, " you may take cold standing here."

" No, no, I must be going, for Lord Ashley is waiting for me at Durham Yard ;† so good-bye till next Thursday."

And the friends shook hands and separated. These prolonged "greetings in the market place" and other quarters, were the natural result of a newsless, because daily-paperless state of society;

---

* This fine, brave, loyal Cavalier, Edward Marquis of Worcester—like so many more—impoverished himself in befriending and defending Charles the First, without obtaining any acknowledgment or recompense from Charles the Second. During the Civil Wars, he was the owner and occupier of Raglan Castle. He had constructed some hydraulic engines and wheels for conveying water from the moat to the top of the castle, or great tower ; and upon the approach of some of the belligerent Roundheads, Lord Worcester determined to startle them by a display of his engineering skill. He accordingly gave orders to set the waterworks playing, of the effect of which he writes as follows :—" There was such a roaring, that the poor silly men stood so amazed, as if they had been all dead, and yet they saw nothing ; at last, as the plot was laid, up comes a man, staring and running, crying out before he came to them, ' Look to yourselves, my masters, for the lions are got loose.' Whereupon. the searchers gave us such a loose, that they tumbled down the stairs, that it was thought one-half of them had broke their necks, never looking behind them till they were sure they had got out of the Castle."

† Durham Yard, so called, from the palace built there by Thomas de Hatfield, Bishop of Durham, as the town residence for himself and his successors. It stood on the site of the buildings, now called the Adelphi, and was, in Charles the Second's time, one of the most fashionable parts of London.

all news was only to be gleaned and inaccurately collected by verbal communication and oral tradition, and so slowly did all intelligence travel in those days that an acquaintance or a person of eminence might die in the next street and their friends and the public not become aware of the fact for ten days or a fortnight after it had occurred, which cannot be wondered at, when it is remembered that that slow, but by no means sure medium, " a private hand," had chiefly to do the work of modern five or six times a day posts, railways, steam boats, and electric and submarine ! telegraphs.

" *Peccavi*," said Master Hartsfoot, holding his hand before his face as he entered Mrs. Neville's drawing-room, " but for the last few days I've had business, imperative, but by no means agreeable, which did not leave a minute at my disposal to come and take your commands, Mistress Dorothy, but to-night there are two novelties, at the Duke's House, a play of Dryden's called ' Evening Love,' a poor thing, I understand though it *is* Dryden's, and he thinks so himself; and at the King's House the first night of Sir Charles Sedley's new play ' The Mulberry Garden.' "

" Well, with my consent," said Mrs. Neville, " any play of Sir Charles Sedley's she'll not go to."

" Nor does she want to go to it ; so *mamma*

cara mia, as consents are of great value *some-times,* you should always keep them for those who solicit them," said Mistress Dorothy, looking exceedingly saucy, as, having pinned her mother with this little impertinence, she turned to her other slave and commanded him to sit down, whereupon she said, as she leant back in her chair and joined the ends of her pretty little rose-tipped fingers together—

" Ahem ! and pray, Master Hartsfoot, do you think that no one has important business but yourself? I have been in no humour for plays or pageants these last two days, I assure you ; but goaded by your base desertion I have been on the highway accumulating bags of money, but as ' conscience makes cowards of us all,' like you I now cry ' *peccavi,*' and want you to help me to hunt out the rightful owner. I have sent advertisements to the newsbooks, but that is slow work."

Master Hartsfoot looked as he felt, completely mystified.

" Nay, Thea, leave riddles, and tell Master Hartsfoot the exact history of that money, which is so much to the credit of those poor people."

" Very well," said she rising, placing a footstool for Master Hartsfoot, a screen between him and the fire, and taking his hat and placing it on a table with a care as regarded the feathers and

the right way of the beaver that would greatly
have modified one of Noah Pump's stock apho-
risms had he seen it, to the effect " that all women
are more or less fools, and delight in destruction
as monkeys do in mischief."   " Very well," said
she, re-seating herself, " it is a long story, and I
must 'settle you,' as I always do myself at
church, when the sermon sets in, for if one is
not comfortable one cannot attend, particularly
when Dr. Stillingfleet preaches, who, I am sorry
to say, generally takes a glass too much."*

" Oh, fie! Thea you are too bad!" laughed
Mrs. Neville, as she shook her head, while Master
Hartsfoot's sides gently undulated for several
seconds.   As briefly as she could, without omit-
ting any of the flemish details by which she had
brought the scene at Audrey Barton's so vividly
before her mother on the previous day, Dorothy
repeated the history of her having taken shelter
at Mrs. Barton's, and the circumstance of Joe
Barton's having found the bag with the money
at Charing Cross.   " Now," added she, in conclusion, " don't talk to me of your Roman virtue
—with all Rome for spectators—after this poor
woman's Christian virtue, with no witness but
God, and His vicegerent her own conscience."

* It was customary at that time, and indeed long after, for
clergymen to preach by an hour glass, and when the sands had
run out without their sermon having come to a conclusion, they
would turn up the time-keeper, merely remarking to the congregation, " Now, my brethren, we will take another glass."

"I won't," said Hartsfoot, as the tears filled his eyes; "but something must be done to put such virtue beyond any more such ordeals."

" Something *has* been done," replied Dorothy, " for my dear good mother has given her the Lodge Cottage, at The Chestnuts; but on going to her with the glad tidings this morning, I found from 'Joe,' that she had been called away yesterday evening to some employment for the next fortnight. So we must wait that time, as well as we can; for I shall have no sleep till I see the trio installed in that bright, pretty lodge out of that dismal dungeon, only fit for rats and toads."

" Audrey Barton you said her name was?" asked Master Hartsfoot.

" Yes."

" Strange! how circumstances dove-tail themselves into one another. I think I can tell you where Mrs. Barton has got employment." And he then told how, on the preceding evening, being in want of a trustworthy person to attend upon a poor friend of his who was ill, Alice Merrypin had strongly recommended Mrs. Barton. " And I think," added he, " I shall be able to rescue the poor boy Barton from the streets, as Pump has long been importuning me to let him have a boy under him, declaring that the ' *saveons* ' make too much work for him."

"Thank you—thank you, dear good Master Hartsfoot," said Dorothy, starting up and taking both his hands, and shaking them. "There! I hope I have not hurt you," she added, resuming her seat; "but the fact is, there is no one in this house to do anything that ought to be done, but me."

Whether it was this announcement that shocked Master Hartsfoot, or any other cause, has never been rightly ascertained; but certain it is, that the blood mounted not only to his cheeks, but to the roots of his hair, and over his ears, so that at that moment he would have made a very good *charade en action* of being "over head and ears." However, as that is a sort of thing that never lasts—except in a case of debt—he soon recovered himself sufficiently to say—

"Do you know I think I can give you a clue to the owner of the bag Joe Barton found at Charing Cross; so far, at least, as knowing a person who dropped a bag there containing £50, in divers coins, angels, Jacobuses, pieces of eight, &c., &c." And he then told them of Roger Marner having two days before dropped such a bag there or thereabouts, when sent by Hollar to Lord Arundel's for the money.

"Oh! that is delightful," cried Dorothy. "I'm sure it must be *the* bag, though I don't know what is in it, having, of course, taken care

not to open it; but I'll go for it, and if you think
it looks like the lost sheep, the best way will be
for you, Master Hartsfoot, to have the goodness
to take it to Mr. Hollar; show it to the man who
lost *a* bag, and before allowing it to be opened,
make him state the amount of money that was in
his bag, and the different coins composing the
amount, and see whether the contents of Joe
Barton's treasure trove answers in every particular, both as to the amount and the different
coins, making up the amount to the bag the man
Marner lost."

" A second Daniel come to judgment!" smiled
Hartsfoot.

" No *persiflage*, Master Hartsfoot; for I won't
allow anyone to laugh at me but myself, although
you may think *that* is undertaking too much
work for one person to do properly."

" But I'm not laughing at you, Mistress
Dorothy; on the contrary, I very much doubt
whether, in Westminster Hall, they would have
come to half so righteous and equitable a decision, and I am very certain they would not have
done so in so short a time."

" Which being interpreted, means—that considering I have no horsehair, I am not after all
such an ass," said Dorothy, pulling both her little
shell-like ears.

" *They* are not evidence," laughed Master Oliver.

" Nothing that *is* evident, ever appears to me to be taken as evidence in your courts of law; but as it is very evident, at least to *me*, that you are a dear, good kind soul, before I go for the bag I must again thank you for promising to take that poor boy Barton."

" No thanks are due to me, as I do so entirely from a selfish motive ; I think the mother such an admirable woman. I don't mean solely from the one act about this money, but from her whole life, for I have a theory, or rather a conviction, that no one ever does a good or noble act, or commits a villanous or mean one, without having long led up to the former by a course of systematic good, or to the latter with a chronic routine of evil. I am quite angry with Merrypin that as she knew of them, she never let me know of these Bartons before."

" It was, I suppose," said Dorothy, as she left the room, " because she knew *you* too well, and therefore knew that if you were made aware of *every* case of distress, you would yourself soon become one of the most flagrant cases, and so, like Othello, *her* ' occupation would be gone.' "

" Indeed, Master Hartsfoot, I fear Thea is right," said Mrs. Neville, as her daughter closed the door, and then, as some persons think that the best way of warding off observation from their own short comings is freely to discuss the faults of others, finding her companion made no reply, she went on to say—" You were good enough to call upon young Broderick about a fortnight ago, the day after his plunge into the Thames to rescue a man from drowning, the night you and Thea went to that horrid Bear Garden; have you seen anything of him since? Odd enough, the person he rescued is the brother of our dear, good vicar at Richmond, Dr. Fairbrace."

" No, I have not; finding him none the worse for his nocturnal bath the day after when I called upon him, and when he returned my visit, I was out; and as I am now pretty well known to be Mistress Dorothy's escort to public places, I thought you would not like—on account of Sir Allen—for me to cultivate too close an intimacy with the young man, which otherwise I should much like to have done, for I never saw a young fellow I liked or thought better of."

" Truly, as you say, on Sir Allen's account— oh! what that horrid, selfish, tyrannical man *will* have to answer for, in the gratuitous way in which he has tortured his whole family. I really believe *literally*, that my dear and inestimable friend Phillida Broderick's death will be laid at his door; I do not think with her fine constitution, her bodily ills would have told upon her for years, but estranged from all she loves by her detestable brother's petty tyranny, she is pining away from a broken heart; of all heart complaints it may be the slowest, but it is unquestionably the surest. I dare not show Thea her last letter which I got yesterday; it is, despite all her exalted spiritual resignation, written in such a hopelessly depressed strain."

"I often think," sighed Hartsfoot, "what a stupendous history might be written of the unlegislated for murders, spoliations, perjuries, and cruelties committed within the safe, because as custom makes them sacred, precincts of private life, perpetrated by those irresponsible domestic Herods, Neros, and Caligulas, the heads of families, whose only audit begins and ends in getting themselves up well, ' to strut and fret their hour' on the stage of public life. But then, to be sure, such men are invariably furnished with an inexhaustible store of hypocrisy. Hypocrisy! the only evil which remains invisible to all but God."

"Yes, and which was the only sin that God when on earth had no toleration for," said Mrs. Neville.

"I'm glad," sighed Master Hartsfoot, "that Mistress Dorothy makes such a brave fight against her adverse fortune."

"Nay, 'tis but woman's bravery at best; more appearance than reality, as in besieged castles, strategy will often send one poor sheep twenty times a day to make its entrance into the keep, so as to deceive the enemy into supposing the garrison is well supplied. But there is in Dorothy's nature a deep well of love and trust, where love and trust can never be betrayed, and as she herself says, when wincing under the pain, it is but like an unreasoning dog, to bite the stone instead of succumbing to the hand which aims the blow, or else why say, ' THY WILL BE DONE ?'"

" Why, indeed," said Hartsfoot, " and she is—"

But he could not finish the sentence, as that moment the subject of their conversation returned with the bag for which she had gone.

" I don't think there can be any pieces of eight in this bag," said Master Hartsfoot, first feeling and then weighing it in his hand; " the coins seem to be two small, all like Jacobuses and Angels."

" Well that can be soon ascertained by Thea's plan of asking the man at Mr. Hollar's what were the different coins in the bag he lost; and as you are good enough to go about this, and to come back and relieve our anxiety, or what you men, I suppose, would call our curiosity, you must add to your kindness by dining with us,

as we shall not dine before two to-day; and I'm
sure Mrs. Merrypin would not like your dinner,
or rather *her* dinner, as artists in her department
always call it, to incur any such ruinous delays."

"Thank you; but to-day I fear I cannot,
for—"

"Fear nothing; and but me no buts; or
tremble at my vengeance, Master Hartsfoot, if I
do not see you at *my* dinner," laughed Dorothy,
holding up her finger menacingly.

"Well I certainly don't fear anything so gentle
and *gentille*, as you, Mistress Dorothy."

"Ah!" said she, shaking her head, "don't pin
your faith upon either of those, but remember
what Mr. Butler so truly says in his inimitable
Hudibras—

> " ' As thistles wear the softest down
>   To hide their prickles till they're grown,
>   And then declare themselves and tear
>   Whatever ventures to come near.'

"But as bribes should always accompany threats,
the one being quite worthy of the other, I may
as well tell you that I have some of your favourite
Katherine pears for you, and such grapes! both
from Hampton Court, made to pay toll on their
way to Whitehall."

"Nay," smiled Hartsfoot, "after your terrible
threats I should fear they were prickly pears;
besides, knowing how the King values that vine

at Hampton Court, I'm not sure that the grapes
would not be a case of *lèse Majesté*."

" Not that; only the King sometimes finds
the grapes sour as well as other people, and that
reminds me that I am very happy to tell you that
the Duchess of Richmond* is *not* disfigured, and
very little altered by the small-pox."

" I am delighted to hear it."

" So ought every one," said Mrs. Neville, "for
we have so much to be ashamed of that we may
well be proud that the most beautiful woman at
Court is also the most virtuous; but after having
withstood so long a siege, I confess I was sorry
to hear that she was sworn in of the Queen's
Bedchamber yesterday."

" So am I," said Hartsfoot, "and I wonder at
the duke's consenting to it, more especially after
last Tuesday's scandal?"

" What was that?" asked Mrs. Neville.

" Why, the state coach was ordered, and a de-
tachment of guards to escort the King to Hyde
Park with the rest of the Court, when his foot
was on the step of the coach, he turned back,
suddenly dismissed them all, and going down
White Hall stairs threw himself into a barge,
and had himself rowed to Somerset House to
visit the Duchess of Richmond; but on arriving

* La belle Stewart, Charles the Second being unable to obtain
her, had her effigy as Britannia engraved on the coin of the
realm.

at the garden gate he found it locked, whereupon
he clambered over the wall."

"He was only going to the park in state,"
said Mrs. Neville, "but clambering over walls to
visit ladies I suppose is a *scale* of royal magnificence more suited to his taste."

Here Jessop came into the room with a note
for Mrs. Neville, there was also a parcel on the
salver, which she was about to take first, when
he said—

"That is for Mistress Dorothy, madam," and
handed it to her accordingly, saying to his
mistress—

"Upton waits an answer, madam."

"Oh!" said Mrs. Neville, turning to Hartsfoot, "it is from my father, who says he'll dine
with us to day.   You have no objection to meeting him, have you?"

"On the contrary I shall be delighted.   Eow
is Sir Charles?"

"Quite well, thank you, indeed surprisingly so.
My love and duty, Jessop, and we shall be truly
glad to see Sir Charles.   But we don't dine till
two to-day, though of course we shall be delighted to see him as much sooner as he can do
us the favour of coming."

"Ill send an answer," said Dorothy, adding,
as soon as Jessop had left the room, "for one
cannot send kisses by a servant, and I must give

him a dozen at least for his presents—a pair for every pair of stockings."

And she laughingly displayed six pairs of emerald green silk stockings.

" And now I'll read you his note, for your true cavalier cannot be *cavalier*, but must be *galant* even to his granddaughter."

" My Dear Thea,—

" As the Duke of York says, ' *qu'il n'y a point de salut pour une jambe sans bas verts,*'* I herewith send you some, at the risk of your putting your foot in your salvation! I know nothing about the leg, but can vouch for your having the prettiest foot and ankle, out of Fairy Land, where I suppose they all wear green stockings, with daisy cloaks. So pray wear these for the sake of your faithful servant,

" And affectionate grandfather,

" Charles Wheeler."

" Now, don't you think that a charming *poulet* for seventy-eight ?"

" He is, indeed, a dear old man in every way," said Hartsfoot.

" Once a gentleman always a gentleman," said Mrs. Neville; " and my father was born, and

---

* See Memoirs de Grammont about Lady Chesterfield's green silk stockings.

flourished in the days when there *were* gentlemen,
and when the Court had not degenerated into the
Bear Garden, and something worse that it is
now. Just fancy a peer of the realm in Charles
the First's time, boxing a gentleman's ears in
the presence! Well, last Wednesday, my Lord
Rochester, irritated at Tom Killigrew's *persiflage
at dinner*, gave him a ringing box on the ear before the King."

"Is it possible! Well, I hope he was sent to
the Tower for it?"

"Oh! dear no; anything that amuses the
King—no matter how great or indecorous the
liberty taken with himself in doing it—is sure to
find favour in his eyes. So my Lord Rochester's
only reprimand was to be seen walking arm-in-
arm with the King the next morning, on the
Mall; and I verily believe, that it would have
been just the same, had he boxed the King's own
ears."

"Well, really it is too bad; and where it is
all to end Heaven only knows. I sometimes
think that Evelyn is right, and that such a satur-
nalia, *en permanence* in a Court, must drift us
into a republic," said Hartsfoot, as he rose to
go.

"Would you have the goodness to ring the
bell, Master Hartsfoot? I forgot to give Jessop
a message about dinner."

Hartsfoot rang, and then taking his hat off the table where Dorothy had so carefully placed it, said—"I shall go now to Hollar's directly, and hope to bring back good tidings about the found money."

As he was about to leave the room, Jessop answered the bell.

" Tell, Butson," said Mrs. Neville, " to be sure and have some quilted pigeons for dinner, as my father dines here; and tell Ruffle, in addition to the other swects, to make a pupton of quince. You know that '42 claret of Prince Rupert's that Sir Charles likes, and be sure the Steinberg is sufficiently iced, which it was not the last time."

Dining at such matutinal hours as they did in those days, exclusive of what modern refinement would think their unquestionably coarse and dirty habits, people, of course, did not dress for dinner; but Dorothy, on this occasion, in order to wear and do honour to her grandfather's present, went to exchange her dress for one more in keeping with her green stockings and their silver clocks.

At the expiration of an hour Master Hartsfoot returned radiant with the good news of which he was the bearer. Hollar had made a mistake as to there having been pieces of eight in the lost bag, for upon sending for Roger Marner and closely questioning him—before showing him the bag Joe

Barton had found—as to the amount and species of coin the one he (Marner) had lost contained, he at once distinctly stated that it held fifty pounds, that there were no pieces of eight, only twenty-five gold Jacobuses and fifty angels; and no sooner did he see the bag Master Hartsfoot had brought than he exclaimed—

"Why that's the very bag as Master Ellis give me, and inside there are the two letters of his name—G. E., for George Ellis—in red," which, when the bag was then for the first time opened, was found to be the case, and the fifty pounds, half in Jacobuses, half in angels, as he had stated. And although the sum was by no means sufficient to have realised Joe Barton's golden dreams of his mother ceasing to work, his sister "walking in silk attire," and himself fluttering as "a captain in lace," yet, small as it was, the lawful owner, poor Hollar, was as delighted at its recovery as if he had really found a gold mine.

CHAPTER XIII.

IN this world of cross purposes and wrong people in wrong places, it is not always from those in authority over us that we suffer; but much oftener from the tyranny of those who *should* be in subjection under us—but who, like many other things that should be, are not. Of this sort of inverse tyranny, bachelors, those supposed "birds of freedom," *par excellence*, and denizens of Liberty Hall, are more especially the victims, and Master Hartsfoot was no exception to the rule. The frequent assemblage of learned and scientific men at his house, *savans* in fact, or " saveons," as Noah Pump called them, were as springs and oasis in his desert and solitary life. But like all deserts, his was by no means exempt from Siroccos and Simooms, now caused by the subterranean fires in the nether regions, over which Mrs. Merrypin ruled; and then, again, from certain hydraulic difficulties with Mr. Pump touching the proper icing of the fluid, contributed

by his namesake to these " feasts of reason," as
also that of the different vintages about which he
was not quite so learned as his master. So the
combined humours of the lar below and the
penate above, though they could not check, yet
were a sad drawback to Master Hartsfoot's hospitality. However, it so happened that on this
particular Thursday in October that he had con-
vened his friends, the domestic barometer was
not only " set fair," but there was a halcyon
suaveness diffused through the atmosphere, that
amounted to a sort of moral ozone, for it so fell
out that in the way of *pièces de resistance*,
Mrs. Merrypin had achieved a swan pie, a venison
and also a salmon pasty, and a baron of beef,
which she thought quite worthy of her talents,
while *chaud-froids* of partridges and gallantines
of pheasants were " trifles light as air" to her;
and as for her stewed lampreys, any king that
might have had the good fortune to taste them
would not have deserved to live had he not been
content to die after having so feasted. Then,
among her sweet things, were whole Alps of
whipped cream, with rugged foundations of
brandied greengages and guava jelly; but with
regard to her fortifications of puff, pastry, and
spun sugar, I am not engineer enough to venture
to speak; but she, who was artiste, connoisseur,
and amateur, was satisfied, quite satisfied, the

pleasing result of which was, that her master might have with truth repeated the last line of that charming epitaph which some model husband wrote upon his wife, and have exclaimed in the gratitude of his heart—

"Now she's at rest, and so am I !"

While above stairs, Mr. Pump having in the person of Joe Barton, become possessed of his long coveted *souffre douleurs*, who, so far as *work* went, out of sight, and—

"Unsuspected, animated the whole,"

was in an equally amiable and condescending mood; so that as slaves never are fit for sudden emancipation, but are apt to let liberty degenerate into licence, the proper spirit of subordination in his master really ran great risks on this occasion, for he had actually the audacity, without any beating about the bush, or circumlocution, to find fault with some of Mr. Pump's arrangements on the supper table, and desired, in quite a master of the house tone, that they might be altered, and ordered that screens might be placed on the backs of those chairs near the fire. Pope Pump stared, but obeyed; while his master looked with greater complacency, or rather greater comfort, than he had ever yet done on his magnificent collection of *Henri deux* ware and his *buffet* of twelfth century plate, and walked through the rooms with a sort of Alexander Selkirk air, as if he had really been—

"Monarch of all he surveyed,"

till his guests began to arrive. First came Lord Worcester and Mr Oldenburgh ;* next Mr. Sheres,† poetaster and *dilettanti*, and immediately in their wake, Mr. Locke, Mr. Evelyn, Lord Arlington, a Mr. Plume, and Mr. Pendarvis, a Cornish gentleman, which completed the party.

Their greetings over—" Now, my Lord," said Hartsfoot, to Lord Worcester, leading the way to his sanctum, a room within the " Cedar Parlour," where they had assembled, " we shall have time, before supper, to witness the experiment you promised to show us, of igniting water by means of certain chemicals ; but first I will take the precaution of locking the door, for if once

---

* Henry Oldenburgh, at that time Secretary of the Royal Society.

† This was the person who so excited Mr. Pepys' jealousy, by being always, "by a fortuitous concurrence of circumstances," beside Mrs. Pepys at public places. On going to see the play of " The Generous Portingales," Mr. Pepys enters in his diary— "Here, by accident, we met Mr. Sheres, and yet I could not but be troubled, because my wife do so delight to talk of, and to see him." Then the next day comes this entry—"April 24th, 1669. Mr. Sheres dining with us, and my wife, which troubled me, mighty careful to have a handsome dinner for him ; but yet I see no reason to be troubled at it, he being a very civil and worthy man I think, but only it do seem to imply some little neglect of me." More especially as Mrs. Pepys not only read Mr. Sheres' own effusions, but everything else that he recommended, till Mr. Pepys seems to have had a sort of prophetic *inverse* knowledge of homœopathy, and thought that as his father, the tailor, had been made by the Shears, he, Samuel Pepys, was to be undone by the Sheres. Mr. Sheres was also an engineer, and employed by Lord Dartmouth to blow up the Fort of Tangier.

my man Pump should discover your proceedings, nothing would convince him that we had not dealings with the devil, and he would take to his heels, and we might get our supper as we could."

" To say nothing," laughed Mr. Oldenburgh, " of the ignition of water being really a dangerous discovery for every pump in the kingdom."

There was a small fountain in this room, which was in fact, a kind of laboratory, and Hartsfoot now turned the tap, and filled the large marble shell under it full of clear, cold water.

" The matter is very simple," said Lord Worcester, putting his hand into his pocket and taking from it a small phial. " I shall not even turn up my sleeves like a conjurer, as there is no hocus pocus about it."

" Very simple to you, my lord," said Locke, as they all flocked eagerly round the fountain, " who have gone through fire and water to discover all the secrets of science, but a very good imitation of a miracle to us ignoramuses."

" And one that, even in these days, might cost you your head," put in Mr. Evelyn, " were you to play any tricks with the conduits of the New River Company."

" Yes, only I'm not so mad as to think of benefiting the public by my discoveries, or I should have offered my really wonderful phenomema about the conduct and warfare of ships to the Government to patent."

"As a present, you mean, my dear fellow," said Lord Arlington, "for we are in such a blessed state of bankruptcy that we have scarcely money for pattens—which would be of more use to our old women in the legislature—let alone for patents."*

"I *should* like," said Mr. Oldenburgh, "to hear your lordship's discoveries about ships."

---

* This would have been a most extraordinary speech for the Chief Secretary of State to have made in the present day, but everything was extraordinary and anomalous in those days, and one of the most so that the members of the legislature were always among the first to cry withered roses, and point out the nakedness of the land. This arose perhaps, from their despair-engendering position, that of responsibility without power; and even had full powers been vested in them, legislation with a bankrupt exchequer is an impossibility, and at that time seems to have been as confused and uncertain as their orthography, and as bad as their grammar, in short, "a mighty maze without a plan." The only wonder is, that instead of the Dutch invasion, we were not invaded by every European power, with the amphibious muddle that then existed of generals and admirals being "rolled into one," and our sailors mutinying from want of pay and insufficiency of food, and others, rather than be pressed into such an inglorious and unprofitable service, committing suicide. It is a still greater wonder that the outbreak of national discontent should have waited till James the Second's time to manifest itself, only Charles the Second, with all his vices and disregard of his *sovereign* duties, was personally popular. But what a state of vulgar extremes meeting was the society of that day. It was not only the poor queen, who had to associate with her husband's mistresses, but such was also the universal custom in an age when "great people" (?) dined occasionally with their own servants, and ladies took their maids with them to the play, and took the patches off *their* face to put on their own !! as Lady Castlemaine is represented by Pepys to have done at the King's house one night; while Pepys, the tailor's son, had his *entrées* at White Hall, and ran in and out of the King's presence and the Duke of York's dressing room like a pet spaniel, independent of Court Chamberlains, and dined one day with the Cabinet Ministers at the Palace, and the next was with his wife and servants at high jinks, at some baker's or butcher's wedding.

" In a moment, when I have shown you this experiment."

And he poured the contents of the phial into the marble basin of water, and immediately it was overspread by a brilliant flame, bright blue at the base, exactly like the flame produced by brandy or any other spirit when set fire to.

" How beautiful !" they all exclaimed, " but how long will the flame continue ?" asked Mr. Oldenburgh.

" Till it has literally burnt up the water, which, being in so small a quantity, it might succeed in doing by this time to-morrow ; but a large body of water would continue burning for years and years, as the water feeds the fire as oil does that of an ordinary lamp, so that a lake or river would by ordinary means, once so ignited, be unextinguishable."

" And how can you extinguish this fire, now ?"

" Not by water, for that would add fuel to the flame ; but I will extinguish it before we leave the room, by other chemical ingredients. It is on the same principle as the ever burning lamp I gave you, Hartsfoot, which unlike servants and Cabinet Ministers, never goes out."

" Ha ! ha ! ha ! and about the ships, my lord? I am so anxious to hear about them," again interposed Mr. Oldenburgh.

" Well, it is rather long to describe, and I fear I shall tire you."

But there was a unanimous negative to this, whereupon Lord Worcester said—

" I have constructed a portable engine to fit in the pocket, which may be carried and fastened to the inside of the largest ship, *tunguum aliud agens*, and at any appointed minute, though a week after, of either day or night, it shall irrevocably sink that ship. I have also constructed a like engine which, at a mile's distance, a diver may fasten to any ship, so that it will punctually work the same effect, both as to time and execution ; but that would be nothing if I had not also discovered a method of protecting a ship against any such attempts or results, such as I have just described to you ; in fact, a way of making it impossible that a ship should be sunk, though fired at a hundred times between wind and water by cannon, and though the vessel should lose a whole plank, yet by this plan it would, in half an hour's time, be made as shipshape and fit to sail as before.   I have also another invention how to make false decks, which in a moment should kill and take prisoners, that is, as many as should board the ship, without blowing the decks up, or destroying them from being reduceable ; but on the contrary, so that they should in a quarter of an hour's time recover their former shape, and be rendered fit for any employment, without discovering the secret of their construction. I have a further discovery, of how to weigh an anchor, or to do any other forcible exploit in the narrowest or lowest cabin of any ship, where few hands shall do the work of many, and many hands applicable to the same force, some standing, other's sitting, and by virtue of their several helps, a great force augmented in little space, and as effectual as if there was sufficient space to go about with an axletree and work far from the centre.

"I have also a way to make a boat work itself against wind and tide, without the help of man or beast; yet so that the wind and tide, though directly contrary, shall force the boat against itself, and in no point of the compass, but it shall be as effectual as if the wind was in the poop, or the tide actually with the course it is to steer; according to which the oars shall row, and the necessary motions work and move towards the desired port, or point of the compass.* I have also many other nautical inventions, too long to describe now; and I have lately constructed a small engine, whereby may be taken out of the water a ship of five hundred tons, so that it may be caulked, trimmed, and repaired, without any need of the usual way of stocks, and as easily let down into the water again."

"Wonderful!" said Mr. Oldenburgh.

* This would clearly be invaluable for a lifeboat if the secret of its mechanism could be discovered.

"Ah! my dear lord," cried Mr. Evelyn, "what an amount of disgrace! to say nothing of loss, would your marvellous inventions have saved us in the Dutch invasion, had our government practically possessed itself of them; as that of France or Holland would have been sure to have done, had either been able to boast of such a genius as your lordship."

"Aye, truly," said Locke; "and our first gain would have been that we should not have lost Sheerness by sheer imbecility."

"Only I am afraid we are taxing your lordship too much, I wish you would tell our friends of that wonderful hydraulic invention you were explaining to me the other day," said Hartsfoot.

"Ah! that, without vanity, I think I may call the most stupendous work in the world; but, by-and-bye, after supper. I have inflicted enough of my doings on you for the present, gentlemen."

"Well, after supper then be it," said the host. "Any news stirring, Mr. Evelyn?"

"Well, I heard one piece of news, which I don't believe—to wit, that Captain Broderick is to marry Lady Jemima Montagu."

"Nor I neither," said Mr. Sheres, "for I heard the story with a variation; that is, that she had refused him (not very likely, I should think, if he ever offered), and that in consequence of this rejection he goes out to Tangier in a month, to join my Lord Dartmouth—in which case he would be my *compagnon du voyage*, which I should be very glad of—but think it is too good to be true, as I'm sure if there had been any match on the *tapis* between him and Lady Jemima, I should have heard of it from the Pepys'; and on the contrary, Mr. Pepys told me in confidence the other day, that everything was arranged, with Lord Sandwich's perfect consent, for her marriage with Sir George Carteret's son."

" Pish! I lay anything that this report, and young Broderick's being consigned—for that's the proper word—to Tangier, is some fresh scheme of that cutter,* Sir Allen's," said Lord Arlington.

" I shouldn't be surprised," said Mr. Evelyn.

Here the handle of the room door was turned in no very gentle manner.

" The fire! the fire!" said Master Hartsfoot, pointing to the flaming fountain in almost as much alarm as if the house had been really on fire.

Lord Worcester took the hint, and pouring the contents of another phial on it, in one moment extinguished it, leaving the water *looking* as cold

---

* Cutter, an old English word, meaning a swaggering, hectoring fellow.

and impassable as if it had never " felt a flame."
Fortunately the extinction of the fire left no tell
tale odour, so the master of the house flew to
the door and opened it with all possible alacrity,
when Mr. Pump announced that " supper was
on the table," but not without casting a scrutinising glance round the room, accompanied by
an inquisitorial sniffing, as if he fully expected
to detect brimstone and other infernal agencies,
for at the time he remarked to himself, and after,
in council, to Mrs. Merrypin, " There was no
knowing what them ere *saveons* wasn't up to;
and all he was afeared on was, that poor Master
Hartsfoot warnt deep enough for 'em, and might
be dragged down goodness, or rather badness, only
knew where; afore he seed where he was a going
to."

" By-the-bye," said Lord Arlington, as he un-
folded his napkin, " I suppose you have heard
that the Duke of York's dressing-room was broken
into last night, the locks of two of the cabinets
picked, and several papers of some importance
stolen, but neither money nor jewels (of which
there was much) touched."

No, of course they had not heard it; people
seldom had new laid news, only twenty-four hours
old at that time, which may account for the extraordinary stories that were hatched from stale
reports.

" What a pity, Lord Worcester," said Hartsfoot, " that there was not one of your marvellous locks that would have detained the hand of the thief just as a fox is springed in a trap."

" Yes," said Lord Arlington, " that would have been satisfactory in every way, and have prevented all the surmises now afloat as to Popish and other plots, and our being on the brink of another rebellion."

" And is it to be wondered at ?" said Mr. Pendarves, " with the pay of our soldiers and sailors all in arrears since the Restoration, the country actually swamped with profligacy, dishonesty, and disaffection everywhere ; the very King without a sixpence in his pocket, while he has always thirty thousand pounds ready to pay Lady Castlemaine's ever recurring de bts, and seven hundred guinea rings to give to Moll Davis, and others of her tribe."

" I have long thought," said Mr. Evelyn, " that we *must* end in a Republic."

" I don't think so," said Locke, " human nature, more especially in the aggregate, seldom returns to pick up the burden it has just laid down ;* moreover men, perhaps from a fellow feel-

---

* Locke was right, and in our own times, as recent events in France have so bitterly proved, M. Philarète Chasles is more right, who has so truly said, in his own terse, quint-essential style— '' Stimulants do not give strength ; comets do not give out heat ; and revolutions do *not* give liberty."

ing, much more easily condone vice and malad-
ministration, than they do tyranny, even when it
insures perfect order. Individuals have long
memories for oppressions or aggressions, and
thus it comes, that family feuds are often per-
petuated through several generations. But there
is an elasticity in the concrete life of nations,
which renders their memory remarkably evanes-
cent, so that the most devastating revolutions
and sanguinary civil wars, are in a marvellously
short time consigned to oblivion, covered, as it
were, like all other fresh made graves, by the
verdure of natural changes, and ever-growing
successions; add to which, the world is ruled by
words, much more than by deeds or by facts, or
even by experience, and as the King's words are
never at fault, despite all he does, he *is* popular."

"I fear," said Mr. Plume, whose brother was
the Incumbent of Cripplegate, "that after what
he said the other day upon refusing to let the
temporal power of the bishops be curtailed, his
majesty is stooping to take a leaf out of the Protector's *grimoire* of pious hypocrisy."

"What was that?" asked Hartsfoot, "I have
not heard what he said, yet generally his sayings,
which are all *mots*, travel pretty quickly."

"Why his answer was sufficiently terse, and
coming from a person of irreproachable morals,
might have been deemed both pious and orthodox.

He said, 'No, take one stone from the Church and you take two from the throne.' "

" I don't see any hypocritical pretension to piety in it," said Locke, " and coming from the *King*, whatever Charles Stuart's *lèse morale* may be, it was *extremely* orthodox ; for as Church and State are incongruously bound up together, each clogging and impeding the other, something like the Mazentian punishment of the living body bound to the dead, Church and State, of necessity become the creed of princes ; consequently, an English sovereign, however impious, irreligious, or even sacrilegious, must of necessity, and in all truth and sincerity, be great sticklers for the Church, as by law established, and having been made, as it were, the lynch pin of the wheel of State machine, all English monarchs do of course conscientiously believe, that take one stone from the power of the Church, and you take two from the power of the throne."

" Ah ! I perceive ; I did not see it in that light before ; but of course it is as you say, Mr. Locke, and the King really meant *bonâ fide* what he said."

" Ha ! ha !" laughed Mr. Evelyn, " I'm glad you're not as unteachable, Plume, as the parishioners of a *curé* in Dauphiné that I encountered last autumn."

" I am sure thereby must 'hang a tale,' not to

say a tail, perhaps the devil's," laughed Lord Arlington, " so pray let us have it, Evelyn."

" Why, I, and my wife, and daughter made a little tour in Dauphiné last autumn, a part of France we had not been in before ; among others, we at last came to a place called DIEULEFIT. Under the sign board at the entrance of the village announcing this name of DIEULEFIT, some wag had written—*Dieu le fit, et le planta là !*—perhaps the *Curé* himself, who was evidently a humourist, as we found out after, upon strolling into the village church to hear the sermon. *Monsieur le Curé* had been lecturing his parishioners upon their backwardness and ignorance in all things, but more especially did he animadvert upon the little spiritual progress which they had made during the five years he had laboured so hard for the good of their souls. ' What,' said he, ' shall I say—what *can* I say to the Almighty at the great final Audit day, in parading before Him such a congregation ?' And he paused for a reply, as is the wont of French preachers, and then added, with a groan—' *Helas ! je lui dirai, Seignieur, bêtes tu me les a donnés, et bêtes je te les rends !* '"

As soon as the roar of laughter this story had caused had subsided, Lord Arlington, in helping himself to a peach (for the dessert was now on the table, and Mr. Pump had withdrawn to

regions where he was more appreciated), said—
" I should not wonder at the Duke of Buckingham's embarrassments if he gave such banquets
of the gods as you do, Hartsfoot."

" Whom the gods deign to visit, must needs
be Amphitryon," smiled Hartsfoot; " but had I
the Duke of Buckingham's £20,000 a-year, I
don't think I could contrive to get into debt; he
really must be very clever."

" Of course he is, for he is very wicked; and
in modern parlance they are synonymous.   But
he *has* not, though he had, £20,000 a-year; here
is his rental," continued Lord Arlington,
" £19,000 a-year, but owes £10,000 ; pays away
£7,000 in interest, about £2,000 in fee-farm
rents to the King, about £6,000 in wages and
pensions, and the rest to live on—I mean to run
in debt upon."

" His Grace's financial system," said Hartsfoot, " appears, Lord Worcester, to be stolen
from your invention of how to make a weight
that *cannot* take up a hundred pounds, and yet
shall take up *two hundred*, and at the self-same
distance, and so proportionably up to millions of
pounds !"

" Very like it," laughed Lord Worcester; " a
pity I never thought of utilizing the invention
in *that* way.   May I trouble you for the sack ?"

" No—no," laughed Hartsfoot; " I'll give you

anything but the sack ! particularly as your lordship promised us an account of what you justly
consider your greatest scientific achievement."

" But of what use is it? or any of my other
inventions, when there is no getting them
patented, in order to utilise them.   One very
simple invention of mine, one would have thought
might have found favour with the fine ladies, if
only to save their pretty faces and their fine
clothes, when taking the dust in Hyde Park,
which literally prevents their getting any air, and
sends them home as if sacks of dust had been
showered upon them.   It is nothing more than a
large box upon cart-wheels, and shafts for a horse
to draw the cart, the said box being about the
size of a spinet, and a foot and a half deep ; in
the centre is a plug, which can be taken out to
fill the box with water, while the back, which
faces the road, is perforated with small holes,
like a watering pot ; but that the water may not
come through till the cart is in motion, there is
a board to slide over these holes, which, as soon
as the cart is filled, is withdrawn, and then, as
the cart is driven on, the road is thoroughly
watered as it goes, and all the dust laid ; the box
being, of course, re-filled whenever the supply of
water is exhausted."*

* Evidently our modern watering-carts, now used in every vil-
age.

" Capital ! " said everyone ; " it would, indeed, be a great boon, and as you say, so simple, that one wonders necessity has not made it occur to minds less inventive than yours ; but now, my lord," continued Hartsfoot, " I want you to have the goodness to describe your *chef d'œuvre* to us."

" Oh ! but I really fear I shall tire you with all my long descriptions, particularly as I have not the engines here to show you the principles when in action."

" No—no; if we don't tire you, pray let us hear all you can tell us."

" Well, you must know, after many years' experience and great labour, I have perfectly succeeded in constructing an engine that the strength of a mere child could bring up a hundred feet high an incredible quantity of water, even of two feet diameter, and that so naturally and easily, that the working of this engine would not be heard, even in an adjoining room, and with such great facility and geometrical symmetry, that though it work day and night, from one end of the year to the other, it would not require forty shillings' worth of reparation to the whole engine, nor hinder it one day from working. It would serve with little charge to drain all sorts of mines, and furnish cities with an abundance of water, though built on ever such great heights, as well as to purify them by running through every street, alley, and suburb, and so performing the work of many scavengers, as well as supplying all the inhabitants with plenty of water for their own particular use; but it would likewise supply rivers with a sufficient body of water, to maintain and convey them from town to town, and enable them to irrigate lands as they went, with many more advantages and profitable results. So that deservedly, I deem this the crowning invention of my labours, and look to it to indemnify me for my expenses, and direct my thoughts in the channel of further discoveries."

They all listened with the greatest attention, and declared that it was indeed truly wonderful; but as an engineer, Mr. Sheres was the most appreciative of his audience, and as a poet, said—

"In fact, my lord, this is your iron epic?"

"It must needs be, since I cannot, like you, Mr. Sheres, pretend to golden numbers."

"At all events, I think your lordship will make a great many others pretend to them, since you have invented an instrument for writing in the dark."

"No, no," laughed Locke; "that must be intended for writing history."

"Wrong for once," replied Lord Worcester; "for my instrument is so *true*, that it writes perfectly straight, and never deviates a hair's breadth."

"Oh! then it will be of no use to those great fictionists, the historians."

"Poor wretches! What would they do if TRUTH was made a *sine quâ non* before they put pen to paper," said Evelyn. "I have lived long enough to be convinced that no one knows the real truth—that is, the whole truth of anything, but God. Is not the town talk we bring from Heaven, or the club, the coffee houses, or Westminster Hall, one day, often contradicted the next? or else considerably either added to, or curtailed? And let two persons, of even the most scrupulous and unimpeachable veracity, write a description of a Lord Mayor's show, or any other pageant, and both accounts shall differ materially, and yet both be strictly true, so far as the writers are concerned, for both relate the truth so far as they saw, but they saw from different points of view; that is, they did not both see the same things, nor at the same time, yet the things that both narrate were to be seen, and did occur. This holds good, even with regard to the four Gospels. Then again, circumstances alter cases; suppose, for instance, any foreigner, collecting materials and intending to write a book upon England, had spoken to poor Lord Essex five years before his execution, of his brilliant but base *protégé,* my Lord Bacon, Essex, in his enthusiasm—for all generous natures are enthu-

siastic—would have taken his measure merely
intellectually, and have described him as a gigan-
tic perfection.   So far, so true.   But let another
have applied to poor Lord Essex a day or two
before his execution, when he knew that the
viper he had warmed had so basely betrayed, and
so assiduously wrought his ruin; then he would
have guaged the wretch morally, and where was
the black—sufficiently black wherewith to pour-
tray him?   Yet both these individuals would tell
the exact truth, in stating that they had these
traits of Lord Bacon from Lord Essex; and both
characters, though differing so widely, would be
both equally true.   How then can we reasonably
expect truth from history? when all history is
not only written at second, third, and fourth
hand, but is of necessity coloured by the individual bias, moral, and political, of the writer.
And there would be no histories written at all, if
historians, as a rule, were too much staggered at
atrocities, and did as De Thon did, when writing
his history, in his house in the Rue de Bétizy,
where, when he came to the St. Bartholomew,
he threw down his pen, and filled up the hiatus
with this exclamation—

> ‘ Excidat illa dies arve,
> Nec postera credant,
> Sarcula, nos certe faciamus,
> Et obruta multâ
> Notce tegi patiamur crimina gentis !’ ”

" Too true," said Locke ; " but it amounts to this, that we must not examine into anything too closely, nor sum up the results of things too generally, or nothing would ever be undertaken, or rather finished ; and so there would be no such thing as progression, and the world would come to a dead lock, were we to preface every human effort with a *cui bono?* For instance, we should all start in life by saying, ' What is the use of my doing, or attempting to do anything? for I *must* die, and do not even know how soon that inevitable event may cut short my labours ; and at best, the world is but a thankless, unappreciative, oblivious, and ungrateful master to work for.' Very true ; but the world is not, or rather should not be our master, for we are, one and all (great and small, splendidly endowed with TEN talents, or straitened by the pauper pittance of ONE), equally GOD's servants. So that, in fact, · our highest aspirations and most ambitious efforts should, on this side Eternity, be ever bounded by that nucleus of all wisdom, enjoined by the Catechism, to ' do our duty in that state of life unto which it has pleased God to call us.' Besides, example does not always act either as precept or precedent—when of an evil kind it quite as often acts as a warning ; and thus, in the wondrous chemistry of nature, both in the moral and physical world, are substances trans-

muted, and pernicious things neutralized. So
that even the very errors and mis-statements of
history have their uses, for they put the more
advanced intelligences of succeeding ages, upon
detecting and analysing its fallacies, and thus
mens digitat molem."

" Then, verily, Mr. Locke," said Lord Arlington, " what a debt of gratitude future generations
will owe our times ; for what a splendid collection
of errors, fallacies, vices, and blunders, we shall
leave them to whet their intellect upon."

" All ages do their little possible for posterity
in that way, and when posterity, with its new
brooms, has swept the byegone rubbish into a
corner, and sets up on its own account, it thinks
it has done great things."

" Pray, my lord," said Evelyn, " do you think
that the King will, as so many persons believe,
make a great push for a standing army, and so
try to rule by military force ?"

" Nay," said Hartsfoot, " that is scarcely a fair
question to put to the Chief Secretary of State."

" It is perfectly fair, inasmuch as that I cannot
possibly answer it in one way or the other," said
Lord Arlington, " for in the present state of
affairs it would be utterly impossible to predict
what may or may not happen from one month to
another, unless one had the gift of second sight,
which I don't pretend to."

" By-the-bye," said Mr. Oldenburgh, " *àpropos* of second sight, what *is* that story, my lord, about some Scotch gentleman, possessed of second sight, having in a most extraordinary manner predicted Lady Cornbury's death ?"

" It's only last year I was asking Lord Cornbury about it, and I'll tell you what he told me, as nearly as I can recollect them in his own words. He said—' Five or six years ago, one day—I know by some remarkable circumstance that it was towards the middle of February, in 1661 or 1662—the Earl of Newborough came to dine with my father at Worcester House, and another Scotch gentleman with him, whose name I cannot call to mind. After dinner, as we were standing and talking together in the room, says my Lord Newborough to the other Scotch gentleman, who was looking very steadfastly upon my wife, " What is the matter, that thou hast had thine eyes fixed upon my Lady Cornbury* ever since she came into the room ? Is she not a fine woman ? Why dost thou not speak ?' " She's a handsome lady indeed," said the gentleman, " but I see her in blood." Whereupon, my Lord Newborough laughed at him, and all the company going out of the room, we parted, and I believe none of us thought more of the matter; I am sure I did not. My wife was at that time

* Theodosia, third daughter of Arthur Lord Clyde, of Hadham.

perfectly well in health, and looked as well as ever she did in her life.   In the beginning of the next month she fell ill of the small-pox.   She was always very apprehensive of that disease, and used to say if she ever had it she should die of it.   Upon the ninth day after the small-pox appeared, in the morning, she bled at the nose, which quickly stopped, but in the afternoon the blood burst out again with great violence at her mouth and nose, and about eleven o'clock that night she died, almost weltering in her blood."*

" Strange, most strange," said every one.

" Truly there *are* more things in Heaven and earth than are dreamt of in your philosophy," said Hartsfoot.

" I only wish," said Evelyn, " we could find out this prescient Scotch gentleman to prognosticate to us what our political future is to be."

> "Omnibus hostes
>   Redite nos populis, civile avertite bellum,"

said Lord Arlington.

" Amen," responded Hartsfoot.

Here Pump announced my Lord Arlington's coach.

" Can I have the pleasure, gentlemen," said

* Several years after this, in 1701, Lord Cornbury, then Lord Clarendon (Henry Hyde, second Lord Clarendon), related this story verbatim as above in a letter to Mr. Pepys, and adds that the great grief he was at that time in, for the loss of his wife prevented his trying to find out the Scotch gentleman who had made so terribly true a prediction.

he, bowing courteously round the table to the assembled guests, " of taking any of you home ?"

" I fear," said Mr. Oldenburgh, " it would be trespassing quite too much on your lordship's kindness, for the way to Durham Yard is so bad and so dirty."

" Can any ways be too bad or too dirty for a Secretary of State ?" laughed Lord Arlington, " as we are the real secretaries of the *Royal Society*. And you, my dear Lord Worcester, will you not let me set you down at your own door ?"

" Many thanks, but I have had too many sets down in my time, and do not want any more, and it is fortunate we cannot be deprived of our feet, however we may be of our footing," and the gallant old Royalist sighed as he thought of the Psalmist's advice, " Put not thy trust in Princes."

The sigh was echoed by all present, who thanked him and the host for the agreeable evening they had passed.

" You have nothing to thank me for," said Hartsfoot. " Mine are all pic-nics ; you bring your own entertainment with you, and I it is who have so much to be obliged for." And always anxious to do any kindness that he could, he said to Lord Arlington, *sotto voce*—

" If it is not crowding your lordship too much, as Mr. Sheres goes out in an official capacity to Tangier next month, it might be a help to him to have received this little civility from you."

"Oh! thank you for telling me; he really seems a very sensible, modest young fellow. I'll give him some private despatches to take to Lord Dartmouth, which may help him more."

And then, turning to the subject of his little parley, he said—

"As all but Mr. Oldenburgh have rejected my offer, I hope, Mr. Sheres, you will take compassion on me; for you know two of a trade can never agree, and recollect Mr. Oldenburgh and I are both secretaries."

Of course Mr. Sheres was too happy to accept the invitation so kindly given, and as soon as he, Lord Arlington, and Mr. Oldenburgh had departed, Mr. Locke and Mr. Evelyn, having offered a seat to Mr. Pendarvis, followed, so that only Mr. Plume was left to accompany Lord Worcester, who produced from his pocket a small lantern with an ever-burning lamp, exactly similar to the one he had given Hartsfoot, with whom he now shook hands, and their adieux over, the former let them out by the glass door that opened on the Mall, at which he stood uttering a final "Good-night," and watched them till they had turned the corner, and cleared the iron gates, at which a drowsy watchman challenged them and rang his bell after them, informing the sleeping inhabitants in the adjacent houses that it was "Past twelve of the clock, and a cloudy night."

CHAPTER XIV.

DOROTHY was lying listlessly on a couch, reading Robert Ascham's "*Scholemaster*," pitying poor Lady Jane Grey, the girl martyr, and wondering what sort of a wretch—instead of a saint and a martyr—she (Dorothy) would have become, if instead of ceaseless kindness and constant care, and every wish anticipated, she had been subjected to the "nips," "bobs," and "pinches" of poor Lady Jane, the breaking of her spirit over the ruts of systematic restraints and preventions, and the grinding her brains under Greek mill stones?

Being now the middle of October, though the sky was bright, the trees were nearly bare, and the Mall was strewed thick with "sear and yellow leaves." Mrs. Neville sat working near the window—plain homely work; in short, a set of garments for Bridget Barton, who, with her mother, was now installed at the lodge gate of The Chestnuts. Every now and then, Dorothy looked off her book and over at her mother, in whose face she thought she detected an unusual expression of care and preoccupation ; she longed to know, yet felt a delicacy about inquiring the cause, as there were no secrets between them ; and, therefore, she knew that had her mother thought fit to tell her, she would have done so. Still, this silence between them oppressed her ; so, addressing Mrs. Neville, she said—"Listen to this, mother darling ; it is a letter of Roger Ascham to Sir William Paulet, about his (Ascham's) wife, and substituting mother and daughter for husband and wife, it is exactly your case and mine.　He says—' God, I thank Him, has given me such an one, as the less she seeth I do for her, the more loving in all causes she is to me ; when I again have wished her well rather than done her good, and therefore the more glad she is to bear my fortune with me, the more sorry am I that hitherto she hath found rather a loving husband (daughter) than a lucky one to her."

Mrs. Neville put down her work, walked over to the sofa, and seating herself beside it, took Dorothy's hand in hers, and rubbed it gently up and down, as she said—"Nay, dear child ; you have always been the best of children to me.　So it's not at all a case in point ; and as for luck, I consider it the greatest of all good fortune to have such a daughter."

Dorothy all this time was carefully reading her mother's face, to try if she could decipher the carking hieroglyphic that was behind the tears that filled her mother's eyes, but in vain; so she merely said—" Then what must I think of *my* good fortune in having such a mother? I know I often think as I *was* to lose one of my parents, how good it was of God not to take you; for what are fathers at best to their children? — merely appendages; they are never part and parcel of them, as a mother is."

" Hush! Thea. You must not say such things."

" Well—but, dear, you know I was only seven years old when my father died, and I have not the slightest recollection of him. If he was like that picture of him at Clumber Chase, that belonged to Sir Reginald Mortimer, and was left with the place to dear Mrs. Broderick, he was certainly very handsome; but what's that to me?"

" I think it has been a great deal to you," smiled Mrs. Neville.

" Humph! Well, one thing I *cannot* under·stand, which is, what you could have been about, mamma, when you refused poor dear Master Hartsfoot?"

" I was about eighteen, and as foolish as most girls of that age generally are, not excepting Dorothy Neville."

" I admit the impertinence, but not the truth of that assertion, Mrs. Neville."

" I suppose you will think me more impertinent when I tell you that I have two offers of marriage for you; one from Sir Charles Slingsby, for his son, the other from Lord Henry Howard for himself."

And Mrs. Neville drew a deep breath, as if she had been relieved from a heavy weight.

Dorothy looked at her for half a second, and then said, " No; not *you*, dear mother, but them."

" I cannot return that for an answer.　What am I to say ?"

" Why don't you know that the truth should be spoken at all times ?　So tell them first the usual falsehood on such occasions, that I feel highly honoured, &c., &c., but that I intend being an old maid, as fools spitefully call sensible women."

Mrs. Neville looked down upon the little hand she was still rubbing, and was silent for about a minute, but she did not smile; on the contrary she looked graver and sadder than before.　At length she said—

" You know, my dear child, were I to consult my own selfishness, I should rather you never did marry, and I'm sure you also know that never will I, by word or deed, try to influence you

to marry anyone you don't care for; at the same
time, I think it not only a pity, but derogatory to
any woman's proper pride, to waste her life in
regretting one who has ceased to—care for—or—
or—even to remember her."

"Mother!" cried Dorothy, half starting from
her recumbent position, leaning on her elbow,
while with her disengaged hand she almost con-
vulsively clasped her mother's wrist, her cheeks
flushing crimson, and the pupils of her eyes dilat-
ing, as she darted her searching glances into Mrs.
Neville's eyes, looking like a deer at bay, "Mother,
what do you mean?"

"Well, my poor child, you must hear it at
last, so better sooner than later; Captain Broderick has made an offer of his hand to Lady
Jemima Montagu, has been refused, and is going out to Tangier to be on my Lord Dartmouth's staff in consequence."

"And *you* believe it?" said Dorothy, with a
look of magnificent scorn."

"It is the town talk."

"Were it the world talk it's false!"

"I fear not; at least it is quite true that he
goes to Tangier."

"Lady Jemima Montagu! Ha! ha! ha!
Why not Bridget Butson, your cook maid, at
once, when they were about it?"

"She is certainly very plain," said Mrs.

Neville, mildly, quite alarmed at Dorothy's feverish excitement.

" Plain ! it's not that ; perhaps he don't think her plain, but so uneducated, so uncouth, so downright vulgar, so unkempt even, never having had as much care or culture as she would have come by in her father's house, and truly *that* would have been so little as only to have half filled the eye of a bodkin ; but first sent to board and lodge with one set of tradespeople and then with another, with no other companions but them and her maid, till even Mr. Pepys, who is neither very *exigeant* nor very refined, used to be quite shocked at the way in which she used to romp with these people, who used to think it very good fun to make her merry with wine."

" Well, but, my dear love, you know what a worldly time-serving man Sir Allen is, and if she were ten times less attractive and less estimable he only thinks of her as Lord Sandwich's daughter ; and he also knows that the King has done more, not only in conferring titles and high appointments, but in hard cash, for that family than he has done for so many others, who have served not only him but his father before him, so much longer and so much more devotedly,— take poor Lord Worcester for instance ; and Sir Allen also knows that my Lord Sandwich still possesses the King's ear, from being even more

convenient and subservient to him than Colonel
Titus, or than the Duke of Buckingham himself.
Therefore, were Lady Jemima his Satanic majesty's
daughter, and a little blacker than her sire, that
would make no difference to Sir Allen."

" Then why don't he marry her himself?   And
if she *were* his Satanic majesty's daughter, then
Sir Allen would be all the better matched."

" I don't suppose there is a woman in England
who *would* marry him."

" Don't be too sure ; English women, as a
rule, would marry anything that had a title and
a rent roll ; let alone both ; and the exceptions
that would not, are too few to be worth mention-
ing.   But the question is not of Sir Allen
Broderick's marriage, but of his son's ; and do
you suppose the latter is such a complete machine,
that his father has only to wind him up and set
him to execute any purpose *he* may design ?"

" Habit is proverbially called second nature,
and the second nature that springs from custom
is unfortunately invariably stronger than the
original nature, which it has completely paralysed,
if not utterly annihilated. And the grinding and
subjective process exercised by all domestic
tyrants, more especially when it has the warrant
of parental authority, generally ends by taking
the muscle and sinews out of the character of
their victims, and reducing them to a mere mass

of malleable and plastic weakness. You have
seen the manner in which even the most fero-
cious wild animals are tamed by the loaded whip
of their keeper, and quite as much are they cowed
by the irresistible power of that inquisitorial
human eye so constantly fixed upon them, and
which alone is quite sufficient to insure the most
abject obedience, even when the loaded whip is
not brought into play. And if such is the result
of indomitable human will and coercive power,
upon even the fiercest natures, what must it be
on the gentler and more affectionate ones of
lambs or dogs? and I look upon poor young
Broderick under the ferule of his paternal keeper
exactly in this light; there was no ferocity to
tame—no savage instincts to cow, but a gentle
nature to crush, and a clinging and affectionately
confiding spirit to quench into perfect nullity,
and it has been done."

"Oh! mother, it is not like you to turn
people's very virtues against them, and place
really the most admirable trait in Gilbert Broderick's character—his child-like submission to so
unloveable and unesteemable a father, in the
odious and contemptible light of inane and in-
sentient weakness."

"Alas! my dear child, all our virtues and all
our vices are placed so closely together, that like
parti-coloured silks, under the influence of wet,

when the colours run into one another, each dis-
figures its neighbour, and the whole fabric is
spoilt.   It is these terrible collisions of extremes
meeting, that flaws and jars the whole world ; in
fact, as John Bunyan more terribly and tersely
says—' At the gates of Paradise itself, there is a
bye-way to hell.' Were our virtues and our vices,
our good and our evil qualities assorted and re-
strained within perfectly separate vessels—as the
poisons and the antidotes are in a chemist's laboratory—life would indeed be easy : so easy, that
it would be almost as difficult to miss the right ;
as it is now to hit it ; but, no—I must return to
my homely simile of the parti-coloured silk.   All
the good and all the evil in us is woven into the
same tissue, and is thus rendered so liable to be
injured by extraneous and external influences.
For instance, how rare is it to see very mild and
even tempered people who are not apathetic, and
wanting in energy and quick perception ? or very
sensitive, impulsive people, who are capable of
calm dispassionate judgment?   Very generous
and unselfish natures who are not improvident ?
or intensely prudent ones who do not culminate
in selfishness and parsimony? and so on to the
end of the chapter.   For it is rare—very rare, to
find great consistency and decision of character
that does not amount to obstinacy, or extreme
amiability, and yielding to others, that does not

degenerate into weakness.   But such an alterna-
tion and reciprocity is there in *all* things ; and
were there not, no doubt the gravitation of the
world would be endangered.   That certain it is,
that some virtues lead to vices, just as some
faults lead to virtues, and I confess I ever prefer
the latter to the former.   There are but two vices
which leave their possessors no hope of redemp-
tion—VANITY and HYPOCRISY ; the first sacrifices
everyone and everything, and violates every law
divine and human, to minister to its own insa-
tiable cravings ; and the latter erects an altar over
the carnage, and affects to be offering incense to
Heaven.''

" Well, I certainly don't think Gilbert Broderick can be accused of either of those.''

" Indeed, I don't think he can ; or of any other
fault but what at first sight has a *faux air* of
virtue, poor young man, and that it is which
makes me feel for him with all my heart.''

" Then how *can* you, mother, believe in the
story of his wanting to marry Lady Jemima
Montagu ?''

" I never thought, and still less did I ever say,
that *he* wanted to marry her.   I only thought,
and still think, that Sir Allen would make him
do so had Sir Allen so decided.''

" Oh! mother, mother, you know that Sir
Allen is an Atheist—at least, people say so—yet

do you, can you think that if he *ordered* his son to publicly swear that he believed there was no God that he would do so ?"

" Sir Allen is far too great a hypocrite and too worldly wise, like all hypocrites, to do anything of that kind, depend upon it; but that's a very different thing to his son's making a sordid and worldly marriage to obey his father."

" A very different thing, indeed ; still, when Gilbert Broderick publicly abjures his God, then, and not till then, I'll believe he intends, or ever intended, to marry Lady Jemima Montagu."

This was all Dorothy said aloud, while in her own mind she added, " or any other woman but me."

" And Lord Harry Howard and Mr. Slingsby, what am I to say to them ?"

" Oh ! hang them," said Dorothy, pettishly, as she gave such a violent pull to her hanker-chief both ways, the border of which she had been examining very minutely, that she tore it.

" Nay, dear, 'Do unto others as you would they should do unto you.'   And suppose Captain Broderick had made an offer of marriage to any young lady, and *her* courteous reply had been, ' Hang him !' how should you like that ?"

" And so she or anybody else might hang him if he *had.*"

And Dorothy turned her face quickly and with great energy to the wall.

" Well, love, I won't tease you now; but, indeed, Thea, it grieves and frets me, to see you wasting your life upon a will-o'-the-wisp, which, with such a man as Sir Allen, Gilbert Broderick must ever be to you."

" Why *ever*, mother? In the first place Sir Allen will not live for ever," said Dorothy, now again turning suddenly round, " for do you suppose that the devil *never* forecloses his mortgages? But even assuming Sir Allen Broderick *should* enter into partnership with the Wandering Jew, I don't consider not marrying, wasting one's life at all."

" Well, for you, who hate anything mean or cowardly, Thea, it's quite as bad ; for it's running away from the battle, and seeking safety in an inglorious ambush."

" Ah ! mother, mine," said Dorothy, trying to laugh, while the tears were in her eyes and the colour had left her cheeks. " *It's pretty to see*, as Mr. Pepys said at his cousin Joyce's wedding, ' how glad all the old springed birds are to see the poor young ones got into the net.' But I am sorry I cannot furnish you with that amusement, as I *never* intend to marry."

" Vows on such subjects are silly things."

" I make no vows, for I think they are worse than silly; they are wicked, for when all things about us change, how can we expect to remain unchanged and unchangeable ? . Neither do I coincide with Mr. Milton's convenient morality, that—

' Oaths made in pain are violent and void,'

" So, ' Swear not at all,' is a safer rule."

" Very true; therefore it is that we Protestants think monastic vows so wrong in principle, and so terrible in practice."

" Ah! and how about the other still more terrible matrimonial vows? Does it not seem to you rather impious to *swear* to love and honour a person all your life whom experience may teach you is hateful, and everything that is dishonourable? And as for men, we know what a mere mockery the most solemn of the vows *they* make in this contract are to most of them? But having made a code of *honour* (?) suited to their actions, called custom, the said custom upholds them among their peers in violating the laws of God, and agrees to ignore *their* perjuries. Now to submit, however reluctantly, to all the pains and penalties our lords and masters might think fit to impose upon us, *that* would be another affair, and however tyrannical and unjust, there would be nothing impious in it, for it *would* be within our power to perform, but to ' love ' and ' honour, ' what is odious and despicable is *not*."

" You know Master Hartsfoot called you Councillor Neville the other day," smiled Mrs. Neville, " and I always avoid litigation, so I won't argue with you on that point, more especially, as I could not conscientiously argue against you. But I am looking upon the matter in its mere natural and mundane aspect, and I think women who do not marry are incomplete; that is, they fail to receive the full complement of existence their Creator intended, by their natures not being fully developed; in as much as their affections and capacities, instead of being strengthened and enlarged by diffusion among many objects, are narrowed and weakened by being concentrated within the chilling and restricted sphere of isolation."

"Now, ' Out of thine own mouth will I condemn thee,' for take all the wives and mothers you know, or ever read, or heard of, and make a Pelion upon Ossa of their devotion, their utility, and their self-sacrifice, and it would not make such a large heart, such a noble mind, such a blameless and extensively useful life as dear Mrs. Broderick's, nor one, which so far as SELF is concerned, has been one great Lethe."

"True; but exceptions don't make—they only prove rules."

"Indeed, mother darling, except yourself, I don't know anyone who lives so completely in, and for others as she does."

"Oh! Thea, it's rank blasphemy to compare me with Phillida Broderick! Nothing *can* compare with her but her own dear, loveable, matchless self. I declare I feel almost as much shocked as if you had compared Solomon Eagle to St. John !"

" Well, I don't ; but," added Dorothy, looking towards the window at the leafless, dismantled trees, " we must accept our blights and our desolations in this life, as well as our sunshine and our greenery."

" Aye, truly must we ; but only as they come —not by forestalling and anticipations. We cannot by ' searching find out God,' but we *know* He neither slumbers nor sleeps.   And how silently, invisibly, but ceaselessly and surely, His great handmaid, Nature, works ; under the winter snows the roses are still growing, despite the bleak wintry winds—she is ever weaving garlands of flowers, spreading over the plum that sort of pulverised, purple air, that we call bloom, and giving a ruddier tint to the peach, of which ever progressing work there is neither sign nor hint to our dense perceptions, till, as Master Herrick has it—

  ' Spring from her green lap throws,
   The yellow cowslip and the pale primrose.'

And depend upon it, dear child, our fates are always weaving in the great loom of Time—overlooked, planned, and directed, by the same unerring Intelligence ; though while the tissue is being woven, we can neither trace the pattern nor see the beauty of the design, nor is it intended that we should. And to us the shuttle may often seem thrown with unnecessary force, but He who aims it must know best."

"At all events, dear mother, as you have ever taught me, we should trust where we cannot trace, and we *must* submit; so it is not only wrong, but useless to 'kick against the pricks.' But I think I *could* submit better at The Chestnuts, with my dogs, and pigeons, and birds, and flowers, and all my other subjects about me, than I can here. Moreover, in the country winter, however poor and miserable, *is* clean and respectable, and does not give way to such squalid filth as it does in London, where the snow itself is ever wrestling with chimney sweeps, and so has to go into mourning for the loss of everything belonging to it. Besides, my incarnate sermon, Audrey Barton, will teach me how to behave myself, for after all, her burden has been ten thousand times heavier than mine, and look how she has borne it!"

"Yes, and also look, how in His own good time God has lightened it for her."

"Oh! dear mother," said Dorothy, throwing her arms round Mrs. Neville's neck and bursting into tears, "what an ungrateful wretch I am to murmur at anything so long as I have you!"

END OF VOL. I.

T. C. NEWBY, 30, Welbeck Street, Cavendish Square, London.

ERRATA OF CLUMBER CHASE.

Vol. 1.

At page 3, for "léze majesté" read "lése Majesté."

At page 5, for "flaçon" read "flacon."

At page 11, for "Jules Caezar" read "Jules César."

At page 11, for "qui mangait toujours, et ne dine jamais;" read "qui mangait toujours, et ne dinait jamais."

At page 130, for "tangled secrets" read "tangled sects."

At page 236, for "Date Olentum Belisario" read "Date Obolum Belisario."

At page 297, for "daisy cloaks" read "daisy clocks."

At page 303, for "souffre douleurs" read "souffre douleur."

At page 816, for "Héias" read "Hélas."

Vol. 2.

At page 21, for "C'en est que l'éolat" read "C'en est que l'éclit."

At page 278, in foot note, for "pink-white lute string," read "pinked-white lute string."

At page 304, for "Me, exit regneo" read "ne exeat regno."

Vol. 3.

At page 52, for "plat de lionnes nouvelles" read "plât de bonnes nouvelles."

At page 91, for "J'ai mais pauvres" read "j'ai mes pauvres."

At page 209, for "Carcomet" read "Carconet."

At page 218, at "n'ayez pas peur," after the word "peur," there should be a comma.

At page 250, for "Hélas l'est clair" read "Hélas ç'est clair."

At page 310, for "covered with perfect velvet" read "covered with purple velvet.'

At page 312, for "also his brother James" read also "his brother Jambres."

At page 51, for "prestonpaus" read "Prestonpans."

For "it's on a great many persons' minds, for that Master Noah's,' read "for that matter, Noah."